HOUSEWIFE UP

In September 2004 *Richard & Judy*'s Executive Producer, Amanda Ross, approached Pan Macmillan: her production company, Cactus TV, wanted to launch a major writing competition, 'How to Get Published', on the Channel 4 show. Unpublished authors would be invited to send in the first chapter and a synopsis of their novel and would have the chance of winning a publishing contract.

Five months, 46,000 entries and a lot of reading later, the five shortlisted authors appeared live on the show and the winner was announced. But there was a surprise in store for the other four finalists.

On air Richard Madeley said, 'The standard of the finalists is staggeringly high. All are more than worthy of a publishing contract.' Pan Macmillan agreed and published all five.

The winning books were *The Olive Readers* by Christine Aziz, *Tuesday's War* by David Fiddimore, **Housewife Down by Alison Penton Harper**, *Journeys in the Dead Season* by Spencer Jordan and *Gem Squash Tokoloshe* by Rachel Zadok.

ALISON PENTON HARPER lives in rural Northamptonshire with her husband and two daughters. Her debut, *Housewife Down*, was a finalist in *Richard & Judy*'s 2004 'How to Get Published' competition. This is her second novel.

Also by Alison Penton Harper

Housewife Down

ALISON PENTON HARPER

HOUSEWIFE UP

PAN BOOKS

First published 2006 by Pan Books
an imprint of Pan Macmillan Ltd
Pan Macmillan, 20 New Wharf Road, London N1 9RR
Basingstoke and Oxford
Associated companies throughout the world
www.panmacmillan.com

ISBN-13: 978-0-330-44638-9
ISBN-10: 0-330-44638-X

1 3 5 7 9 8 6 4 2

A CIP catalogue record for this book is available from
the British Library.

Typeset by SetSystems Ltd, Saffron Walden, Essex
Printed and bound in Great Britain by
Mackays of Chatham plc, Chatham, Kent

For my sister:
Every little breeze

Contents

Prologue

TRAUMA

THE TELEPHONE PURRED through the early-morning pillows and I answered it sleepily to Leoni's cheerful voice. 'Happy birthday, gorgeous!'

'Thanks,' I yawned.

'Do you feel any different?'

I held up a sleeveless arm and checked my semi-fledged bingo wings, then looked down to inspect the pale pair of legs poking out from the bottom of my cotton-rich nightie. Little mousy weed patches nestled untidily around each wrinkled knee. Those could really do with a shave. Still, why bother? Leaning sideways to catch the reflection of a shockingly mature face in the dressing-table mirror, I pulled the phone closer to my ear and slumped back lazily against the big pile of cushions. 'I don't think so.'

'So.' Leoni breathed dramatically into the mouthpiece. 'The big four-oh, eh?'

'Good of you to remind me.'

'Why? You don't bloody look it. Anyway, forty is the new black.'

'So long as it's not the new horizontal stripes,' I grumbled.

To be frank, I had ignored the notable birthday looming like a huge black cloud on the horizon in the vain hope that it would just go away. Now that it had presented itself to me in all its seven-signs-of-ageing glory this fine morning, I was feeling more than a little deflated. Forty? Moi? That's just not possible. We had old bags at school who were younger than that. I permitted myself a self-pitying sigh, suddenly noticing that the fine hairs on my arms seemed to be greying in front of my very eyes. The next thing I knew, Leoni was in my kitchen.

'Coffee?' I asked, in a fast-approaching-middle-aged way.

'Don't be so ridiculous.' Leoni dumped her handbag onto a vacant stool, marched to the fridge and helped herself to a bottle of champagne. 'It's your birthday. We're having Bucks Fizz and hold the bloody Bucks, mate.' She brutally tore the cork from the bottle and tried to catch the minor explosion of froth in her mouth. The force was strong, instantly bloating her face into a souvenir puffer-fish. She quickly pulled upright and stuck her thumb in the top instead to preserve the gushing contents, looking away from my laughing face and trying hopelessly to swallow the fizzing mouthful without choking. We mopped up the mess together and she pretended to wring the Spontex out in her glass.

'I can't believe you're forty.' Leoni eyed me with a serious gaze. 'That means I'm next.'

I smiled at her knowingly.

'It's all right for you!' she complained. 'You're not being sucked dry by the twins from hell or being forced to sit through interminable school plays about bloody baby Jesus and caterwauling orchestra recitals with wrist-slitting kazoo solos. I'm telling you – ' she sought a moment's comfort in a lengthy sip – 'there's only so much any woman can stand, and right now, I'm seriously thinking about taking some drastic action.'

'Really? Like what?'

'I don't know yet.' She squinted her eyes at me suggestively. 'But I'll think of something.' Considering the question for a few seconds she added, 'Maybe I'll start drinking heavily. That'll teach them.'

'You are funny.'

Picking up my glass with a smile, I was aghast to see

two large clusters of liver spots creeping across the backs of my hands. I anxiously tried to rub them off without arousing Leoni's suspicion.

'I'm serious,' she said slyly. 'Loads of mothers do it. I've seen them at the school gates. They're the ones who chew gum all the time.' The more I wiped my hands, the darker the blemishes grew. I hid them self-consciously in the pocket of my apron and wished that the awful noise would stop. 'Happy birthday, honey.' Leoni raised her glass towards me and we toasted the death of my youth.

The irascible tone of the telephone grew louder, gradually amplifying to a shrill electronic blare. My eyes blinked into the rumpled duvet and I waved a disorientated arm out of the bed, fumbling for the receiver. Covering the mouthpiece with my clammy hand, I had a good old throat-clearing croak before answering shakily, 'Hello?'

'Have I woken you up?'

'Leoni? Oh, thank God.' Tiny beads of perspiration chilled the skin on my face. 'I've just had the most horrible nightmare.'

Part One

OLDER, BUT NOT NECESSARILY WISER

Chapter One

SITTING PRETTY

WAKING UP TO find oneself widowed at the grand old age of thirty-seven is a peculiarly uncommon phenomenon. Of those unfortunate husbands who have perished prematurely, there is no question that many among them will have left behind devoted wives whose grief and loss was, and remains, unspeakably painful. But, for some of the few others, it has to be said that widowhood is not without its merits.

Fleeing the suburban humdrum and all the ghastly memories that went with it had been an elementary decision. The street on which I had lived was like the valley of the forgotten people, populated by ordinariness, a waiting room where nothing ever happened.

To remain there would have rendered me brain-dead in less than a year.

Leaving was the easy part. It was finding somewhere to go that had proved tricky. After dithering for weeks that stretched into months and listening to the incessant, well-meaning recommendations from all and sundry who seemed to think that a widow of any age should head for the nearest outpost of Aga Central and buy herself a nice green waxed-cotton jacket and a faithful labrador, I had come to the firm resolve that I might as well try to live a little before the sun finally went down on my amuse-by date. It was a no-brainer. I took my life in my hands and decided to head back to the city. I had been happy there once, as a youngster.

As I never got around to having children ('result', as my best friend Leoni frequently reminded me), I was unaware that two local schools had fared remarkably well in the regional borstal league tables, with the direct effect of adding a soaring premium to the asking price of my flying-ducks semi. After a shamelessly ugly scene in the estate agent's between two fathers (under strict instructions from their wives) who almost came to blows over my humble abode, the deal was done and, in a manner of speaking, I suppose I was on my way.

It wasn't all plain sailing, mind. The sudden impact of a large inheritance brings along its own set of problems, let me tell you. Especially when you've been used to hanging around by the meat counter waiting for the chops to be marked down. It took me weeks to get over the initial shock, and Julia insisted that I get some proper investment advice in her regular big-sisterly way. Being as my personal financial experience begins and ends with a couple of ancient crumpled premium bonds wedged in the back of a kitchen drawer, she was right, as usual.

Richard Lomax was the only blind date (*Money Programme* version) I had met who seemed completely unfazed at the prospect of handling my weighty invest-ments. I guess you could say he was reassuringly unflappable. Making it last, investing it wisely, living off the interest, not having to worry about money ever again. That's what the man had said, and it was the first conversation I had understood after drowning in the torrent of jargon from the obsequious little man with piggy eyes at the bank, who had been barely able to control himself at the sight of my impressively enhanced balance. So I took Lomax's advice, went independent, and signed on the dotted line. He took care of everything for me and, true to his word, I hadn't had to trouble myself about any of it since. It's a comforting feeling. A stress-free zone.

The flat was the first I had seen. Impulsive, I know, but from the very moment I stepped through the front door in to the light, airy sitting room with floor-to-ceiling French windows opening out onto a peaceful view of the communal garden below, I knew that this was a place where I could put the past behind me and happily start again. A place where anything could happen. I left the final negotiations to Lomax who, for a not so modest fee, had a knack for brokering a ruthless deal. Not that it was much of a worry. Under his steely gaze my significant lump sum was steadily growing into a Fabergé nest egg of magnate proportions.

As I PULLED INTO the sun-dappled square three months later and wondered why on earth I had chosen to move to an address where you had more chance of spotting an osprey than a parking space, I could hardly contain my excitement. The hazard warning lights blinked a toothless defence against the clear and present danger of clampers, while I quickly unloaded the few belongings I had unfeelingly retained into the hallway behind the heavily lacquered, black front door. Julia had shared with me her homespun philosophy that the most effective strategy for avoiding Her Majesty's Boot was to double park. Her theory is that they can't immobilize your car if it's blocking innocent people in, so they have to call plod and send for a lorry to tow you away instead, giving you about ten minutes' grace to nip back behind the wheel and beat a hasty retreat. Kicking the clampers in the shins before you speed off is optional.

I parked around the corner on one of the busier thoroughfares, feeding the meter the maximum permissible dose and Sellotaping a big hand-written notice in each of the windows. *For Sale. One careful lady owner. Low mileage* (the car, not me). *Tax and MOT*. My asking price was ludicrously low and took into consideration that by showrooming it on a London meter I had accelerated its depreciation by several squillion pounds a second.

The short walk back smelled of lately fallen rain and reassured my battered heart that its new home was going to be just perfect. Key trembling in my outstretched hand, I slipped it in the shiny golden latch and carried myself over the threshold and into a new life with two beautifully appointed bedrooms, the larger one being nothing short of magnificent, living quarters with enough space to entertain should I find myself popular, and a ridiculously disproportionate kitchen with polished teak work surfaces that seemed to go on for ever. I bet they've seen some action.

The clicking thud of the hefty Banham lock closing behind me for the first time echoed around the empty rooms. The thrilling elation of that moment will never leave me. An untarnished blanket of exhilarating white space that was mine and no one else's, to do with as I wished, to live in as I chose. What a feeling it was. Like taking the Olympic gold, falling in love, and winning the rib of beef in the Sunday pub raffle all rolled into one. I shook off my coat, dropped it to the dusty floor, and laughed until tears ran down my cheeks.

BY SATURDAY AFTERNOON I was wondering if I hadn't made a terrible mistake, accidentally immersing myself in the total anonymity favoured by most city dwellers, only to find myself a regular Billy No Mates. This wasn't exactly the kind of place where you could share a cup of tea and a natter over the garden fence. The comings and goings of the building's inhabitants were few and far between. (I hadn't yet got my act together on the curtain-hanging front, so had to flatten myself against the wall while spying from the windows.) It crossed my mind that years might go by without my meeting any of my new neighbours. Perhaps I would become so desperate that I'd have no option but to set fire to the place one night just to orchestrate a group hello on the pavement outside. I would contrive to have canapés craftily at the ready.

That first weekend, I was busily loafing around on my new hippie bed-free mattress with the balcony doors wide open to let in the chilly air, watching an old black and white John Wayne movie on the tiny portable television set while trawling my way stealthily through a packet of chocolate HobNobs, when there came a firm knock on the door.

That's strange, I thought, with a modicum of alarm.

Being on the first floor, one doesn't get knock-knocked. One gets buzz-buzzed. The remote-operated intercom is supposed to give you a sporting chance of identifying a violent criminal before granting them access to the building. Maybe it was an undesirable who had already managed to make it past the first hurdle and was now testing the internal doors to see which flats held the weediest occupants. I stood up and crept towards the door on my silent odd-socked feet, leaning my ear towards the peephole as I approached on tiptoe, waiting and listening for any movement outside. I scanned my immediate surroundings for a defensive weapon. My options were: rather nice newish tweed coat; unopened pack of ready-made curtains (cardboard reinforced corners having potential for a swift Croatian temple jab); wilted prayer plant.

Knock, knock. This time so much sharper that I jumped with a start and held on to my chest with both hands, crushing the half-finished biscuit packet against my sweater. Oat crumbs scraped menacingly against my pounding cleavage. I peered through the spyhole and braced myself for the worst.

Oh my God. It was that gorgeous man from upstairs. Or, at least, I thought it was. I'd seen him leaving for work in the mornings a couple of times, always suited up like Giorgio Armani (but without the Botox) and sometimes I had even caught a wafting glimpse of his fresh citrussy cologne on my way downstairs to check for the post. Very nice too. Now, through the little round window with the fisheye lens that makes everyone look like a Weeble, there he was, knocking at *my* door.

Well, about bloody time. I'd been sitting there for days waiting for something interesting to happen and fantasizing about what that might be. I had even considered joining something local and social, like the residents' garden association, but the thought of having to introduce myself and then go through the rigmarole of the dead husband story put a major damper over any romantic notions I might have been nursing. I was still trying to decide whether or not to just lie about the whole thing and make up a brand new past that would be better suited to the woman I had decided to become. It would have to be something mysterious and intriguing. Glamorous without being too ostentatious.

'Just a minute!' I called out as I rushed around for no apparent reason, realizing there and then that there was absolutely no chance of rescuing my atrocious Stig of the Dump appearance in the available time. I pulled the pink elasticated band off my unwashed hair and shuffled it around a bit with my fingers, rubbed the crumbs off my face, hoped that my eyebrow hairs were all pointing in the same direction, and peeked back through the viewfinder. God, he's good looking. I could see that he was most definitely in his Saturday civvies from the top of the white vest that clung to his broad, tanned shoulders, and decided that this was going to be a very good day indeed. I whipped off my odd socks and quickly threw them behind the prayer plant with the remainder of the savaged HobNobs. Open sesame.

'Hello!' he chirped brightly, smiling widely and proffering his hand. 'My name's Paul and I live upstairs.' He pointed upwards to confirm the whereabouts of his nest, then clasped his hands together excitedly. 'And we just wanted to welcome you to our lovely little household here and wondered if you would like to drop by and join us for drinks later.'

Now, I don't usually jump to conclusions about people, but this man was so obviously gay that he might just as well have had a great big neon sign flashing above his head. One hundred per cent, no doubt about it. The white, silk leisure suit pants with the big floaty pockets fluttered against his legs in the breeze that had followed me to the door. My eyes ran their length and came to rest on a pair of ornately beaded flip-flops and French-polished toenails. And his earrings were nicer than mine.

Chapter Two

ONLY THE OLD KNOW HOW TO BE YOUNG

'ALL SET FOR drinkiepoos tonight?' Leoni was clearly beside herself at the prospect of five hours of pre-booked childcare.

'I don't know if I can be bothered,' I said wearily.

'What? You can't do that,' she snapped. 'I'm warning you, Helen, I've got a babysitter and I know how to use it.'

'So long as everyone knows we're talking more sausage-on-a-stick than Nigella extravaganza.'

'Well, that's what you get for catering your own

party. I still think you should have got someone in to do it for you. If I had your kind of moolah I'd never lift a finger again except to phone out for a twenty-four-hour low-fat gigolo.'

'But it's such a waste of money! And it's not as if I've got anything else to do.' I pulled the twisted spiral of the receiver cord to see how far it would stretch. 'It makes me feel useful in a sad and pathetic sort of way. Besides, it's only you lot.'

'Need any help?'

'Thanks, Leoni, but really I've got it covered.' The cord twanged and snapped me sharply in the face with an audible ouch, which she ignored.

'Sure? I can come over now and give you a hand if you like. It's no trouble.'

Judging by the rising cacophony in the background from what sounded like a miniature army freshly demobbed, instead of her brood of three, this was most definitely Leoni Ipcress Code for get me the fuck out of here before I go on a deranged killing spree.

'You're just looking for an excuse to abandon your adoring family, aren't you?' I teased her.

'Shall I write a list?' she offered loudly.

'I bet you've got your coat on already.'

'Your best crockery? Oh, my God! How on earth did that happen?' There is credible horror in her voice as she turns up the volume, bellowing her alibi through the house for everyone to hear. I'm laughing out loud.

She's trying not to. 'And the cooker? Bloody hell, Helen, how on earth are you going to manage?' Then yelling away from the phone, presumably towards her long-suffering husband, 'Marcus! I've got to get over to Helen's right now, darling. She's had a complete disaster in the kitchen and the poor woman's in pieces.'

'You'll go to hell, you know,' I told her.

'So, WHAT DID you get to mark the grand occasion of your move?' Leoni edged her metal chair towards me on the balcony with a teeth-splitting scrape. I looked at her blankly for a moment.

'I'm sorry, what did you say?' My mind had wandered off to another place where I still looked twenty and I berated myself for having wanted to grow up too quickly. I had gratefully rushed at the first offer of marriage, only to realize my foolishness years later, by which time everything was starting to head south. Perhaps I've learned how to feel young too late. 'Looks good on paper' is not the same as 'looks great in a wet suit'.

'Don't tell me you didn't buy yourself anything!' scolded Leoni.

'But there's nothing I need,' I protested blandly.

'Since when did *need* come into it?' Leoni frowned. 'We're talking sinfully frivolous and totally pointless. The kind of thing that comes trimmed with marabou that you only wear once because you can't be arsed to have it dry cleaned.' She stood up to make her point. 'Good God, Helen. Look at what you've achieved here, girl! Isn't that worth celebrating? I know that you like to birch yourself for some bizarre reason that none of us shall ever understand, but you might get run over by a bus tomorrow and you're still using the same handbag I gave you last year. And it's not even that nice!' She refilled our glasses. 'I think we should go out immediately and treat you to something completely outrageous.'

'You're supposed to be helping me with a house-warming party,' I reminded her. 'Even if I wanted to go shopping with you, which I don't, we haven't got the time.'

'Stuff that,' she sniffed. 'I think you're in denial.' I opened my mouth and went red. 'No woman in her right mind would rather peel a mushroom than treat herself to a new handbag. Face it, Helen. You're sick and you need help.'

I looked at Leoni and thought about it. I had to admit that she had a point. Even after all this time I still felt guilty about buying myself anything, unless it was either essential to my very existence or knocked down to half price in the sales. And it's not as though I'm destitute. Yet I have found that old habits die hard, and the hallmarks of a downtrodden housewife are not so easily erased. As the school report said: must try harder.

'All right then,' I said. 'You're on.'

BY SEVEN O'CLOCK, I was dressed from head to toe in the kind of ridiculous but fabulous things that you could only get away with wearing behind locked doors in your own home. So was Leoni. My proven method to survive the impulse-purchase guilt factor was to buy things for her at the same time, thus neatly deflecting some of the inevitable retail remorse onto my unsuspecting but eager volunteer. 'Buy away, honeybun,' she said. 'Who am I to deny you a good night's sleep?'

We'd been at it for hours. A dress for me, a pair of shoes for her, and so it went until we finally succumbed to Brompton blindness. That's like snow blindness, only with shopping. I'm not convinced that it was a particularly good idea to have the champagne *before* we hit the racks, although it did give us an added sense of adventure with our personal styling experiments. We seemed to have bought things for their individual merits, rather than because they went together, so trying to co-ordinate an entire outfit from the disparate jumble of funky new garb when we got back to the flat was a rather hit and miss affair. The flower-print-headscarf-and-massive-sunglasses ensemble I sported in the kitchen later while impaling irregular lumps of organic Cheddar onto cocktail sticks was indeed Jackie-O fabulous, but I wouldn't have had the bottle to wear it outside the house.

'Why not?' demanded Leoni, looking back at me with her identical scarf and super-shades set. She checked her hazy reflection in the shiny glass of the top oven door and adjusted the neck of her purple sequinned kaftan. 'I think we look bloody great.'

I was glad somebody did.

THE LOW EVENING sun pushed its way into the sitting room across the soft, biscuity carpet as Leoni opened the French windows and stepped out onto the modest balcony that stretched over the portico. 'I love this place,' she murmured.

Seating herself on one of the white wrought-iron chairs by the little table, she rested her arms on the edge of the balustrade and leaned forward to admire the view of the leafy garden square below. Two mothers sat on a chequered blanket spread open on the grass and chattered amiably, ignoring their over-tired toddlers who took it in turns to rip the heads off the fleeting peonies and fight over the remnants of a shop-bought picnic. Every now and then a blood-curdling wail would rise painfully from the otherwise tranquil scene.

We secretly held vigil for a while, watching the women becoming increasingly agitated with their unruly charges until finally an old man wielding a pair of shears came striding up and demanded to know who they were and why they were allowing their revolting little brats to vandalize the garden. Mother number two lost her cool completely and yelled first at the pensioner and then at the howling three-year-old before being forcibly ejected.

'It gets a lot worse, you know!' Leoni shouted down merrily, raising her glass and waving as they glanced up towards the disembodied voice. She turned from them and looked at me mischievously. 'Perfect vantage point up here,' she said. 'Bloody gorgeous. Just look at it.'

I settled myself beside her and shared her bird's-eye view of the surroundings that had become my new 'hood, then leaned my elbows on the cool stone beside her and looked across at the near-identical houses and balconies on the opposite side of the small, verdant space that nestled between them.

'You've got everything a woman could possibly want,' she sighed. 'Fabulous shops and restaurants on your doorstep. A gorgeous garden you don't have to do anything to. Really interesting neighbours, even if they do sound a little weird. I have to say, old bird.' She nudged me gently on the arm. 'I'm really happy it's all worked out for you.'

'I know,' I said, but should have touched wood instead.

THERE'S THAT AWFUL feeling you get when you've asked people over for eight and still no one's turned up by twenty past. Nine, that is. 'No one's coming,' I wittered pathetically to Leoni. 'I knew this was a bad idea. Why did I let you talk me into it?'

'Stop being so bloody paranoid,' she said, face pressed up against the window, her breath steaming the pane. Within moments she spotted a familiar figure and turned to me with a direct told-you-so.

Sure enough, everyone had decided to turn up fashionably late and we soon had something of a rush on. Marcus was first up the stairs, mumbling tetchily about the babysitter holding him to ransom for an extra tenner as he bumbled in through the door. He hugged me briefly, then pulled away with a chuckle, noticing his wife's colourful attire.

'Hi, darling.' He smiled with obvious amusement. 'What on earth are you wearing?'

His wife scowled at him. 'Piss off, Grandad. What do you know?'

I HAD SLIPPED AWAY to lay the guests' coats neatly on the bed in the spare room when Leoni popped her head around the door. 'Dudley's here,' she hissed excitedly. 'And he's on his *own*.' She gave me a grinning, double thumbs up.

'Oh, don't start that again.' I deposited the pile in my arms. 'I've told you, there's absolutely no way. We're just friends and that's as far as it goes.'

'I think you're mad,' she whispered loudly. 'You should have snapped him up months ago while he was crackers about you.'

'He's boring,' I said, switching on the bedside lamp and remembering how my face would ache with the effort of feigning interest in the bottomless pit of painfully dreary anecdotes he stunned me with over the course of our brief dalliance. Spending any length of time with a crashing bore is actually very stressful. You have to bite your lip through acute urges to scream, 'Oh, why don't you just stop talking,' and sit there looking scintillated. I imagine it must be a similar feeling to having Tourette's.

Leoni tutted impatiently and shook her head. 'So? Is that a crime? For Christ's sake, Helen, who isn't boring after the first five minutes? God, I'm so bored I doubt I've still got a pulse.'

'No. I mean really boring. Like – ' I struggled to find a suitable word – 'like, *sanitized*. He's got a rubbish sense of humour, which can get a bit embarrassing after a while. And honestly, Leoni, what kind of man carries disclosing tablets and dental floss in his pocket?'

It was a terrible shame, because Dudley was a truly lovely chap, like Superman in the flesh. Chiselled and dependable. Handsome without being too overwhelming. Smart, but not inconveniently clever. Sure, he had all the makings of an outstanding modern-day Casanova, but the three-pin plug was missing. After four cold-fish dates, I'd conceded that there was no point in trying to hammer a square peg into a round hole and we crossed the invisible divide that signals the death knell to passion. As with all his ex-girlfriends, we remain the best of friends.

'Dudley!' I swept down the hall to greet him. 'I didn't think you'd be able to make it! No supermodel on your arm tonight?' We laughingly kissed each other hello and I caught Leoni squinting at me and frowning a series of semaphore messages before brushing past us to buzz in whoever it was who had just arrived. We all heard the ball of energy rushing up the stairs.

'Wey-hey!' shouted Sara as she bounded through the door like a crazed red setter, closely followed by the boyfriend with the personality bypass – what was it about men these days? – Ian with the unpronounceable surname. Quite what she sees in him we simply can't fathom. (Leoni reckons it must be something to do with the parts we *can't* see.) The nondescript beau shuffled in behind her, dragging his knuckles and grunting some form of Neanderthal greeting before retreating to the far corner of the sitting room with a bottle of beer. Sara thrust a little gift-wrapped parcel in my hand and leaned towards me confidentially. 'I've gone off-piste with your moving-in present. Open it when you're alone.'

Oh no, not another one. She'd already got me one for Christmas, which I was far too embarrassed to throw out with the rest of the rubbish in case the bin men stumbled upon it. Perhaps she was buying them in bulk.

'Can I just nip to your loo?' Sara asked, pulling at her uncomfortable VPL. She caught Dudley eyeing her ungainly tugging and dipped him a cheeky curtsey. 'It's these bloody fishnet tights,' she explained loudly. 'I feel like I've got my arse strung up in a bag of satsumas.' He reddened and watched her disappear down the corridor, hitching her skirt up well before she reached the bathroom.

'I won't be able to stay long, I'm afraid.' Dudley recovered his composure and apologized in a flash of gleaming teeth, glancing at his Piaget. 'Got a video conference with New York at ten o'clock.' He stepped out of the door again for a second, then came back armed with an enormous basket of white lilies.

'Oh, Dudley! They're absolutely beautiful.' I filled my nose with their heavy petroleum scent.

'And so are you,' he smiled. 'I think you'll be really

happy here.' He squeezed my arm gently and nodded into my home. 'It's got you written all over it. All you need now is a man to open your jars.'

'That's very sweet of you, but I've decided I must be getting old.' I wrinkled my nose at him as he followed me through to the kitchen. 'I'm starting to find Jeremy Paxman attractive. Beer or bubbly?'

'Beer's good,' he said, pulling a newly pressed handkerchief from his pocket and carefully wiping the neck of the bottle before lifting it to his lips.

'I still say you got a real bargain here, Helen,' declared Marcus, who was leaning back on the balcony, shouting at us through the open doors and surveying the front of the classic white stucco façade. 'The markets have gone barmy over the past couple of months. What do you reckon it's worth now?'

'Marcus!' barked Leoni. 'Do you think you could possibly think of a topic of conversation that doesn't include the value of everyone's houses? It's so bloody vulgar.'

'What have I done this time?' he complained, voice full of injury. 'I just can't bloody well win, can I?' I stepped outside, moved in between them to break the surface tension and tugged on his sleeve.

'Thanks for the glorious vase,' I said, refilling his glass. Leoni rolled her eyes at me and went in search of more food.

'Leoni chose it,' Marcus confessed. (And here was

me thinking that he had scoured John Lewis's home knick-knacks department all by himself.)

Julia's husband, the divine David, was hanging around by the sink, picking at a bowl of olives, chatting cars and testosterone to Dudley. 'No man again, Helen?' David knocked Dudley's arm, peered mockingly in the kitchen cupboards then leaned towards me. 'I keep telling everyone that you must have one stashed away here somewhere.' Dudley laughed and nodded his agreement.

'All the good ones are taken,' I sighed. 'And the other sort aren't worth having. Although I have to admit a bit of you-know-what might be nice once in a while.'

'I'd be only too happy to oblige.' David smiled. 'But I'm not sure how it would go down with your big sister.'

Sara sprang back into the kitchen and dropped her bright-orange fishnets in the bin. 'Tell you what,' she said. 'If you get really desperate, I'll come round and do the honours, if you like. It's getting very fashionable these days.'

You can always trust Sara to keep you on the right side of cutting edge.

I THOUGHT ABOUT SARA'S cheerful offer. It hadn't escaped my notice that I can go most places now on my own with little or no danger of anyone trying to spin me a corny chat-up line. There used to be a time when I'd feel irritated at not being able to sit quietly in a café alone or enjoy a sneaky day out without some random saddo trying to strike up a conversation with me. That traditional lone-woman-equals-up-for-it assumption that so many men misguidedly labour under. Now the only candidates I catch looking are quite apparently the ones from the reject pile. Or the single fathers looking for a free weekend child-minder. All in all, it doesn't bode well.

It's not that I've deliberately avoided the relationship issue, either. More that I've found myself to be a lot fussier than I used to be. It's cruel, but sadly true, as anyone who knew my late husband will verify. On the odd occasion that I've met somebody who appeared to have some potential, they've soon turned out to be dragging around enough excess baggage to keep the scavenging handlers at Heathrow busy for a good decade.

So I've become accustomed to being on my own now, and I have to say that I rather like it. I don't have to compromise myself over anything any more, which is a fine alternative to having to compromise yourself over everything. And I can honestly say that I'm happy. Is *happy* the right word? I think so. Maybe *deeply content* would be better. Not having to share one's personal space does become strangely addictive. You can be as idiosyncratic as you like, but you do run the very real risk of ending up quite eccentric, if not completely mad.

I like to play loud disco music some mornings and dance around energetically for a while as a cursory nod to exercise. I also like to eat certain food combinations that you wouldn't necessarily want other people to find out about. White bread sandwiches stuffed with salt and vinegar crisps. Mashed potatoes on toast with enough hot mustard to give you a nose bleed. Everything in the fridge, fried. And then there are my curious little habits, although I prefer to call them my foibles. We won't go into those yet.

I finished clearing away the last of the post-party carnage and ran a broom over the loose crisps littering the balcony floor. A half-empty champagne bottle had been left on the ground beside the downpipe, no doubt having been secreted by Leoni, who lived in permanent fear of exhausting her glass. The bubbles were still lively when I picked it up, so I did the civilized thing and finished it off with the rest of the cheese.

Sitting with my feet up on the coffee table, gazing at the generous basket of Stargazer lilies, I wondered if I shouldn't take Leoni's advice and reassess my opinion of Dudley. I thought about it long and hard, disappearing into a temporary overripe brie haze, then snapped to my senses. Nah. It would never work.

ONE UNDENIABLE DOWNSIDE to living *la vie solitaire* is that there is no one around to grab the wretched telephone if it goes while you're in the bath. I'm not one of those highly adapted android people who can just leave it to ring. Far too worried about missing something interesting. I reluctantly heaved myself out of the tub and dripped to the bedroom, wiping the watery conditioner from my ear with the corner of the towel.

'Whoever you are,' I began. 'You have just got me out of the bath.'

'Helen? Keith Jameson. Sounds like I've caught you at a bad moment.'

'Oh, hi Keith! To what do I owe this unexpected pleasure?'

I like Keith. He's exactly the kind of bank manager I need. Keeps an eye on everything for me and never says no.

'Helen, this is a bit awkward,' he said, awkwardly.

'Sounds ominous,' I teased, pulling the damp towel into a more comfortable position under my armpits and sitting on the edge of the bed. 'What's up?'

'Well, it seems that you're quite seriously overdrawn.'

It took a couple of moments for his sentence to register. Overdrawn is not a part of my vocabulary. Even when I was running my husband's own personal Colditz, I managed perfectly well on the insufficient housekeeping by being thrifty, and I never spent what I didn't have. I don't 'do' overdrawn. My brain stumbled around looking for a reference point. Then I remembered the shopping trip.

'Oh my goodness!' I gasped. 'Keith, I should have said! I got a bit reckless with a friend the other day and forgot to call the bank to transfer funds across from my reserve account. It's just that the last couple of times I've spoken to them they said they would move the money over automatically when my account needed it. I just assumed they would do the same this time.'

Keith hesitated for a few moments before answering. 'Well, that's what they tried to do, but it seems there's a problem.'

I'm not big on problems. 'What kind of problem?'

'We're not really sure, but it would appear that there are no funds to transfer.'

I can't say that I was entirely following the conversation at this point. 'What do you mean, no funds?' The rigid smile on my face remained, but goosebumps had risen on my arms. I attempted to laugh his concern away with a meekly casual, 'That's just not possible, Keith. There must be some mistake.'

I waited for him to agree with me, apologize for the error, and reassure me that they would get onto it straight away and fire whoever was responsible for giving me such an awful fright. Instead, the line seemed to expire with a deafening silence.

'There's no mistake, Helen,' he said eventually. Keith sounded pretty certain of his level response. 'The account's empty.'

Chapter Three

A MERRY DANCE

STORM CLOUDS GATHERED ominously and threatened my blue horizon in the guise of a visit from my hitherto friendly and helpful bank manager.

'I don't understand it,' I said to Keith impatiently as he followed me through to the sitting room. (One of the benefits of private banking is that they come to see you, so you don't have to display yourself in one of those awful open-plan booths in the local branch down the High Street while everyone in the queue pretends not to be straining to hear the scandalous details of your scurrilous personal debt and microbe salary.) 'The income from the investments is paid directly into the reserve account so you shouldn't have had any trouble.' I deliberately put the tray down on the table with a frown and poured the coffee, handing one to Keith and taking a seat on the sofa opposite him.

'There's nothing in the reserve account.' Keith took the cup from my unsteady hand and avoided my gaze by concentrating on the saucer.

'I'm sorry, Keith, but there's simply no way that's right.' I had taken to reading the money sections in the weekend papers (okay, sometimes), and you didn't need to be a rocket scientist to know the difference between up and down. Keith's demeanour this morning was a million miles away from his usual sunny disposition, and his discomfiture was more than a little apparent.

'There haven't been any deposits into that account for three months. The funds have been going out, not in.' His newly acquired air of quiet concern was beginning to unnerve me. 'Have you checked with your investment people?'

I knew he was going to ask me that.

'I'm waiting to hear back from them,' I lied, stirring my sugarless cup unnecessarily and attempting to make light of the question. I hadn't meant to fib, but I didn't know quite what else to say. The fact was that I didn't have the faintest idea where Richard Lomax was. I had left messages everywhere. At least, everywhere I could get through to. The main office number was unobtainable, the home number was routing through to a voicemail, and his mobile was constantly switched off. It was only when I sat and thought about it that I realized it was always him who'd called me. Yesterday I went to his office myself only to discover that what had looked like a perfectly respectable and not insignificant company was actually just a rented room in a building that belonged to a serviced business centre. When I challenged the receptionist about the deliberate deception on their part – and I'm not usually one to cause a scene or start bawling in public – she took pity on me and checked her records. They hadn't seen Lomax for months, and the red alert flag on her computer confirmed that I wasn't the only person looking for him. Not by a long chalk.

That feeling which is described as sinking is about as accurate as our common parlance gets. A horrible, dragging sensation that pulls you down into unimaginable depths of worry. I had been consoling myself with the half-hearted conviction that this must surely be a hideous misunderstanding. With all the safeguards these days, you can't just *lose* almost two million pounds, just like that. It was all bound to come right in the end, probably just some grotesque digital mistake. A humungous computer glitch like the ones that send threatening letters from the Gas Board to dead people. Sticking my head in the sand was fine so long as I didn't frighten myself by thinking about Barings bank, or Equitable Life, or the great ongoing twenty-first-century pensions scandal. Those were the kinds of thing that happened to other people.

I resolutely closed my mind to the rest of the conversation with Keith, digging my heels in like a mule and stubbornly refusing either to entertain or allay his concerns about contingency plans and my no doubt having spread my investments sensibly so as to limit my exposure to anything risky. Bastard. I wanted to shout at him and knock the coffee cup from his manicured hands, to ask him who on earth he thought he was, coming around here and talking to me like I was stupid. I wanted to cry and scream and smash plates against walls. This could not be happening. I'd served my time already.

By the time Keith left, I could do no more than sit on the sofa in a silent daze. When I did eventually rise, it was to rush to the bathroom and violently throw up. I splashed my face with cold water and did my best to pull myself together and try to quell the surging acidic pain burning deep in the pit of my stomach. More than anything, what I really needed right now was for someone strong and true to gather me up in their arms and tell me that everything was going to be all right.

ON THIS PARTICULAR occasion, those arms happened to belong to Salvatore, Sally to his friends, and Paul's utterly delightful other half. He was my nearest port of call in a raging storm and took the full brunt of my car-crash arrival at his front door with the kind of sweetness and understanding you could only get from a man like him. Sally scraped me off the mat and hugged me until I nodded okay, you can let go now, then he plonked me down on a kitchen chair and gave me room to settle.

'You know what I think, Helen?' Sally filled a tall glass pitcher with ice from the big American fridge in the corner. I looked at him dolefully through a tear-stained tea towel (the meagre ration of tissues from my pockets having run out by the fourth racking sob). 'I think we should make a big jug of margaritas and get very, very drunk.' He started squeezing a basket of limes on the nine-inch steel Chrysler building and nodded sagely. 'Unless you have a better idea.' The juice collected in the high-walled parking lot. I blew my nose and shook my head forlornly. 'Then we'll watch *The Weakest Link* through one eye and laugh at the stupid people who don't know what a cow is.'

That's the great thing about Sally. Not only does he approach every problem in life with a cocktail in hand, he also works from home, which means that any time is a good time when you need a crushing hug and a shoulder to cry on. Sally is the artist who does those sublime illustrations you see next to the lifestyle section in one of the big Sunday supplements. They're as cool as he is, and each one only takes him a couple of hours. He says he spends half the week thinking about it, then knocks up the artwork on a Wednesday morning. Job done. Charges a fortune.

'Put on some music.' He nodded me towards the stereo as he swung the jug and glasses into the sitting room. 'There's already something good in there. It's from my country.' (That would be Colombia, which to my mind makes Sally far more exciting than your average domestic neighbour.) 'Just switch it on and hit play.'

I DON'T THINK EITHER of us heard Paul come in, and by the time his shrieking cry of 'What in the name of all—' pulled my tequila-addled brain to attention, there was no hiding the fact that I was up to my neck in it. *It* being his neatly starched charcoal-grey duvet cover. I say *either of us*, because I assumed that the other culprit was still there. But there was no sign of Sally, and I found myself the red-handed lone occupant of somebody else's bed. The only thing going through my mind at that moment was whether there was anything at all I could possibly say that might salvage a truly delicate situation. I could tell him that I accidentally got horribly drunk while spilling my guts to his boyfriend, then found myself suddenly taken ill and was kindly put to bed to sleep it off. So, that explains my location, but not my nakedness. I imagined myself being set upon by a gang of marauding clothes moths. Mmm. Unlikely.

Don't ask me how it had happened. True, emotions were running pretty high that afternoon, and after I had finished crying my eyes out, drenching every Kleenex and dishcloth in the house, Sally had determined to cheer me up no matter what it took. All I know is that one minute he was teaching me the basic moves of a common or garden salsa, and the next we became violently entangled in something far less appropriate for a weekday agony visit to my neighbour.

The most sacrificial parts of being (happily) single are those occasional days when you are, well, you know, one doesn't like to use the expression gagging for it, but it does paint the picture rather well. The look on my face must have had guilty written all over it. Paul just stood there and glared at me with folded arms, foot tapping angrily against the polished floor.

'Where is he?' he demanded.

I shrugged hopelessly. 'I don't know. I thought he was here. I mean, oh God, Paul.' I held my hands to my burning cheeks and hid my face in shame.

'Don't bother,' he snapped, striding forward and pounding furiously on the locked bathroom door.

'Sally? You in there? You despicable pile of Colombian trash.' Then back to me, 'And if you're looking around for your clothes, you might want to try your balcony. That's the ones that didn't miss.'

'Paul! I honestly don't know how it happened. We were just—'

'Just what?' He pounds harder. 'You can't stay in there for ever you know! I'm going to count to three. One . . . two . . . Right.' He marched angrily into the sitting room, made some alarming commotion, and came back moments later with a handful of vinyl LPs. Pulling one out from its perfect paper sheath, he yelled, 'Are you listening to this?' then violently smashed it against the door handle, instantly shattering it into sharp fragments that flew like little black daggers through the air. 'It's Astrid! And this one's Tito! Can you hear me?' and he whacked another precious album against the bathroom door with a jarring crash. It swung open immediately.

'Stop!' shouted Sally, emerging from the en-suite clutching a raw silk kimono around himself protectively and snatching for the record still in Paul's hand.

'You can't shower this one off, honey,' yelled Paul. 'She's our fucking neighbour, for Christ's sake!'

'I think I'd better go.' I started to edge off the bed shakily, taking the bottom sheet with me.

Sally moved towards Paul.

'Don't you touch me!' Paul screamed, his eyes closed and hands held high up beside his head. 'If you can't keep your ridiculous fatherly hormones out of our lives, this relationship is *never* going to work.' He turned his face to the wall while Sally looked mournfully at the broken records scattered across the floor and ran his fingers through his hair.

They didn't seem to notice me sidling naked out of the room, and I closed the front door silently behind me.

If only I had remembered my key.

Chapter Four

THOU SHALT NOT GO TO BED WITH THY MAKE-UP ON

DEPRESSION. THE MODERN malady. It crept up on me like a deathly white fog while I wasn't looking, starting one day as I stared blindly at the television set that dank afternoon behind closed curtains and chose to ignore the ringing telephone shortly after the two detectives from the Fraud Squad left. They couldn't have been less interested if they'd tried. The younger of the two looked like a pit bull, chewed on his nails and spat out the shards, and seemed completely unaware of his revolting habit. I handed over copies of the scant paperwork and tried not to lose my temper when the older officer openly sniggered at the contents of one of the documents.

The telephone remained unanswered. I didn't want to speak to anyone. I had absolutely nothing to say. My new life was over before it had begun. An almighty left hook out of a clear blue sky. Then, much later, when the hours eventually became days, I just couldn't be bothered to pick it up. Or the clothes littering the bedroom floor. Or the gathering post from the table in the hall downstairs. I heard Sally come knocking once, or was it twice? He was calling something out, muffled beyond the door, but I stayed put on the couch under an untidy pile of throws and closed my eyes. After a while the sounds stopped and he pushed some letters under the door. I didn't pick those up either, and soon they began to spread, like a wide puddle of printed fear, gradually flooding its way across the gritty unvacuumed carpet.

The calls became more frequent, more urgent, then stopped altogether when the battery on the mobile finally gave up the ghost and I wrenched the plastic sockets from the wall. I preferred the silence. There was nothing for me to answer. Besides, what was the point? I had become addicted to the television, watching it all day, all night, needing it there for company even if I fell into fitful sleep for a while every now and then. The impotence was overwhelming. There's no fighting an invisible enemy, and the frustration was worse than a slow crucifixion. I moved on to the sofa permanently, stopped eating properly, and disappointed myself every day when I woke in the morning.

I don't know how long I'd felt like that. How long I'd been like that. It must have been a while, because when Julia burst in through the door like the seventh samurai, she faltered in her step the moment she saw me. 'Bloody hell,' she whispered softly. 'Whatever's happened to you?'

IT WAS AN easy mistake to make. At least that was the way Julia had talked me off the ceiling when I broke down, painfully vomiting the whole miserable story about the man who had promised to look after my portfolio then promptly disappeared off the face of the earth, taking my savings and my identity with him. Last seen sunning himself somewhere in the Caymans. If I were to join the queue of people waiting to smash his smug face in, I might not live long enough to see the halfway orange-squash checkpoint.

THE FULL, MIND-BOGGLING scale of the epic disaster had gradually revealed itself after some lengthy investigations by the bank and a steady stream of terse correspondence from the various financial institutions where I had thought that the money had been invested. All of them clearly thought I must have been a couple of radishes short of a salad for not spotting the writing on the wall with Lomax long ago, and for missing the widespread news about his well-publicized scams that popped up in most of the national papers from time to time. If I had been expecting something resembling sympathy, they soon put me straight. The general consensus was the same: unlucky, lady, but not our problem. Hard cheese.

Some poor bastards had lost literally everything, whereas I at least still had a roof over my head, albeit one that I couldn't realistically afford the upkeep on any more. I couldn't bear the thought of losing my home. And where would I go? What would I do? But numbers rarely lie, and the gaping deficit between the new household budget that Julia carefully drew up as she coaxed me back to the human race and the reality of my widow's pension made depressing reading.

'What did the police say again?' Julia put a piping-hot mug of tea in front of me.

'I don't want to talk about it,' I repeated. 'And I've decided I'm wasting my time if I thought for a minute that they were going to rescue me.'

'But they're supposed to be fraud detectives. They

must be able to do *something*.' She sighed and tutted. 'I can't believe they'd be that useless.'

'Well, they bloody well are,' I snapped. 'When I dared to complain, the chief detective whatever he was came over, took one look at the flat and made it clear that he thought I was a stupid woman with more money than sense. Said it happens all the time. Took all the details, for the tenth time, and told me not to get my hopes up.' I picked up the mug then put it down again. 'Whichever way I look at it, I've really cooked my goose this time. There's no way out. I'm going to have to sell everything and move to a trailer home. I'd hire a private detective were it not for the fact that I haven't got any sodding money to pay for one.'

'Try not to worry,' she said gently.

'Yeah, right.' I looked up at her bitterly. 'This wasn't supposed to happen. I'm not cut out for this kind of stress. It does my head in. Why didn't I just stay where I was instead of complicating everything? And why didn't you just keep your nose out of my business?' I turned towards her pointedly. 'I could have left the money in the bank instead of getting involved with that shit. It was your bloody idea, not mine.' Julia bridled momentarily but took it on the chin. It was a cruel remark, and Lomax had been my choice, not hers.

'It's nobody's fault,' she said. 'You weren't to know.'

'Well, I bloody know now, don't I? Never look a gift horse in the mouth. It's liable to bite your face off.' I stared into my tea like a wet weekend and sighed a lot.

Julia straightened her shoulders and lowered her tone. 'So. What are you going to do about it?'

'There's nothing I *can* do about it, is there?' I sniped back.

'Oh, really?' she growled sarcastically, getting up from her seat. 'Yes, I suppose you're right. I know that if it happened to me, I'd sit around snivelling into my tea and waiting for the bailiffs to arrive. No point in trying to help myself; after all, the executioner is already on his way, so I'll just stand by my bed and wait for them to take the flat off me, then lie around in the street feeling like a victim.'

I shot Julia a glowering stare. 'I can't believe you said that.' She looked back at me defiantly without responding. 'Well, thanks a bunch for your support. Next time I need a sympathetic ear I'll call the bloody Samaritans.'

'That's up to you,' she said with a barely disguised note of anger in her voice. 'But in the meantime I'd start thinking about how you're going to dig yourself out of this mess. And I wouldn't take too long about it either.'

*

JULIA ANSWERED HER front door to find me skulking on the doorstep behind a battle-fatigued bunch of purple-headed anemones. Trying to get to her house on our crippled public transport system had taken more than two hours and used up every last ounce of my timetable-deciphering ingenuity, but the surprised look on her face was worth it.

'I'm really sorry,' I said, holding out the flowers. She took them from my hands without a word, put her arms around me and held me close for a good long while.

'I'm sorry too,' she said. 'I should never have said those things. It was pointless and stupid. I can't begin to imagine how you must be feeling.'

'No,' I said. 'You were only telling it the way it is. It's just that I don't know where to start.' I followed her into the kitchen, discarding my bag and raincoat on one of the wooden chairs.

'Sit,' she said. 'I'll make us a really good pot of coffee.' She turned away from me and started rummaging about in the top freezer door. 'I've got some Blue Mountain stashed in here somewhere, but don't tell David.' Julia has a knack for making seriously great coffee, but she's rubbish with pastry. It's just the mysterious way in which God moves sometimes. I picked up the gossip magazine lying on the kitchen table and browsed through the first few pages.

'Blimey.' I stared down at one of the pictures. 'What's Fergie done to her face?' Julia reached the sugar bowl down from the high cupboard and looked over her shoulder.

'I know,' she said. 'Scary, isn't it?' She came over and stood beside me while we cocked our heads this way and that at the photograph. 'Why don't we cook a really complicated dinner?' she suggested. 'David will be back in a couple of hours. He can pretend he's got two wives. Men love that.'

SUPPER PASSED AS a comfortable threesome. We ate together like any close family, talking openly about what a right bugger this all was and exploring a number of convoluted but unlikely theories about how best to tackle the wild moose bucking around the kitchen. The free-flowing red wine buffered us all nicely from the severity of the situation, and we brought the meeting to a late close by unanimously agreeing that if I wanted to avoid a serious downshift to some ghastly sink estate twinned with a dustbin in Siberia and feeding myself on dented reject tins from Asda for the rest of my life, there was only one sensible course of action to take.

'You can do it,' David reassured me with a brave smile, 'and if it all goes horribly wrong, you can come and live with us.'

*

'So, Helen, isn't it?'

The woman behind the desk looked up from the dusky pink form to regard her ten o'clock appointment and removed her tortoiseshell-rimmed spectacles with a flourish, leaving them to dangle on the thin gold chain between her sun-damaged breasts. 'Thinking about returning to work, are we?'

'Yes.' I tried to smile, but my throat had dried to a stony riverbed and my mouth seemed to have taken on a personality of its own.

She returned her attentions to my sparsely filled application form. I had struggled with it on an uncomfortably trendy red sofa for the past forty minutes under the super-efficient gaze of the snooty receptionist, who went to great lengths to swan around reminding me that she, unlike me, had a job.

'It's been quite a while, hasn't it?' The lady's smile was friendly, in a successful yet slightly belittling way.

'Thirteen years, or thereabouts.' I sat up straight and tried to look industrious. She set the form aside, put the lid back on her pen and drew her hands together, adopting the tried and tested global interview position. 'So, what is it that you want to do exactly?'

My mind went completely blank. Christ, that's a toughie. I was expecting some difficult questions but come on, isn't that a bit below the belt for an opener? 'I need to get something that's quite well paid,' I answered. Nicely avoided, and neatly coming straight to the whole point of my being here.

'And what skills do you have?'

God, this woman's persistent. Now, let's see. Folding napkins into amusing shapes. Baking big cakes because I'm bored (then eating them). Running up a nice set of fully lined curtains with goblet pleats in about six hours (yes, and I'd like to see *you* do that, missus).

'I'm quite good at organizing things,' I offered hopefully.

She knitted her brow. 'Any computer skills?'

Ah. The million-dollar question I had been hoping to avoid. 'I'm afraid I haven't got around to those yet.'

'Secretarial experience? Typing? Shorthand?'

'Probably a bit rusty,' I mumbled.

She produced a stopwatch from her desk drawer and my heart sank.

IMAGINE TRYING TO describe the colour red to a blind man. The poor woman was almost tearing her hair out by the time I got my head around the blank Word document sitting patiently on the pale-blue computer screen in front of me. 'Just think of it as a piece of paper in a normal typewriter,' she said through gritted teeth.

Three false starts later, I finally tore through the command of 'Go!' and managed to smash in some of the text on the laminated test sheet propped up in front of me. With shaking hands, my fingers landed far too heavily on the hyper-sensitive keyboard, clacking like machine-gun fire from beyond my felt-clad partition. After what seemed like a thousand years, I heard her shout, 'Stop!'

With tear-jerking relief, I ground to a sudden halt halfway through the sentence and hit the carriage return. In the blink of an eye, the entire screen disappeared.

'YOU'RE NEW HERE, aren't you?'

Her name was Sonia, or rather as I was to discover some days later, Silly Sonia Fat Ballerina. The nickname had been bestowed upon her in the mid-sixties when she was a student there herself, then passed down through the folklore of the young ladies who had glided through the Lucie Clayton College over the ensuing decades.

'Yes,' I admitted shyly.

'Well, it's jolly nice to see a more mature face around here for a change! Perhaps we'll be able to have a decent conversation one day that I can actually understand. These young girls these days. Heads full of all sorts of rubbish. Can't fathom a word!' She had the kind of manner that delivers every sentence with a rolling laugh towards the end as though hitting the punchline of a long and tedious joke. 'Wanting to get back to work now that the children are grown, I expect!' Another laugh, and a knowing nudge from her spindly elbow into my ribs.

I smiled back at her. 'Something like that.'

'Well, we'll have you ship-shape in no time. Just you wait and see. Ha, ha.'

She wasn't kidding. They didn't call her old lightning fingers for nothing. Once let loose on the keyboard her hands became a blur. She soon took me under her wing as her pet project and insisted we eat our sandwiches together each lunchtime while she told me, several times over, all about herself and the teach-yourself book she was planning to write. It was a strange six weeks, reminiscent of my final year in the sixth form, when we had been permitted to dispense with the formality of uniform and could even get away with hanging out of the common-room window for a sneaky ciggie without being hauled up in front of the Mother Superior, provided we were discreet about it of course. Only now I looked more like one of the teachers, minus the wimple.

I had elected to invest what little credit I had left in myself, or rather, in *improving my chances on the job market*, as the woman at the agency had put it after I crumbled under the pressure and started snivelling like a fatally grazed five-year-old thirty seconds into the shorthand test. She told me sympathetically how much things had changed 'since my time' and that technology now ruled every commercial environment. Without the required accoutrements, the best I could hope for would be something low skilled, and therefore low paid. The whole thing had been an unmitigated disaster, and by the time I let myself back into the flat later that afternoon after consoling myself with an unnecessarily extravagant food shop, I had felt utterly dejected and went to work on a full-size tub of Chunky Monkey.

SUMMER'S NOT A BAD time to change your life around, I suppose. At least the sun's more likely to be shining and the general population appears a little less depressed than usual. Speaking of which, where on earth do you start on dress code for a college induction day when you're twice the age of your peers? I did my best with a pair of jeans and a newish T-shirt with a bit of a flared sleeve number going on. With the sky clear and bright that morning, I had opted for Shanks's pony with a spring in my step and headed for the first day of my new, self-sufficient future. Then I saw the rest of the summer school intake hanging around near the entrance. Young, fresh-faced, mostly reed thin. Mobiles and midriffs everywhere. Now that really *was* depressing.

On the upside, by week two it had become apparent

that they all seemed to have one particular thing in common: not an ounce of common sense between them. If these silver-spooned young ladies were my main competitors in the job market, I reasoned that I should surely be home and dry. One of them thought 'fiscal' had got Julian Clary the sack, and another threatened to have her daddy sue the personal presentation tutor (that's how to apply your lipstick on the Piccadilly Line) for drawing attention to her T-zone.

Six weeks later, after a tearful departure wave from Silly Sonia and an empty promise to keep in touch, I was certainly feeling a lot more confident and was much better prepared for my interview at the second unsuspecting recruitment agency. They suggested I take some temporary positions to provide an immediate fix to my reduced circumstances and give me an opportunity to dip my toe back in the workplace ethic before leaping straight into something permanent. I could see the words 'commission' and 'refund' flashing across the boss's unconvinced eyes.

MY FIRST ASSIGNMENT lasted for all of four hours as I tried hopelessly to navigate my way through the inscrutable filing system in the archive cupboard of a firm that imported plastic septic tanks. Blurgh. I did notice with some interest that they sell quite a few top halves only to Indian restaurants.

By lunchtime, I had managed to rehome just twelve miserable pieces of paper. They must have rung the agency because Penny called my mobile and said that they no longer required my services. Except that I was so busy being a valuable new employee that I had switched off my phone, worked through lunch with the aid of an energy bar (king-size Snickers), and didn't get the message. The head of department had to come down and ask me why I was still there. I like to think I handled my subsequent ejection with a certain dignity.

The typing job at the big accountancy firm was much better. Sitting there quietly in the corner, anonymously keying in endless rows of meaningless figures, topping and tailing each schedule with standard passages from a predetermined list that had been explained to me by a witch of a woman with dreadfully unkempt hands (you get sent home for that sort of thing at Lucie's). The boredom of the repetition was comforting. The shocking cheque for a measly one hundred and sixty-six pounds at the end of the week was not.

'Is that it?' I wailed at Penny. 'For a whole week's work? I've practically lost all feeling in my fingers!'

'SALLY HAS SOMETHING to say to you.'

I had answered my door to find a deeply tanned Salvatore and Paul standing there in front of me, the first looking sheepish, the other purposeful. Following the afternoon of the ill-fated paso doble lesson, they had stealthily avoided me for almost two months, including going away on holiday without dropping me a key as they had arranged, and I had sadly resigned myself to the inevitable loss of their colourful friendship. It had crossed my mind once or twice to be grown-up about it, go upstairs and knock on their door to clear the air, but I just couldn't face it. It had been one hell of a big price to pay for an accidental coupling that I had little recollection of, and home hadn't felt quite the same way since.

'I'm sorry, Helen,' drawled Sally. He checked Paul's face then turned back to me. 'I took advantage of you when you were vulnerable. I have no excuse. My behaviour was indefensible. I hope you can find it in your heart to forgive me.' He hunched his shoulders in submission and met my stunned expression with a nervous smile.

Paul watched over Sally and seemed satisfied. I was lost for words and more than a little confused. An apology was the very last thing I was expecting.

'And I think you have something to say to me?' Paul eyed me sternly.

Well, there's nothing like being put on the spot, is there? Cue apology, and you'd better make it good.

'I'm sorry, Paul. I mean really sorry.' I truly meant it and tried not to wring my hands like a child. 'And it wasn't Sally's fault. It was me. I threw myself at him. I haven't had a man for so long that I—'

'He's not a man!' Paul snapped angrily. 'He's a poof. And what's more he's *my* poof.' Paul jabbed his finger into his chest and looked at me accusingly before taking a deep breath and exhaling slowly with his eyes closed, palm on his chest, to calm himself, the way he is prone to do when his patience is being tested. 'But I understand that these things happen, so we've come to make friends with you again.' He looked at the door frame defiantly and picked at an imaginary flake of paint. My sigh of relief hung heavily on the air and I stepped out to hug them both.

'But don't you *ever* do that to me again!' howled Paul, then started crying on Sally's shoulder. Sally kissed his head and nodded at me. 'We come back another time,' he said, and he led Paul towards the stairs. I closed the door quietly, leaned my back against it and exhaled.

'Bloody hell, that was freaky!' Leoni had been out of sight in the kitchen when I answered the knock and had silently edged herself towards the unusual doorstep conversation. 'What on earth was all that about?'

'Oh, nothing,' I said to her a little too casually. 'They're always having some drama or another.' I had kept the entire shameful salsa-shag incident to myself and saw no point in fessing up now. It was one of those stories that, however well presented, could only ever sound beyond appalling. Besides, why give your friends that kind of nuclear ammunition? The torment would never cease.

'Anyway, back to me.' She dismissed the other drama as far less interesting than her own. 'So this woman only goes and produces a pair of spiked Nikes from her bag and sticks them on just before the mothers' race.' Leoni is seething. 'She practically gouged my ribs out with her nails as she pulled me out of the way and, I'm sorry,' she didn't look sorry in the slightest, 'but anyone else in my position would have done exactly the same thing.'

'Well, Leoni, I've got to hand it to you.' I switched the kettle back on. 'It's usually the kids who are hauled up in front of the headmaster, not the mothers.'

Leoni pulled a little mirror out of her handbag and fiddled with her hair. 'She's said that if I replace the jacket she won't press charges.'

'So replace it.'

'Sod off!' She snapped the mirror shut and shoved it back in her bag crossly. 'I'm not bloody falling for that one. She's claiming that it was vintage something ridiculous and cost her a fortune in a secret Paris outlet on the Left Bank that nobody's ever heard of. Bloody Oxfam is what it was. Anyway, I've seen her pipsqueak husband and Marcus could knock his teeth out with a single punch.'

'So you'll have to deal with the consequences then, won't you?' I reached up for the teabags.

'Nope. And I'd like to see them try and make me. Shall we break out something cold?' Leoni pulled open the door of the fridge and let out a little gasp. 'What? No wine?' She peered closely at the empty shelves. 'You on a starvation diet or something?'

'No.' I sighed heavily. 'I'm economizing.'

'Oh God, are things really that bad?' Leoni put an arm around my shoulder.

'Don't ask.' I shook my head. 'And next time, bring a bottle, will you?'

'HELEN?' IT WAS Penny from the agency, no doubt calling up to tell me that they wanted me to dress up as a giant banana and hand out leaflets in Oxford Street again for five groats an hour. 'Something's come up which I think might be right up your street.'

'Oh yes?' I tried to sound enthusiastic and focused my mind on the unpaid bills propped up against the bread bin.

'It's working as a general assistant for a man with international business interests. He travels a lot and needs someone to organize his life for him while he's not here and accompany him on the odd occasion when the need arises. But that's not often, apparently.' I heard the faint rustling of her notes. 'He's looking for someone who can be flexible who doesn't have the usual family ties. You know the kind of thing. The hours might be a bit odd. To be honest, it sounds to me like he needs a sort of part-time paid wife-cum-mother, but the salary is very generous considering, and you were the first person that sprang to mind.'

'Really?' I flushed with pride. How incredibly flattering. I don't think I've ever been the first person to spring to mind. Not for anything. Not even once.

'Well, our younger applicants won't have the experience to deal with, er, shall we say. . .' She paused for a moment. 'He can be a bit difficult, according to his current assistant.'

'I see.' Difficult? If I can do psycho-husband-from-hell, I can certainly do difficult boss.

'Yes. They'll only come crying back to us if he so much as snaps at them, and none of our more mature women are prepared to be that flexible.' Hang on a minute. I thought I was the first person that came to mind. 'Can you get yourself to an interview this afternoon?'

I'M BRILLIANT AT interviews now. All you need to do is dress up like a headteacher, wear some extra lipstick, and nod understandingly every couple of minutes. Never say yes to the offer of a tea or coffee. If it comes out of a machine it's an undrinkable concoction stewed from burnt acorns and lavatory water, but you have to drink it anyway. Or else it's a heinous brew bitterly constructed by a disgruntled secretary who's had you in her sights from the moment you stepped into the boss's office. And if the meeting is suddenly curtailed, as so many of my earlier ones were, you end up leaving the building with a badly scalded tongue as a result of having to sling down a boiling hot drink in fifteen seconds. Say things like, 'Really?' and 'How very interesting' often, and answer direct questions about your skills with 'I'm sure I can manage that', even when you know perfectly well that you can't.

I waited anxiously for long enough to play the whole of 'Bohemian Rhapsody' in my head a couple of times over, and stared at the back of the double photograph frame standing on the otherwise clear desk. The angle prevented me being able to see the pictures, and the indiscreet glass wall offered little security for a spot of covert craning. I suspected it held a couple of Testino-quality shots of an unfeasibly beautiful wife with an assortment of high-achieving sprogs. Just when I was making a breakthrough with my attempt at CIA distance viewing, the door swung open and in strode a hefty man, I'm guessing at fiftyish give or take, hair not quite grey with vestiges of its original sandy colour, and a body showing not much regard for healthy eating. I got the impression that he probably had far more important things to do this afternoon than pow-wow with me. His suit looked a bit stressed. Undoing his top button and pulling his tie looser, he nodded me an irritable hello.

'Rick Wilton,' he said, then sat down and stifled a yawn. 'So . . .' He fumbled around shambolically for the piece of paper and looked at the top of the page, then began with a relieved, 'Helen.'

'Yes.' I answered brightly (but not as bright as my coral interview lipstick).

'No husband? No children? No ties at all? Why not?'

Great. He hasn't read the CV. Here we go again.

'I'm widowed.' I waited politely for the standard reaction. He flushed scarlet and started mumbling a pitifully clumsy apology. 'Please,' I started. 'It was a long time ago now. No harm done. Don't worry about it.' But he worried about it anyway and looked painfully embarrassed.

'Would you like a coffee?' He started searching around for any form of distraction.

'No, thank you.'

'Tea?'

'Really. I'm fine.' I wondered if I shouldn't just get my coat now rather than sit through another twenty-minute horror matinée before being ejected with just a little too much relief.

'I'm sorry. That wasn't a very good start, was it?' Nervous laugh from both of us. In a matter of seconds, the so-called great man in front of me had gone from being barely able to make time to know my name to trying really hard to make amends for his terrible faux pas. I knew why. He felt sorry for me. Everyone does when they first find out. I stopped trying to stem their bleeding some time ago. It only leads to confusion. Now I just wait for the flustering to finish. He eventually started to relax and I gave him my most efficient, warm Employ Me smile.

'What did the agency tell you about the job?'

I thought about it for a moment. 'They said that you need a woman to organize your life.' The words were out of my mouth before I had fully engaged my brain. 'I mean, they said you need someone who can be completely flexible and—'

'No. No.' He raised his hand defensively. 'If I'm honest, you were spot on the first time.' He sat back in his chair and looked at me properly. 'I'm a very successful man, Helen. In business, that is. As for my private life, well . . .' He moved a pen from left to right, then back again. 'Let's just say it hasn't been all that.' I nodded understandingly. 'I'm divorced.' I nodded again. 'Twice.' Nod nod. 'And I have five children.' My neck is starting to ache. 'Although not all of them with my two ex-wives, and some of them live abroad.'

'How very interesting,' I said.

'Yes, well. Things can get rather complicated around here, and I'm away a lot, as you can imagine.' He frowned at the top of his pen. 'It's more of a personal role than a business one. I already have a secretary who takes care of all that at the office. It's more about keeping things the way I want them at home. The personal stuff, you know.' He looked up at me briefly. 'I don't want my staff knowing everything.'

'Really?'

'And until I find and marry the next ex Mrs Wilton, I need someone who can look after all those things I don't have time for. The little extras that a man gets used to then misses. A bit like a housewife.' He winced at his mistake. 'Sorry, er, house manager, with knobs on. Think you can handle it?'

'I'm sure I can manage that.'

'Excellent.' He put his pen down with a satisfied nod and I got the distinct feeling that this housewife was definitely on the up.

Part Two

OLD DOG, NEW TRICKS

Chapter Five

ALL CHANGE

'I'M SO SORRY about what happened, Sally.' He and I were standing together in the far corner of their sitting room while Paul busied himself preparing authentic Cuban missile refreshments for the half dozen or so other guests. It was one of those let's-put-this-indiscretion-behind-us-and-have-a-few-people-over-for-drinks evenings. This was the first opportunity I'd had to talk to Sally after he and Paul had knocked on my door the other day, and it seemed to me that we had one or two issues to resolve before we could get our friendship back on an even keel. I had thought better of popping in to see him while Paul was out just in case he came home unexpectedly and found me, well, *there*.

'It wasn't your fault,' Sally assured me softly. 'It was me.'

'No, not at all,' I insisted. 'You don't even *like* women. I threw myself at you like a harlot and you were kind enough to well, you know . . .' I made a rapid circular gesture with my hand, partly to indicate the unspeakable act and partly to encourage him to wind up this area of the conversation quickly before Paul got back from the kitchen.

Sally put his hand on my arm and checked that there was no one within earshot. 'I put a Quaalude in the margarita jug,' he whispered.

'You did *what*?'

'Well, you don't think that I could sleep with a woman without getting a little high, do you?' Sally leaned in to my ear discreetly. 'I know it sounds ridiculous, but all my life I wanted to have a little baby, a beautiful child of my own I could raise with pride who would call me Papa.' He looked up at the ceiling fan and touched his chest with feeling, my bemused expression probably betraying that, from where I was standing, the conversation had just gone from slightly awkward to totally surreal. 'And it's never going to happen unless I sleep with a woman.' He shrugged his explanation. 'So now and again that's what I do.' Sally looked ashamed and shook his head sadly. 'But I only sleep with someone who is very nice. A respectable woman who I know would be a good mother to my child. Not just *anyone*.' He switched the weight on his hips and smiled tenderly, embarrassed at having just given away the high esteem in which he held me.

'No,' I said. 'I mean what's a Quaalude?'

JULIA LET HERSELF into the flat, slamming the door hard behind her, and delivered her bombshell with a face like thunder.

'Sara's getting married.'

Leoni and I were propped up on the high stools in the kitchen, planning her next move in the Oxfam Jacketgate scandal. We greeted Julia's news with a chorus of 'No!!!'

'I kid you not.' Julia's dark expression was not even slightly amused as she stood there, stony faced and more than a little flustered. 'And that's not the half of it. Guess who she's marrying?'

'That's not very charitable,' I said to her. 'We all know that Ian's a bit of a knob, but I'm sure once we get to know him better he'll improve upon—'

Julia cut me off. 'Dudley.'

Our jaws dropped in unison and Leoni and I stared at each other.

'*Dudley?*' We didn't mean to squeal like guinea pigs, but sudden shock newsflashes do tend to have that effect.

Julia threw her handbag onto the worktop and

stared back at us knowingly. 'Which means she's no doubt planning to swan off and live the life of Riley, dropping me right in it.'

Well. There's nothing like a nice juicy nugget of twenty-four carat gossip to set the cat amongst the pigeons on an otherwise slow Saturday afternoon. Leoni had brought Little Miss Millie along to put her through module one of how-to-spend-the-afternoon-gossiping-and-drinking-Pimms-with-your-girlfriends. She considered this essential basic training for any daughter of hers, although at just six years old, Millie clearly found it all rather boring and kept asking when they were going home.

'I'm stunned,' I said. 'Of all the people in all the world, I would never in a million years have put those two together. I mean, if I thought Dudley was dull, then surely he wouldn't even register on Sara's radar?'

'They've been having it off on the side for months,' Julia revealed bitterly. 'At it like rabbits apparently and completely nuts about each other. Sara told him that she wasn't even slightly interested in leaving Ian for him, because she knew he had absolutely no intention of ever getting married, so there was no future in it for her. She said he'd have to make do with sharing her.'

'I don't believe it,' said Leoni. 'The devious little . . .'

'Dudley went out of his mind with jealousy and bloody well asked her to marry him. You should see the size of the ring. She's christened it Gibraltar and declared it an independent tax haven.'

'What about poor old Ian?' Like we cared all of a sudden, but my sympathies always tend to fall on the side of the injured party.

'Sara sent him a text and told him to bugger off.' Julia helped herself to a sip from Leoni's glass and delicately picked out one of the apple slices.

'That's our Sara,' said Leoni. 'Ever the diplomat.'

Chapter Six

IT'S WORK, JIM, BUT NOT AS WE KNOW IT

FIRST DAYS AT a new job are always a bit of a baptism by fire. That feeling that everyone is staring at you and making bitchy comments about your clothes/hair/shoes, or, worse still, about you. Not being able to remember a single person's name despite being told several times over. Then you eventually build up sufficient courage to have a stab at addressing someone correctly and go wading in with a confident 'Morning, Maureen', only to find out later that her name's Marisa and she's having a love tryst with the head of human resources and suddenly you're doing the Walk of Shame again after being fired for insubordination.

Monday had come around not a moment too soon according to the bank statement that landed heavily on the mat the preceding Saturday morning. I had got up earlier than usual to assemble my executive assistant outfit (sombre, but not quite funereal) and put my best sensibly heeled foot forward. The 'office' I had been dispatched to turned out to be a Tardis of a house somewhere behind Victoria in a potentially very nice street that had up-and-coming written all over it despite the peeling plasterwork and political graffiti.

Rick answered the door in a dark-blue towelling dressing gown, cigar in hand. As I chirruped my most efficient good morning and waited for him to invite me in, he launched into an aggressive tirade about why it wasn't good enough and who the fuck did I think he was, and did I think he had the c-word written on his forehead, and if not, why was I talking to him like one? The blood drained from my face as he stormed away. It wasn't until he went off into another toxic stream of barbaric expletives that I realized he was talking to somebody else through an ugly electronic carbuncle attached to his left ear. I demonstrated my incredible initiative by walking in confidently and closing the door behind me, then stood there in the hallway like an obsolete spare part.

The heated rally continued, leaving me hanging

around conspicuously for seemingly ages. I spotted what looked suspiciously like a bachelor's kitchen (a sterile, untouched operating theatre of stainless steel with floor-to-ceiling gadgets and not a scrap of food in sight), so really pushed the boat out and went off in search of his kettle. He saw me from the open doorway and gave me a thumbs up.

'MUST THINK I'M effing stupid,' Rick announced as he came striding into the kitchen fifteen minutes later. I'd have given it a quick once-over with a bit of detergent and a damp sponge if I could have found a single speck of dust, and hadn't yet managed to pluck up the courage to come out and show myself.

'I see you've found the kitchen, which is a good start. You'll need to learn how to use that thing over there.' He pointed at a bus-sized Gaggia coffee machine. 'And you'll have to make yourself a duplicate of my diary, both business and social, so that you know what to—' His phone blared the James Bond theme into the room. 'Hello? Chris! Yes, mate.' And he disappeared out of the door again shouting like a barrow boy.

I waited patiently for him to finish the half-hour conversation. 'I thought your assistant was going to be here for the first week to show me the ropes,' I levelled.

'Er, yes.' Rick scratched his head and rumpled his

face. 'She told me to fuck off actually, so it's in at the deep end for you, I'm afraid.' I tried not to look as alarmed as I felt. 'But I'm sure you'll get the hang of it.' His phone rang again loudly and he glanced at the screen before yelling, 'Spud! Where have you been all my life?'

'I THINK I'D FEEL a lot better if I actually knew what I was supposed to be doing.' Leoni's kitchen was filling with smoke fast as she incinerated another batch of bacon. 'I like to get the rind really crispy,' she said distractedly as she squashed the sizzling rashers down hard with the back of a heat-deformed fish slice. 'There's nothing worse than a soggy bacon sarnie. Here.' She waved a hand over her shoulder. 'Pass me those mushrooms.' I held out the little blue plastic punnet and watched her pull the skin off a couple while the fat caught fire in the pan. 'Perfect,' she said, hauling the flaming frying pan off the stove and setting it down on the wet draining board with a raging hiss. 'Avocado with that?'

'Oh, go on then.'

'So, what's this Rick bloke like?'

I pictured my curious new boss with the ruddy complexion and tried to paint an accurate picture. 'Chaotic. Difficult. Fat.' Sounded about right.

Leoni bit into her sandwich and seemed oblivious to

the steady trail of buttery mayonnaise dripping into her lap. 'Yeah,' she attempted with her mouth full. 'But you haven't been fired yet, have you? So what's the problem?'

I eyed the terrifying carbonized snack on the plate she slapped in front of me and wondered if the enamel on my teeth was up to it. 'I'm just getting a bit fed up with the phone calls at all hours of the night and day asking me where his underpants are and checking which woman he's supposed to be meeting.'

'He phones you to ask where his pants are?'

'Well, no, not literally, but you get the general drift. He's got me out buying presents for his girlfriends and lying on the telephone about where he is and dealing with screaming ex-wives and trying to communicate with a communist cleaner who doesn't speak a word of English and mutters to herself threateningly all day. I'm sure she shouldn't be at large in the community. God knows what goes on in her head.'

'Really? Bloody fantastic!' Leoni absent-mindedly squeezed a dollop of tomato ketchup on the side of her plate and dipped the remaining corner of the sandwich into it, before finishing the last quarter in a single mouthful and mumbling, 'Sounds really interesting.'

'I'm not so sure I agree with you. Although the money's been a godsend. At least I'm no longer staring vagrancy in the face.'

'Thank heaven for small mercies,' she said, polishing

off her Scooby snack with a noisy slurp of truckers' tea. 'I don't mind telling you, Helen, we were all pretty worried about you for a moment there.'

The back door opened with a crash and in fell the twins, locked in some kind of double Nelson, ankles bound together with a school tie, and trying to take each other apart limb from limb. Leoni ignored them and raised her voice to be heard above the din, but I lost track of the conversation anyway and thought it pointless to try and compete with the noise.

'Mum? Can we get a dog?' William had Joshua pinned to the wall by his shoulders while Josh kicked out wildly at William's free leg.

Leoni bawled at them. 'Does it know how to cook lasagne and clean the bathtub?'

The boys exchanged a Mum's Gone Mad glance, saying 'No,' and 'Don't be so stupid, Mum.' She dropped the plates into the dishwasher and let the door swing back with a glass-shattering slam.

'Well, there's your answer then.'

The boys hung their heads like a pair of snipped marionettes, moaned bitterly and protested about the unfairness of it all, and I got up and made my excuses, declining Leoni's offer of a lift to the Tube station with three screaming, fighting children strapped in around me.

*

'HELEN? IT'S RICK.'

The glowing green numerals on the bedside alarm clock yawningly blinked two a.m. What now? Lost your toothbrush? Run out of cigars? Dead prostitute in a hotel room? I rubbed the sleep from my eyes and propped myself up on one elbow.

'Are you all right?' I asked. He sounded panicky, if not a little the worse for wear.

'Er, well, yes and no. I'm all right. The car's not all right, and I need to get both myself and it out of here pronto.' These strange late-night conversations no longer surprised me, and I waited to hear the set of no doubt bizarre instructions that were certain to follow. 'You drive?' he asked.

'Yes, but I don't have a car.'

'Good. Now listen.' The listen came out more like *lishen*, and he hushed his voice down to a whisper. 'My car's parked on a double yellow just around the corner from Green Street. I've left the keys on top of the tyre under the front wheel arch on the driver's side. Can you come and move it and stick it in a car park or something?'

I should probably mention at this juncture that I had felt obliged to speak to Rick within the first week of my new role to point out that there was a big difference between flexible hours and taking the piss. He had responded by upping my salary by a few thousand quid, and I had sold my soul to the devil. Pulling on my coat and searching around for my keys, I reasoned that getting up in the middle of the night to shift the boss's car off a double yellow line was at least a welcome change from the hysterical phone calls from jilted women and playing find-Rick's-lost-property after a crazed night out somewhere in deepest Hoxton with a teenage stick insect he'd picked up on the internet.

I didn't mind really. It was nice to get out of the house with a sense of purpose. Thinking about it, I supposed that my life prior to the direct hit by Lomax's cruise missile had become overly comfortable, slothful even. Having the freedom to spend each day any way you want to does actually become a bit samey after a while, and I'd had to go to great efforts to structure myself into some kind of routine, no matter how loose. Up, tea, bath, a bit of rubbishy daytime television, make something complicated to eat, go out if I could be bothered, that kind of thing. Had I known it wasn't going to last I'd probably have made better use of my time. Indeed, had I realized I'd be queuing up at the local Job Centre Plus with the skills set of an air-fed house plant, I might have trained to do something a little more impressive.

The taxi rumbled comfortably along, the soothing sound of its diesel engine resonating around the empty streets, and rocked ridiculously from side to side as it hit the cobblestones in one of the narrow Dickensian short cuts. I pulled up my coat collar and glanced sideways out of the window, imagining that I was on an important mission for MI5 as we slowed down and I bought the driver off on the next corner with a used note. Squinting into the dimly lit middle distance, it took a few moments for the sight to register.

So, crashing your car into a concrete bollard in the middle of the night, then running off and abandoning it is what you call parked, is it, Rick? The car was half on, half off the pavement, and the front offside headlight was smashed and partially hanging down with a spaghetti of wires spilling out from the fractured bodywork. He had come a cropper in one of those tiny little side roads built to accommodate horses' hooves rather than Maseratis, which only a lunatic would try and take at any more than ten miles an hour.

I found the keys where Rick said they would be, and spent the next God knows how long trying to decipher the bridge of the Starship Enterprise. When I had eventually sussed out how the ignition worked, the engine sprang agonizingly into life with a teeth-shattering rattle. As I gingerly reversed the screeching metal carcass away from the broken bollard, the front bumper fell off and clanged into the road. Well, that's just bloody marvellous. What am I supposed to do now? Retrieve it and try to shove the thing into the back seat of the car? Leave it where it is? Perhaps not. Someone might come along and have a fatal accident. I decided best to go and get it.

Had I noticed the policeman loitering with intent next to the car I would have taken more care swinging the door open. It caught him square in the guts.

'Right! Get out of the car!' he commanded, roughly grabbing hold of my coat collar to drag me out and pointing a limp-wristed martial law signal at his colleague in the patrol vehicle that had snaked up silently behind me. Copper number two leapt out from behind the wheel and piled towards us with grave determination. The next thing I knew I was being pressed up painfully against the side of Rick's car having the cuffs slapped on (proper chafing government issue) and my rights read out.

'I'm arresting you on suspicion of dangerous driving and attempting to leave the scene of an accident,' said the over-excited constable before parroting the standard caution. His burly number two with the red beard and grim expression was trying to get a good look inside the vehicle while holding onto my arm.

'But . . .' I tried to turn around to face him but was forced to resume the position by Captain Birdseye.

'And resisting arrest,' he added before radioing in the registration number in fluent Romeo Kilo Quebec. I looked down at my pink fluffy slippers and cursed myself for having left my nightie on under my coat.

*

I DON'T KNOW IF you've ever had the pleasure of being carted off to the nearest nick in the early hours of the morning to be breathalysed and manhandled into a cell. It's quite an unusual experience, and not one that I would readily recommend. They smell worse than a men's public latrine, echo with inhuman wailing and banging noises, and all the officers seem to think they're auditioning for *The Bill*, acting like overcooked hams and delivering predictable lines like 'We've got a right one here, Dave.'

During my interview (which the monstrously rude younger officer had obviously elevated to my *interrogation* in his alarmingly dramatic head), my perfectly reasonable explanation had been dismissed as 'a likely story', so I pointed out patiently that I clearly wasn't driving around central London rolling drunk as the breathalyser was green, and it was highly unlikely that I would have chosen to go out 'on a job' in my slippers, anyway.

My normally faultlessly polite manner when dealing with anyone in a position of authority (or any kind of uniform at all for that matter) was eventually worn so thin in the face of a pugnacious little upstart with the IQ of a bathmat, that I finally folded my arms and refused to answer any more of his outrageous questions. 'This your pimp's car, is it?' (he was salivating), 'Who's he supplying the drugs to?' (they claimed to have found a half-smoked joint in the ashtray), before I was led back to my revoltingly stinky accommodation and left to sweat it out. The door slammed shut and my mind turned to Steve McQueen bouncing a base-ball against the wall, hand in glove, as he settled into the cooler for another month whistling Dixie.

HOURS LATER I HEARD the big key turn in the heavy metal door and looked up wearily from the edge of the bunk to see a slightly dishevelled, unshaven man stand-ing there beside the kindly duty officer who had kept me company. He had been quite sweet really, bringing me cups of tea now and then and smiling at me not to worry. Showed me some pictures of his wife and kids at one point. God, they were an ugly family.

'Helen.' The man with the stubbly chin stretched a hand towards me and gave mine a cursory shake. 'I'm Michael Rowles, Rick's lawyer. There seems to have been a bit of a misunderstanding. If you can bear to hang on there for a little longer I'll see if we can't get this all straightened out and then we can get you out of here.' Thirty minutes later I had been sprung, and emerged blinkingly into the early morning light with my impressive brief by my side. Michael hailed a pass-ing taxi and opened the door to help me in.

'I lost the contents of my pockets somewhere along the way,' I told him apologetically. 'I'm afraid I haven't got any money.' He looked up to the sky, pulled a black wallet from his inside pocket and handed me a twenty. The driver took me home in silence, dropped me off outside my house and eyed my less-than-fresh appearance suspiciously, raising an eyebrow at my inky fingertips. I squinted at him menacingly and chose not to leave a tip.

STIRRING THE ICE in my water glass, I looked up at Rick from the menu. 'I didn't know what else to say.'

Rick had insisted on taking me out for lunch when I failed to turn up to work for the next couple of days. I had been far too cross to return his calls initially, but after the first flush of anger settled, I was actually feeling criminally pleased with myself for having told the police where to shove it and spending the best part of a whole night locked up in the slammer. Makes you feel like one of the hard nuts at school. Perhaps inside each one of us there is a tiny little anarchist just dying to get out. The enormous floral apology that Rick had sent to the flat the next day was nothing short of film-star fabulous.

After some consideration, I had decided that a whispered public sacking in an expensive restaurant was probably going to be less humiliating than another of those it's-not-working-out-and-here's-your-P45 conversations from a smug sub-manager in a shared office.

My plan was to head him off at the pass the moment the conversation started edging towards the inevitable bullet and resign first, but hopefully not before pudding. I had my eye on a slice of the New York baked vanilla cheesecake. With lashings of extra thick cream. After all, I may have to prepare for lean times ahead.

'That was a close call,' he said, motioning to the waiter for service. 'I told plod I'd had a couple of sherbets to steady my nerves after the accident.' He had also said that he must have been suffering from temporary concussion because all he could think about was getting himself to hospital, so he had staggered out of the car and put himself into a passing taxi then phoned me because he was worried that it would be causing a dangerous obstruction. I looked at him disapprovingly.

'Oh, come on, Helen!' he implored me. 'Don't look at me like that! I get enough of those lecturing glares from my two ex-wives. You're supposed to be on my side, remember?'

'You put me in a very difficult position.' I wasn't going to let him off the hook that lightly. Maybe I'd order an ounce of Beluga and kick him right in the wallet. He looked remorseful, then brightened instantly as he played his unbeatable trump card.

'How about another rise?'

I narrowed my eyes at his vulgarity. Ker-ching.

Chapter Seven

CROUCHING TIGER, HIDDEN DRAG QUEEN

'I'VE LEFT HIM.' Leoni's voice distorted its way through the intercom and I buzzed her in immediately. I stood and waited at the open door while she huffed her way up, dragging something heavily behind her, bumping it along the stairs with the reassuring clank of full glass bottles. Maybe she'd brought the body with her and the wherewithal for us to construct a do-it-yourself acid bath.

'Whatever's the matter?' I completely forgot about the homemade avocado and oatmeal mulch mask packed onto my face, met Leoni on the landing in my dressing gown and took the bulging case from her hands. She went into the sitting room ahead of me and flumped heavily on the sofa, wearily pulling the Hermès scarf from her neck.

'I can't live like that any more.' She looked up at me. 'My life is just a living hell and Marcus refuses to listen to anything I say, so he can bloody well do it himself and see how long he lasts.' She couldn't be serious. But the luggage and the look on her face indicated that she was. 'I'm just a bloody unpaid lackey with no rights and it does my head in. The same thing, day in, day out. It's so boring. *I'm* so boring. I'd rather be dead than live the rest of my life like this.'

I didn't want to sound like a killjoy, but couldn't help but ask: 'What about the kids?'

'They're in Cornwall with Granny Meatloaf for a couple of weeks.' She kicked off her shoes and started rubbing her feet.

'Yes, but I mean *what about the kids*?'

'What about them? What about *me*? My whole house is a filthy, disgusting tip all of the time, no matter what I do. It's like painting the bloody Forth Bridge. It stinks of feet and farts, no one gives a toss about my feelings, and I am *so* sick and tired of saying the same old thing over and over again.' She exhaled loudly. 'Well, they can all just piss off. I'm not doing it any more. I should go on *Mastermind*. Name? Leoni. Specialist subject? Wasting my breath.'

This was obviously not a good time to try and have a rational conversation. Leoni rummaged around in her big straw basket and produced an enormous bottle of wine and a corkscrew. 'I assume you've still got glasses or did you have to sell them on eBay?' She got up and wandered off to the kitchen, returning a few moments later with a couple of tumblers, an open bag of Doritos and the little bowl I had left on the side by the fridge.

'This dip's a bit of an acquired taste, isn't it?' She screwed up her face and I pointed at mine.

HALF A LITRE LATER, it transpired that Marcus had refused to agree to get a nanny in to help, and told her that if millions of other mothers managed without a hired hand *and* went out to work, then she was obviously quite seriously lacking in the basic housewife-and-mothering skills department. Inadequate, selfish and spoilt. That's what he had called her. Leoni described how the red mist had descended. She had spent hours cooking that buttering up dinner, and it broke her heart to pour it over Marcus's head. The ensuing category five row had destroyed virtually everything in their kitchen and dining room, and she admitted somewhat ruefully through a nervous giggle that she had gone for his hair at one point (Marcus is very sensitive about his maturing hairline), ripping some of it out by the roots.

'I just lost it,' she said. 'Well, let's see him deal with it. I bet there's a nanny there within twenty-four hours of the kids getting home, and I'm not going back until he's got one.'

'Does he know where you are?'

'It's okay.' Leoni poured herself another glass of wine. 'He'll never take me alive.'

IT'S ONE THING to enjoy the company of a good friend, but having them come to live with you is quite a different kettle of fish altogether. I wouldn't go as far as to say that a friend in need is a bloody nuisance, but it was mighty strange to have someone else living in my space. Take eating, for instance. It goes from grabbing yourself something easy when you fancy it, to 'Are you hungry?' or 'What are we going to do about dinner?' All of a sudden you can't just do whatever you want when you want. It just doesn't feel, well, *polite*.

More worrying perhaps was the realization that Leoni was straining at the leash so ferociously that she was in serious danger of doing something rash. She had been captivated by Sara's methodology in stalking and staking a suitable husband, and was now hell-bent on snaring herself a magnificent new man to whisk her away from all this. She would deny the existence of a husband or children and call herself something intriguingly exotic like Petronella de Havilland. Romance was bound to ensue, and she would never have to so much as look at another pair of stinky sock balls ever again. The separation from her children would be painful at first, but she would get over it in time with the help of her spectacular lover and no upper limit on her credit card.

With me out at work for at least part of most days, I shuddered to think what she might be getting up to in my absence. Rearranging my closet (after trying everything on) was pretty high up on her list of amusements, but she kept suffering anxiety attacks about her rebellious walkout, which she habitually quelled with a couple of enormous Camparis stacked with plenty of ice. As she rightly said, it beats sticking it in a dishcloth and holding it across your throbbing frontal lobes.

THE NEW HAIRDO was the first sign of trouble. I went out the next morning after saying bye to Leoni with the neat, shoulder-length chestnutty hair, and arrived home later that same day to find a blunt-cut copper and blonde wino collapsed on the sofa. Thank God she had gone to one of the better salons, and what could have been a shocking disaster had actually turned out sensationally well.

The best news was that Leoni seemed to have brought her entire housekeeping budget with her, so the leviathan fridge was once again creaking under the strain of female-orientated chilled supplies. Cheese, wine, chocolatey things, and a bag of salad in case we should get spot-checked by the vitamin police. I banned her from the cooker after she managed to set fire to the kitchen roll and its holder while boiling midnight noodles. (Bear in mind that this is the woman who makes grilled cheese sandwiches with an iron.) She's a terrible cook, and I suppose it was nice for me to have someone to feed again. We made quite a cosy pair, in an odd-couple sort of way.

On the second morning I came into the kitchen to answer the telephone and caught Leoni suicidally trying to unwedge a waffle from the live toaster with a large bread knife as I gave my distracted hello. She looked apologetic, shrugged her shoulders and gave up on trying to hide the evidence. I held the receiver towards her. 'It's Marcus.'

She fixed me with a determined expression, got up from her stool, wiped her hands and came to take the phone from my palm. Covering the mouthpiece for a moment, she took a deep breath, then put the telephone to her ear, her eyes locked with mine. 'Have we got a nanny?' she demanded. He can't have been more than three words into his reply before she hung up on him.

LEONI AND I WERE lounging around together on the sofa that evening basking in the armchair anthropology of *Big Brother* and wondering how on earth the programme makers had managed to unearth such a grotesque mix of freaks and flakes. I'd never seen it before, but Leoni was well and truly hooked and the nightly parade of damaged under-developed adults suffering from ADHD had been a non-negotiable part of her terms for becoming my new, self-appointed flatmate. Perhaps all the infantile arguing and screaming over nothing made her feel at home. An urgent pounding on the door interrupted our scathing commentary. Leoni got up and went to the spyhole, taking the little bowl of peanuts with her.

'It's bloody Tinkerbell from upstairs,' she whispered loudly.

'Well, open it!' I said, and went to the door to join her.

Paul lurched in the moment he heard the latch go, and flustered an excitable, 'Get dressed! We're going out!'

'Paul,' I started. This had happened before. I don't know what they get up to, those two, but sometimes one or the other will arrive on my doorstep in the middle of the night and insist that it's the perfect time to paint the town red.

'Paul, it's nearly eleven o'clock and we were just thinking about turning in for the night.'

Paul noticed Leoni standing behind the door munching nuts, then gave me a little inquisitive smile.

'You remember my friend Leoni,' I reintroduced them.

'Of course. Great *hair*!' He reached out and squeezed her hand. 'Having a little quality girlie time together, are we?' He tried to look past us to see if there was anyone else in the party.

'Leoni's staying with me for a little while to get a break from home, and she needs to catch up with some well-earned beauty sleep,' I explained by way of an excuse.

Leoni stopped eating. 'Do I bollocks?' she snapped. 'Give us five minutes.'

'WHAT'S THAT YOU'RE drinking?' I returned from the packed ladies' room to find Leoni propped up against the bar, nursing a family-sized green cocktail with a huge slice of pineapple impaled on the edge of the pink sugar-frosted glass.

'Flash,' she said, manoeuvring the two long-stemmed straws back into her mouth. We were all squashed into a tiny, dimly lit, smoke-filled cellar, together with a twelve-piece salsa band, a raging pizza oven and a couple of hundred people who had apparently dressed for the Rio Carnival, most of them transvestites, and all of them far more attractive than your average female.

'I reckon we're just about the only women in here.' Leoni was scanning the room.

'Looks like it,' I said. 'But I wouldn't bank on pulling if I were you.'

'Don't just stand there!' Paul sashayed to my side, spilling some of the orange liquid he was carrying in an enormous glass salad bowl. 'Dance!' He stretched his arms and shimmied his shoulders to show off his red and gold flamenco sleeves to their full ruffling effect.

Leoni grabbed at my arm. 'Helen! Look!' she said. 'Over there in the corner!' I squinted in the direction she was fixed on but could see nothing. 'Through my fingers, Tonto,' she said, and held her fingers in a V in front of my eyes. The thick smoke burned my viewfinder as I squinted across the dingy room. There was no one there I could recognize, and the back of some bloke's head. He turned profile.

'Oh, my goodness. Is that Dudley?'

'Never mind that. Look who he's with!'

Leoni and I looked at each other. 'No way!'

*

'My ears are still ringing.' Leoni sat on the lid of the loo, pulling at her lobes anxiously while I brushed my teeth. 'Do you think he saw us?'

I shook my head and rinsed my mouth, reaching for the towel she was holding. 'I doubt he would have noticed a bomb going off.'

'Do you think we should tell Sara?'

'Absolutely not. It's none of our business.'

Leoni raised her eyebrows at me, unconvinced.

The weekend arrived just in time. Leoni abandoned her room as soon as she heard me moving about, crept into mine and slid into bed beside me for a tea-fuelled slobs-R-us lie-in.

'Let's put on Saturday morning cooking,' she said, reaching for the remote control and wrecking the peace of the big newspapers with BBC2 at full volume. After my initial protests, I relaxed into it and we lay back and watched two hours of notable telly chefs chopping Kung Fu vegetables and knocking up various artery-clogging delicacies. By midday we were half starved out of our minds, having been tormented with a pornographic pageant of Delia's stickiest puddings. We headed for our lunch appointment with ravenous appetites and grumbling tummies.

*

'AREN'T YOU THRILLED for me?' Sara arrived late at the restaurant. We (being me, Leoni and Julia) had all got so fed up with waiting for her that we were already halfway through our entrées.

'We've nearly finished,' said Julia without apology. 'Do you want to order something?'

'I don't eat food any more,' Sara announced. 'I intend to look spectacular on my wedding day, so the only calories I consume now are the ones in the plastic bubbles around my mineral supplements.'

'That's me screwed, then,' Leoni observed dryly as she piled her remaining piece of bread with half an inch of butter. The date had been set for the first available Saturday at St Mary's, just three weeks away, and Sara had that peculiar air about her which told all those who crossed her path that she didn't have a care in the world.

Leoni kept giving me furtive glances then doing Action Man eagle eyes towards Sara. The wine was already breaking down her flimsy discretion barriers and I knew it was only a matter of time before she sang like a canary about our illicit Dudley-spotting session. You could tell from her face that she was just dying to let it all come tumbling out. I placed my hand over Leoni's, although I would have been far happier putting it directly over her mouth.

'We couldn't be more pleased for you,' I beamed at Sara on behalf of us all, squeezing Leoni's hand until I felt her knuckles crack. She squirmed under the pain with a shocked but fixed smile.

'Absolutely!' Leoni's shrill expression began to take on a twisted grimace. She seemed to have got the message loud and clear so I relaxed my grip.

I LOVE A GOOD WEDDING. There's a big patch of life's great diary where nuptial invitations are pretty thin on the ground. A whole lot come winging through when all your friends start getting married in their twenties, then you have to wait for a few divorces and the inevitable second-time-arounders (usually a lot less fun as they're done on a pinched budget as a result of the crippling settlement), after which there's nothing for it but to hang on until everyone's kids start getting married. You then take the place of the next generation up, and the whole cycle kicks off again. One's life as a wedding guest goes through a series of stages, ranging from too young to remember, to too old to dance. The grannies in the room always provide some decent entertainment, either by losing their teeth in the trifle or rolling out carefully guarded family secrets to complete strangers because they don't recognize anyone any more anyway, and are working on the assumption that everyone here must surely be a relation.

'How many people have you got coming?' Leoni asked.

'Don't know. Don't care. My mum's doing everything. She and Dad are in seventh heaven since Dudley insisted on paying for the whole shooting match. I think my mum's fallen in love with him. She hangs on his every word and laughs like a hyena at the smallest remark.' Sara's fork wandered towards Leoni's plate. 'It's a bit embarrassing really.' Leoni discreetly shielded a potato with her hand and effected a coughing diversion as Sara sneaked it away.

'And what about your new in-laws?' I asked.

'Oh. They haven't spoken to Dudley for years.' She popped the potato into her mouth and smiled. 'They're really religious and denounced him publicly for his capitalist pagan lifestyle a long time ago. Wanted him to be a minister, apparently.'

Julia sprayed wine everywhere and launched into the most raucous laugh, before breathing in too quickly and choking. She held her hand up to indicate that she was okay and dabbed the tears from her eyes with the edge of her napkin. 'Now I've heard everything,' she spluttered with a smile.

'TRY THAT ONE!' Leoni pointed to a purple mink-trimmed monstrosity perched high up on one of the displays as she balanced her own wide-brimmed lace-edged spectacular on her head. We were playing that perennial favourite of games, Find the Most Ridiculous Hat in the Store, and rudely ignoring the two sales assistants who very openly wished that we would just get out. I pulled down the furry monster and plonked it like a tea cosy on top of my head. We all fell about laughing and I won the heat hands down.

'It's nice to be out shopping again, isn't it?' I nudged Leoni and she grinned at me.

'And it's nice for me to be out at all,' she replied. 'Honestly, Helen. I've been having such a great time over the last few days. Not having to think about all that shit at home or deal with a screaming rabble. I actually feel human again, for the first time since I can't remember when. All hell's broken loose with Marcus, and the parents are having kittens.' She gave me a triumphant nod and I tried to disguise my look of concern. 'It's all right, you know.' She put her arm through mine. 'I'm just teaching him a lesson. Should have done it years ago.'

'I can't believe how skint I am,' I said, picking up the sleeve of an unremarkable dress and clucking at the exorbitant cost on the ticket. 'Now all I can think about when I look at a price tag is whether or not I want it more than I want to eat for the next fortnight.'

'I'd be gutted,' said Leoni sympathetically. 'That was like winning the lottery and losing the ticket.'

'I know.' I nodded. 'Makes me wish I'd just blown the whole lot on clothes, fast cars and loose men. There must be a lesson in there somewhere.'

'Yeah,' she said. 'Spend it all on yourself as fast as you can. Come on!' She tugged on my arm. 'Let's pretend you're still loaded.'

Chapter Eight

HOUSEWIFE AHOY

YOU WOULD HAVE thought that I might have learned by now not to count my chickens or tell God my plans. As the dust settled around my latest incarnation, I found myself spending a great deal of my downtime reflecting upon the events that had got me here. Sometimes you only feel the deep impact of a sudden shockwave when the danger has passed. That terrible sense of what might have happened had you been placed a mere degree to the left or right a split second sooner or later. You realize that you've survived, but still the tremors of the near miss rumble a sinister warning around your rudely disturbed roots.

Not only had Lomax neatly swindled me out of my

entire fortune, there was also the not insignificant matter of the gargantuan overdraft that had resulted while I blithely went about my daily business in blissful ignorance of the imminent crisis heading my way. Thank God I had bought the flat outright, although that had been more by luck than judgement, because I hadn't understood the convoluted scheme that Lomax had suggested instead of a straight cash purchase. But my status at the bank had been swiftly demoted from VIP customer to major pain in the backside when the debacle was properly unveiled, and the Mexican stand-off finally resulted in my having to take out a mortgage on the flat. It felt like a twenty-year sentence. I'd be on nodding terms with the prospect of a free bus pass before I saw the light of day again, working on the chain gang to bring home the tendercure. It was the bitterest of pills.

Had I wondered a year ago where I would be twelve months hence, I think this would have been the very last pickle I could have guessed at. But despite everything here I was, alive and almost well, and inside, for the first time, there was something else. I wasn't afraid any more.

'WHAT DO YOU think of her?' Rick shouted. I looked up to see him kitted out in full naval regalia with white rubber-rimmed plimsolls, arms proudly held wide open on the deck of a fifty-something footer steel ketch with a gleaming black hull. I was standing on the jetty, open-mouthed and completely unprepared for whatever fiasco today was obviously about to bring. The garbled text message that had beeped its way to my phone the night before had told me to get the first train to Portsmouth that morning, and I'd then had to decrypt the rest of the directions myself after the taxi ran out of land mass. Nobody mentioned anything about a bloody boat and I'd been wandering around for ages looking for a pub or café called the Sundowner. My empty stomach rumbled impatiently reminding me of my red-eyed five o'clock start.

'Meet my new wife!' he announced with a grin. 'I'm through with women for good. From now on, it's just me and this baby!' Rick stuck the over-chewed cigar back in his beaming mouth and motioned at me to hurry aboard, or whatever the appropriate nautical term is.

'Come and have a look below deck and I'll tell you what we're gonna do,' and he disappeared backwards down the steps that led into the galley and living area, issuing instructions while I was still trying to negotiate my way down the awkward flight in a knee-length linen skirt and a wholly unsuitable pair of cream slingbacks.

'I'm gonna rip all this shit out, see.' He started waving his arms around. 'Then we're gonna do it all up in cherry wood with a big sound system.' I wondered if I should get a notepad out, 'and that bit up there in front I want a big . . .' what, Jolly Roger? '. . . bed and a power shower with all the gadgets.' He stopped and strained his ears with a frown. 'What's that noise?'

'I'm sorry,' I apologized. 'It's me. I haven't had anything to eat yet today.'

'What? Well, why didn't you say something?'

THE YACHT CLUB at the end of the marina was filling up rapidly with people who must all buy their outfits from the same place. Men with leather faces stood alongside pretty young things in not much clothing and waiting-list handbags, telling salty dog tales about hedge funds and helicopters they used to know. The girls smiled a lot without speaking and checked out each other's bleached teeth and silicone. Rick and I were shown to a table by the panoramic window overlooking the harbour and he craned his neck to check that his new toy was still there and admire its curves.

'Bring us a bottle of Cristal,' Rick yelled at the nearest waiter, then leaned towards me. 'I feel like celebrating.'

And celebrate he did. Rick proceeded to get completely plastered and poured out his whole slightly dodgy life story to me, detailing the rackets he had started running while still at school, and the double life he had managed to fabricate while married to one woman and expecting his second child with another. He'd made his first fortune trading Italian cars, put some money into a board game that took off like Ariadne and gave him the kind of return people like you and I can only dream about, and now got involved in pretty much any deal that took his fancy. Nice work if you can get it. He'd set his aged mother up for life and had never really got over her untimely death while playing poker on an American cruise ship five years ago.

'She loved her cards, the old biddy,' he said respectfully, with a small sniffle. 'I did warn her about cheating but she insisted it was all part of the fun. They never should have tried to tackle her like that. Where else was she going to run except over the side?' Rick pulled at the hairs on the back of his hand. 'Still. It's the way she would have wanted it.'

'She was lucky to have such a good-hearted son,' I reassured him. 'And I can see where you get your chutzpah from.' Rick's head was starting to dangle a bit and he was having trouble relighting his cigar, match swaying in his hand. I took the burnt-out stick from his fingers, struck another and held it steadily for him.

'I've got the Midas touch,' he hiccupped from behind a big puff of smoke. 'Bloody shame every woman I touch turns into a gold digger.'

'I'm sure it's not that bad.' I patted his hand sympathetically for a moment. 'You just haven't met the right one yet. You'll see.'

'But what about you?' he moaned, suddenly springing up in his seat. 'You meet mister right, get married, and before you know it, bang, it's game over. Wallop. Gone. Just like that.'

'Well.' I played with my glass uncomfortably. 'I was married for quite a long while, you know. It's not as though we hadn't had our time together.' I cast my mind back. 'We certainly had plenty of that.'

'Must be pretty difficult for you.' He shook his head sympathetically.

'Not really,' I said. 'I like being on my own.'

'Seeing anyone?' Rick inspected his empty wine glass with one eye closed then looked around for the waiter, who was diligently doing his best to avoid our table.

'I'm perfectly happy with the way things are,' I told him firmly. 'And I don't think you'll be needing any more wine.'

WHEN I OPENED MY eyes, I had absolutely no idea where I was. You know that fleeting feeling you get sometimes upon waking, when for a few misplaced seconds you don't recognize anything, then you realize that it's morning and you're safely tucked into your own bed. Except that this time I wasn't. I had helped Rick stagger into the big berth at the bow end of the boat after lunch finally caught up with him, and he fell into a deep, snoring sleep moments later. It had looked as though he might be there for quite a while, so I decided to take a sneaky little nap myself. Well, when in Rome and all that.

I looked at my watch. Ten thirty, it said. *Ten thirty?* But it's still light outside! I looked out of the porthole, and up there in the luminous sky hung an enormous shining moon the size of Jupiter, seemingly just a touch away. On finding Rick's bunk empty, I hastily made my way up on deck. He was standing at the wheel, gazing upward and watching the gentle wind fill the ghostly silver-white sails. Portsmouth was nowhere to be seen.

'Rick?' The chill in the damp air raised the hairs on my arms. Or maybe it was the alarm. 'What on earth do you think you're doing?' I demanded. He winked at me and returned his eyes to the softly gusting canvas. I threw my hands into the air. 'And where the hell are we?'

THINGS RAPIDLY WENT from weird to worse. My complete sense of humour failure upon finding myself an unconscious stowaway sobered Rick up in no time, and I then had to stare death in the face (again) when we started heading into an unfamiliar port at an alarming rate of knots while Rick wrestled ineptly with a vessel he clearly found completely unmanageable, shouting a panic-stricken, 'Fenders! Get the fenders out!'

Well, it wasn't my fault, was it? How was I supposed to know what a bloody fender is? By the time he had dashed momentarily from the wheel to grab one of the big white plastic balloons and throw it over the side there was no avoiding the row of neatly parked yachts looming towards us as the wheel spun out of control. Still, the damage was fairly minimal when you consider it in the grand scale of how much paint is actually on a boat. Or should I say several boats.

Feet now squarely back on terra firma, my head started swimming almost immediately I disembarked and I felt myself swaying unsteadily from side to side, so I sat down on one of those big black concrete cotton-reels on the jetty that you tie your crew to, and tried to settle my mounting queasiness while Rick went off to deal with the furious international yachting fraternity he had ploughed into as the finale of his grand entrance. You should have heard the noise it made. He emerged from the unimpressed harbour master's office a while later and found me with my head bent to my knees, feeling very sorry for myself indeed.

'There's a decent hotel about five minutes from here,' he said quietly. 'A taxi's on its way to take us there now.' I fired a scowling warning shot over his bows and was about to read him the riot act when he stopped me with an out-turned hand. 'Don't worry, I'm sleeping on the boat. I'll just make sure you get checked in safely, then I'll come back for you in the morning.' He looked genuinely remorseful. 'Sorry, Hell. I guess I just got a bit carried away.'

A few minutes later a car pulled up. The taxi light on the roof looked different, and when the driver called out rudely from the half-open window, I couldn't understand a word he said. For a moment, I thought I must have suffered some sort of mild stroke, suddenly unable to comprehend normal language and everyday occurrences like an impatient cab driver. I looked at Rick questioningly. 'Where did you say we were?'

He took the cigar from between his teeth and smiled broadly. 'France, Hell! We're in France!'

THE HOTEL WAS truly lovely. I took a long soak in a hot bath to wash the salt out of my hair and sank into the deeply sumptuous comfort of the beautiful oak four-poster bed. The linen was thick and crisp, and a small, ribboned lavender pouch had been left on one of the pillows, its therapeutic fragrance inducing an immediate sense of calm and wellbeing. I drifted off the moment my head hit the fresh cotton, feeling my body lilt and sway with the memory of the undulating sea.

The following morning after a pot of intensely rich coffee and a nibble on a sweet, freshly baked croissant, I rang down to the desk and explained my delicate predicament in my best ancient schoolgirl Franglais. Although I had definitely become more flexible in my outlook over the past few months, there was absolutely no way I was going to don the distinctly skanky clothes I had been wearing since cock crow the previous day. In the usual tradition of our Gallic friends, I was answered by the receptionist in perfect English.

Not ten minutes had passed before a stylish stick-thin woman arrived from the hotel boutique wheeling a selection of show-stopping daywear and various other critical essentials in a glossy black carrier bag. If you ever get shipwrecked, do try to do it near a good quality and reasonably large hotel. Chances are they will have absolutely everything you could possibly need from lipstick to liposuction. And you can say what you like about the French, but their women really know how to kit out a sister in need. I didn't need much encouragement to pick out more than was strictly decent (an outfit without the appropriate foundation wear and accessories? *Quelle horreur*), and then charged the whole lot to the room.

'Wow!' RICK LET out an inappropriate and preposterously loud whistle as I approached him in the grand reception. My outfit was pretty incredible. All Paris and no Purley with a neatly swaying hemline and a strange but chic loose-knit half cardigan slung around my shoulders.

'I needed a few essentials,' I started defensively, suddenly riddled with guilt by my sensational appearance. 'What with being stranded in the middle of the night in a foreign country without so much as a handkerchief.'

Rick raised his hands and hung his head in submission. 'No. Absolutely. You're perfectly within your rights to be cross with me. You go ahead. It's the very least I can do.'

Actually, I'd had a pretty fantastic time, apart from the scary bits. Breakfast in bed watching a catty fashion programme on the television that I couldn't understand. New clothes, new cosmetics, new *shoes*. And there's nothing like a spanking pair of new peep-toes to soften even the most hard-nosed jury.

'Lunch?' Rick offered hopefully. 'I'm bloody starved.'

I psyched myself up in preparation for another hard day at the office. 'All right then,' I said. 'But definitely no wine.'

He put his hand on his shirt. 'Agreed.'

'And if you think I'm going back to Blighty in that pirate tub of yours, you've got another think coming.'

THAT EUROSTAR SERVICE is pretty impressive, which is more than I can say for the Schumacher taxi driver who somehow got me to the station in one piece without mowing down half the population of Brittany. He grunted rudely when I handed him the fare plus a more than generous tip and shot off at such a speed that he almost ran over the open toes of my new shoes. Now that *would* have made me cross. Less than four hours and one French *Vogue* later I was slipping my key into the familiar latch. There in the kitchen was Paul, sitting on a stool reading the *Standard* and picking at a carton of takeaway chop suey.

'Paul?' I closed the door behind me and looked around for Leoni. He put down the chopsticks and folded his paper.

'Okay,' he started, clearing his palate with a sip of mint tea. 'Now I know this looks a little strange but . . .' He got up and walked towards me, then rested his hands gently on my shoulders. 'Congratulations,' he said. 'I'm your new roomie.'

IN THE THIRTY-SIX hours that had passed while I was doing the Duke of Edinburgh gold award, something of a seismic shift had taken place back in the leafy square. Leoni had answered the door to a panic-stricken Sally (now that I would have liked to see), and while I was on my way to Portsmouth, she and Sally were hacking their way down the M4 corridor towards Heathrow.

Sally had received the phone call he had been dreading for years. It was his sister, Jolanda, just touched down in the UK, because she was fed up with waiting for him to go and visit their mother, who flagellated herself about his absence every single day and thought that the sun shone out of his jacksey. So now she was bringing the mountain to Mohammed and so, say hello to Ma.

'Salvatore!' the mother had cried into the payphone. 'You never come to see your devoted Mama, so now I come to you before I die and you can introduce me to your wife!'

Poor Sally was beside himself. He had cooked up a fairytale story about his amazingly successful life here in England, and finally put paid to the rumours that his father was calling him unholy things (may he rest in peace) by sending home the wonderful news of his marriage, but that his new wife was afraid of flying so, sadly, they would not be able to visit. Ever. His mother had been so relieved that she collapsed on the spot, the letter from Jolanda reported. She had been begging God's forgiveness ever since he started drawing strangely anatomical flowers and customizing his own clothes.

But what were they doing here? She was seventy-eight if she was a day and had never before set foot outside of their village somewhere west of Bogotá. And as for Jolanda, well, let's just say that they've never really seen eye to eye ever since he rebuffed two of her best girlfriends and she had told him that she knew what he was and she thought he was disgusting. Sally had responded by putting as much distance between himself and his family as the world stage would allow. He had meant to go back and visit, honestly he had, but the time just never felt right.

Leoni made a snap decision, grabbed her coat and sprang into action. Finally, something exciting. Something *unexpected*. And it was happening to *her*. Within minutes, they were in a taxi together heading for the airport. By the time it pulled up at arrivals, Jolanda, mother and a whole heap of luggage were standing outside on the pavement waiting impatiently. Sally pointed them out to the cabbie and he pulled up alongside.

Sally threw open the door and leapt out towards them. 'Mama!' he called, bending down and wrapping his crying mother in a bear hug as she reached up to pull down the back of his head to hers. Jolanda glared at him angrily, hands on her hips, then looked away in exasperation muttering something in Spanish as the sight of her weeping ma started to upset her. Sally straightened himself up, kissing and clasping his mother's hand as he turned to his sister.

'Jolanda,' he said, and after a few terse words and her initial point blank refusal, she reluctantly accepted his open arms and they hugged each other hard. Pulling away from her a moment later, he motioned his arm towards the open taxi door. Leoni bent forward from the back seat of the cab to reveal her face, smiled, and offered a shy little wave.

Sally looked at his family proudly. 'Mama, I want you to meet my wife.'

PAUL RAN ME a delicious bath, scattering in freshly cut orange and lemon zest with a handful of rosemary from the herby window box, lit candles everywhere, and poured himself into some black silk pyjamas. After bathing like Cleopatra, I joined him in the sitting room and we settled on the sofa in front of the television and watched *Newsnight* like an old married couple. It must have been Paxman's night off, because instead there was some woman being far too lenient with the Teflon-coated politician in the hot seat. Paul and I voiced our mutual disappointment over a mug of hot chocolate and wondered how things were going upstairs. 'But if he sleeps with her – ' he wagged his finger at me – 'I swear I'll be moving in with you for good.'

IT HAD NEVER occurred to me to advertise for a paying flatmate to ease the burden of my monthly standing orders, and Leoni's constant presence had done little to improve the attraction of the idea. Let's just say that she has a different approach to household management from me, which includes things like hiding coffee rings on polished tabletops under strategically placed magazines. Paul, on the other hand, turned out to be a completely different proposition. He is as meticulous with home cleanliness as he is with his personal grooming, and that first morning he presented me with breakfast in bed and cleared away every last crumb of kitchen mess before I had even emerged from my pit. I could get seriously used to it.

'Helen!' shouted Paul through a mouthful of apple. I peered out from the bathroom door, frothy toothbrush in hand. 'There's a man downstairs wants me to buzz him in.'

'Who is it?' I pulled my dressing gown closed and went to the balcony, SAS style, sticking close to the wall as I strained to see who it was. There on the street below with an enormous ribbon-wrapped bouquet of flowers was a very dejected-looking Marcus. I rushed back towards the door.

'It's Leoni's husband!' I panicked. 'What are we going to do?'

'You want me to get rid of him?' Paul suggested, munching on the core. 'I can do that.' He turned back towards the intercom all efficiently.

'No!' I reached forwards to cover the little red self-destruct button with my hand. 'He'll get suspicious. We'll have to tell him something.'

Paul looked at me and shrugged casually. 'Well, don't look at me,' he said. 'Hetero guidance counselling isn't really my thing, and from what Leoni's been telling me, we should pour a vat of boiling oil over the balcony and do the whole world a favour.'

'Just a minute!' I chirped brightly through the intercom before turning back to Paul. 'Get upstairs now and tell Leoni that he's here. I'll stall him.' I watched Paul disappear up the stairs before buzzing Marcus in and tried to look normal by leaning up against the door and casually twiddling my hair as he reached the landing.

'Oh, Marcus darling, you shouldn't have!' I avoided Marcus's gaze and rushed in dramatically for the flowers.

'Er,' he looked embarrassed. 'I didn't. They're for Leoni.'

'Of course they are.' I hugged him. 'I was only teasing. Come on in.' I held the door wide open and he stepped inside. 'Leoni's not here at the moment.' Quick, think of something that doesn't sound completely implausible. 'She just popped out to get a breath of fresh air. Should be back any minute.'

Marcus went straight to the sitting room, sat down on the sofa and breathed an exasperated sigh. 'I don't know what to make of it, Helen. One minute everything's just fine and the next she's dousing me in red-hot boeuf bourguignon and calling me every name under the sun.' He shook his head. 'I don't know what's got into her. Just how difficult can it be to look after three children? It's not as though she's said anything and I'm not a bloody mindreader.' I couldn't help but feel sorry for him, sitting there glumly looking like a confused schoolboy in his Sunday best. 'Has she said anything to you?' The telephone rang and saved me from the pathetic explanatory speech I was desperately trying to cobble together in my head.

It was Paul. 'She's not here.' Oh, that's just perfect. I pressed the receiver hard to my ear to keep his shrill voice from escaping into the room.

'Right,' I said, smiling inanely at Marcus. 'Any more information than that?'

'I've tracked Sally down and they're in the queue for the London Eye, then they're going off on one of those open-top sightseeing buses.'

'Great,' I said, still smiling like an idiot and raising my eyes to Marcus casually.

'So, what do you want to do now, smartypants?' he whispered loudly. While I racked my brain, Paul started humming the *The Dam Busters* theme.

'I have absolutely no idea, but thanks for ringing anyway.' I hung up and tutted at Marcus. 'Bloody double-glazing salesmen.'

There was nothing for it but to hold tight and wait. I busied myself in the kitchen while I tried to gather my thoughts and come up with a reasonable excuse. All I had to do was to find a nice straightforward way to explain to Marcus that his wife was currently living under an assumed name with a strange Colombian family, playing the role of a gay man's wife. It was all perfectly innocent and he should just go home and wait for her to call him. But no matter how I looked at it, I couldn't imagine anything other than an extreme reaction, so Marcus and I sat on the sofa together and politely drank a lot of coffee that neither of us really wanted. Not a particularly good idea if you're one of those people who is prone to caffeine palpitations after two espressos. (That would be me.) He's not much of a one for small talk either, and the conversation dwindled painfully as Marcus became increasingly agitated and checked his watch every few minutes. Just when I was about to concede defeat and blurt out the whole story regardless of the consequences, I was saved by a sharp rap on the door.

'Paul!' Just in the nick of time.

'Hi, Helen.' He spoke extra loudly and flashed his eyes at me while pointing through the half-closed door towards the sitting room and mouthing, *Is he still here?* I nodded furiously and pulled an ugly grimace. 'I was wondering if you could let me have your baked Alaska recipe,' he shouted. *What?* He shrugged his shoulders and put his hands up in a sorry-but-I-couldn't-think-of-anything-else-to-say gesture.

'Yes, of course! Do come in.' Paul followed me towards the kitchen, deliberately averting his gaze from the open sitting room door as he delivered his speech at full volume.

'Oh, by the way, I saw your friend on my way back from the shop a couple of minutes ago – you know, the one who's staying with you at the moment?' His eyebrows were raised high and he kept nodding his head sideways towards the elephant in the sitting room. Thank God. He's got a plan.

'Oh yes?' I encouraged him.

'She said she was on her way to the Natural History Museum because it's such a nice day and then she might go and have a look around the shops.' Paul was wide-eyed and flapping his hands around by way of an apology for the weak excuse. Marcus silently appeared behind him in the doorway and I grabbed hold of Paul's arms to interrupt his outrageous mime.

'Paul, this is Marcus, Leoni's husband.' Paul turned and looked Marcus up and down, then smiled nervously as they shook hands. We all stood around uncomfortably for a brief moment. Without warning, Marcus suddenly turned and headed straight for the bedrooms, marching in and shouting, 'Leoni!' He went to each room bellowing, 'I know you're in here. This has got to stop right now.'

It took him all of two minutes to finish searching the premises. Finding nothing, he reluctantly threw in the towel and returned to the pair of us loitering guiltily in the kitchen.

'She's not here, Marcus,' I said to him gently. 'But I know she'll be pleased that you came and I'll make sure she calls you as soon as she gets back.'

Marcus eyed me suspiciously. 'I don't know what's going on here, but I'm bloody well going to find out.' He tossed the flowers on the worktop and left in high dudgeon.

'Now what?' I wailed at Paul.

He thought about it for a moment. 'What say we bake that Alaska?'

Chapter Nine

LOVE THY NEIGHBOUR

EARLY MORNING IS probably my very favourite time
of day. I try to make a point not to miss it if I can.
Getting up in the silent stillness before the noise of the
traffic starts in earnest. Mooching around the kitchen
quietly in bare feet to make a pot of English Breakfast.
Sitting with the tea tray in bed and looking out of the
window waiting for the day to open its eyes. I like to
think that I've got the whole world to myself for an
hour or so, although the minutes seem to pass far
more quickly than they do at any other time. One
moment it's only twenty to seven so you get involved
in a mind-boggling real-life story in *Heat* magazine,

and the next you're horribly late for work and sprinting towards the bathroom door.

Rick was away on business for a few days, so I had little more to do that week than to replenish his household supplies and see to his list of subservient tasks which, this time, included replacing the half dozen smashed Baccarat crystal goblets that his latest ex-girlfriend had hurled at his head when she discovered an earring in the bed that definitely wasn't hers. I wrapped the lonesome survivor in tissue paper and took it to the glass department at Harrods for identification. While waiting for the heavily starched assistant to come back from the incident room, I felt a hand grab hold of my elbow.

'Gotcha,' said Julia brightly. I almost had a heart attack on the spot. 'What are you doing in here? You're supposed to be boracic. Don't tell me I've just caught you in a moment of retail weakness!' She eyed the expensive glassware teetering precariously on the tall display stand beside her.

I kissed her on the cheek. 'They're for Rick. I get to do all his shopping these days.' The goblet pathologist emerged from behind the counter and told me they would have to order them in, so I paid for the goods and asked for them to be delivered.

'Well, that's me done for the day then,' I told Julia.

'Good,' she said, linking her arm through mine. 'You can come and help me choose an anniversary present for David. I was thinking along the lines of a set of oyster silk lingerie with six-inch stilettos and a Hollywood.'

'A what?'

Julia opened her handbag and showed me a picture torn out from the pages of a dubious magazine, featuring a woman of questionable morals without so much as a landing strip in sight. My cheeks burned instantly. 'You'll never get one of those in here,' I said.

ONE OF THE great shames of living way up in the northern hemisphere is that it's normally much too cold for pavement dining. When the faint-hearted English sun eventually deigns to show its pasty face for a few merciful weeks in the summer, which it doesn't always do, there is a mad stampede for the scant places that dare risk putting a handful of tables outside. We nabbed an early spot and awarded the third chair to Julia's impressive collection of carrier bags. She arranged them carefully to prevent anything tipping over and ordered a cold bottle of house plonk.

'No work for you this afternoon?' I asked her.

'Uh-uh.' She shook her head and smiled at me as she settled the napkin into her enviously trim lap. 'I had a very upset Marcus on the phone last night and I think this is going to be one of those lunchtime conversations that goes on for hours.' She raised her glass towards me and winked. 'So, go on then. Spill the beans.'

IT'S NOT OFTEN that I see Julia literally roar with laughter, but she made up for lost time that sunny day as I gave her a blow-by-blow account of the ridiculous Brian Rix farce that was being played out with such gusto in my homestead. She said it was the funniest thing she had ever heard, with my bizarre new occupation coming in a close second.

'So, how are Sara's wedding arrangements coming along?' I nibbled on my tenth bread stick.

'Oh, thank God you mentioned it.' Julia reached for her handbag and pulled out her organizer. She tapped the screen with a little black plastic stick and checked her diary. 'What are you doing on Friday night?'

Now let me see. Would Friday night be the same as any other night? Probably. I felt reasonably confident as I answered without checking my schedule.

'Nothing.'

'Well, that's settled then.' She put her diary back in her bag and picked up her coffee cup.

'What?'

'Hen night, silly! And you'll be needing your passport.'

*

ALTHOUGH I HAD FOUND my life fuller than it had been for fifteen years, I was also feeling something else. I never considered myself a loner, but it seemed clear to me now that that was precisely what I had accidentally become. Leoni had been with me for four days, Paul for two, and in less than a week I was already weighing up the ramifications of being left all by myself when things returned to normal.

'Start off with one of these once a day in the evening with food,' said Dr Brown. I had gone there for something else entirely, which I won't bore you with. It was only my second visit since registering after I moved, and on that occasion I had seen a fossilized old man who was deaf as a post and should have retired ten years ago. Dr Brown was standing in while the surgery went computerized, and ran through some routine questions, cursing at her cursor and clucking testily whenever a prompt appeared on the screen. It was when she asked me about my stress levels that the trouble started. I tipped my hand in a so-so gesture and smiled. Except the smile failed and I had to reach for a tissue.

She was nice enough about it at first, even though she pointedly looked up at the clock on the wall urging me to hurry it along, but by the time I finished explaining what I had been through over the last few months, her jaw was literally hanging open. She nodded sympathetically, told me she thought I had done jolly well to keep out of the psychiatric department, and reached for her fountain pen. I felt thoroughly defeated that I should have been reduced to a prescription for anti-depressants, but she assured me that a short stint on the Right Stuff wouldn't do me any permanent damage and might just be the emotional crutch that I needed right now.

Paul noticed me looking decidedly glum when he got in from work and pursed his lips when I told him about my day. 'Are you absolutely sure that you want to get involved with the international pharmaceutical drugs cartel?' he warned me. 'They're the most powerful corporations in our entire galaxy, Helen, and your GP is almost certainly collecting club card pill points towards a beach holiday in Maui. Although they'll call it a convention.' He narrowed his eyes at me. 'She's probably dishing those things out like Tic Tacs.' Wagging his finger, he turned to go to the kitchen. 'Be warned. That's all I'm saying.'

Now that he came to mention it, Dr Brown had looked a little wired. I put the unopened packet at the back of the bathroom cabinet and Paul knocked up a gravity-defying cheese soufflé instead.

'ARE YOU COMPLETELY out of your mind?' When Paul had mentioned something that morning about the dinner he was planning, I must have either misheard him or he had neatly left out the finer details of his guest list. Leoni had become completely incommunicado since Sally had declared his national state of emergency and cordoned off the area, so we'd resorted to sliding envelopes under their door in the hope of raising her. I had more or less given up on the girl and resolved to hide on the floor next time Marcus came knocking.

'I miss Sally,' Paul said dejectedly, drooping his face in his hands. 'I miss the way he lies around, his voice, his . . . you know, stuff. And if I don't see him soon, I'm going to get all unnecessary,' he threatened. 'We're not supposed to be apart. It's like we're two halves of the same thing.' Paul dovetailed his fingers together and suppressed a small sob.

'Like Tommy Steele in *Half a Sixpence*?' I suggested understandingly.

'Puh-lease.' Paul closed his eyes against my offence. 'And I need to remind him how adorable I am before he starts getting any ideas.' He patted the side of his cropped hair with one hand and opened the fridge door with the other. 'Nobody knows how to look after him like I do, and I just know that he won't have been eating properly.'

Paul had skipped work for the afternoon to cook a traditional roast beef with all the trimmings. He insisted I leave the kitchen while he made his Yorkshire pudding batter and charmingly ushered me away with excuses about his age-old family recipe and the hex that would befall anyone who should try to steal it. I found the instant-mix packet in the bin later. Despite his canny shortcut, the mouthwatering aromas of perfect English Heritage comfort food permeated every brick in the building, and the South American faction arrived spot on the stroke of seven thirty for eight.

Sally, Leoni, Jolanda and the mother bundled in through the door, talking all at once in a flurry of rapid-fire Spanish and English (except Mama, who stuck rigidly to her mother tongue), and Sally leapt in to make the introductions.

'Everyone, these are our lovely neighbours, Paul and Helen.' I nodded hello as we shook hands. 'My sister Jolanda and my beautiful Mama.' Sally kissed her hand. Paul took the mother's coat, although why she had thought she needed it to get down one flight of stairs heaven only knows. 'And of course there's no need for me to introduce Geraldine.' Gales of schizophrenic laughter from Leoni, who immediately gave herself away as having taken on board a little Dutch courage before dinner. *Geraldine?* Oh, come on!

'Gerry, darling, come and give Helen a hand for a minute, would you?' said Paul, then started looking at me and doing that bizarre pointing with his eyes thing to get my attention. I followed hot on Leoni's (or should I say Gerry's) heels, while Paul guided his unsuspecting in-laws towards the sitting room and offered them an aperitif.

'Leoni!' I whispered loudly at her as she shoved me into the kitchen. 'Just what the bloody hell do you think you're playing at?'

Leoni turned and looked at me desperately. 'I don't know how to get out of it,' she hissed. 'It's like being cooped up with the fucking Munsters in the middle of the Spanish Inquisition. I'm having to sleep with one eye open in case mother Teresa over there tries to come in and check my ovaries while I'm unconscious.' She helped herself to a glass of wine and went at it like a woman possessed. 'The decrepit old crow's an evil witch and she doesn't even attempt to hide it, especially when Sally's out of earshot. Mummy's boy. And as for that bloody sister of his . . .' Leoni drained the glass. 'She's been watching me like a hawk ever since we picked them up from the airport. I've even caught her sneaking photographs of me with her phone. I think this could all get seriously dangerous.' She paused to come up for breath and leaned heavily against the worktop.

'Marcus is doing his pieces,' I told her. 'He turned up here while you were gallivanting around tourist land and now he thinks you've run off with another bloke.'

'What?' Leoni went pale. 'What the hell did you tell him that for?'

'I didn't! But he's a sodding man, isn't he? What else is he going to think?'

'Shit.' Leoni grabbed my shoulders. 'You've got to help me!'

THE MOTHER WENT on like a broken record throughout dinner, speaking emotionally about all kinds of stuff we couldn't understand, wiping her face with her increasingly grubby gravy-stained napkin and reaching out to pinch Sally's cheeks and waggle them hard while she murmured motherly nothings to him with her mouth shockingly full. I've never seen an old person eat so much. If our pensioners had appetites like that, Meals on Wheels would have had to switch to a fleet of pantechnicons long ago. She turned her nose up at the Yorkshire pudding, describing it as unnatural, but unashamedly piled her plate with three enormous helpings of beef and potatoes.

'You make baby,' she finally spluttered to the table, pointing a gnarled index finger at Leoni and nodding savagely. Sally masked his exasperation well, put his cutlery down quietly and rested his hand on top of his mother's.

Addressing the table, he said, 'My mama is getting old and she doesn't understand that we will not be having any children. She wants a grandchild more than anything in the world.' He looked at her tenderly.

'Mama had a dream that we gave her a grandson. She says that she is never wrong and that it was so real that she had to come and see for herself. Mama says she knows that Gerry is having this baby, but I have explained to her that,' he cast down his eyes, 'as the good Lord knows, it cannot be the case.' Sally shook his head sadly and looked at his mother. 'Because my poor wife cannot bear us the miracle of children.' He took Leoni's hand. 'We have to accept that she will never be blessed.' A pitiful hush fell upon the room, but only for a second.

'What?' boomed Leoni furiously, picking up her plate and banging it back down on the table with both hands. So, she'd finally snapped. 'How do we know it's not you, big fella?' She clicked her fingers in the air and sneered at Sally with a knowing nod. 'That's just typical of you exotic foreign types. Always the woman's fault. Never the man's.' Leoni had finished her wine so she swiftly took charge of Jolanda's. 'Your brother's a real male chauvinist pig,' she told her. 'He might come across all sensitive and understanding, but believe you me, he's just like all the rest of them.' She turned back to face a blanching, wide-eyed Sally. 'I've stuck by you all this time when we both know very well that you're firing blanks, mister. Every day I think about what it might have been like to have a little baby . . .' Then Leoni started crying. It was brilliant and utterly convincing, if a little sozzled. 'But enough's enough. I can't take it any more.' Leoni got up from the table and stood her ground. 'Salvatore. I'm leaving you.'

There was a gasp from the table. Even Paul was completely taken in, hand flying to his mouth. Jolanda was busily translating the general gist of the conversation to the mother. Twenty seconds after the rest of us, Mama's gasp rose to a full-volume scream of abuse at Leoni. She stretched angrily across the table, slinging the contents of her wine glass in Leoni's general direction and shouting, 'Puta! Puta de madre!' before wailing something involving Jesus in Heaven and collapsing heavily into Salvatore's arms. He stumbled momentarily under the sudden weight of all those extra roasties while Leoni ran off sobbing hysterically and locked herself in the bathroom.

'We knew it!' shouted Jolanda. 'From the moment we see her we say she no good for you! Mama say she big whore, she bad woman, she frigid.' Sally was dragging the maternal dead weight, still sobbing and gagging, towards the door.

'Now you see what I am putting up with,' he replied wearily. 'And you wonder why I haven't been able to visit? She's a crazy woman. It's like this all the time.'

Jolanda's face filled with deep sympathy for her persecuted brother. She retrieved the mother's coat from the hat stand beside the door, thanked us for the dinner, and helped Sally manhandle their supersize mother back up the stairs.

I waited until the coast was clear, then tapped gently on the bathroom door. 'You can come out now.'

Leoni's head appeared. 'How did I do?'

Paul flashed his eyes in admiration and stretched his arms wide open. 'Meryl Streep, eat your heart out.'

'ALL RIGHT, HELL? Don't mind me saying so, but you're looking a bit peaky, love.' I had managed to jam one of the steam jets on the ridiculous coffee machine and Rick was watching me do my impersonation of the Chernobyl meltdown as I started to lose my temper with it. God forbid he should offer to walk over and give me a hand. Had he not been there I would have given it a good old kick and smashed it a few times with my fist in frustration. Take a deep breath. Count to ten. One, tomato, two, tomato. Now is not the time to lose your cool, or your job.

'Can't you make do with a cup of tea?' I complained. 'Or I'll make you an instant.'

'I've got a better idea,' said Rick. 'Get your coat on and we'll go out for one instead.'

RICK QUEUED UP at the counter, waiting to relay the order while I sat miserably at a messy table in the window. The staff appeared to be strictly forbidden from wiping them over or clearing away the previous customers' used cups. He returned to find me rankled and watched with amusement while I tore open two little pouches of brown sugar, poured their contents into the froth then waited for the soft sparkling mound to sink through the milky cloud. I stirred the liquid in my corrugated paper cup absently with the useless wooden lolly stick and rested my head on one arm.

'Man trouble?' he asked.

I laughed bitterly. Chance would be a fine thing. 'No, Rick, it's a whole lot more complicated than that.'

'Oh,' he said, and shifted uncomfortably on his seat. He tried again.

'Women's things?'

'Only if you're a woman like me.' I smiled thinly at him. 'Did you ever stop and wonder how you got here? Life used to feel so simple. Now –' I sighed helplessly – 'now I don't know what to think.' And before I knew what I had done, I had gone and told Rick all about my life as a suburban housewife with an abysmal marriage, the missing millions, the gay hussars and my domestic *ménage à trois*. By the time I picked up my coffee it was stone cold. Rick must have been bored senseless. His expression had changed from his usual cheeky chappy to something altogether more serious as he reached for his jacket.

'You're a dark horse, Helen,' he said.

Chapter Ten

SPACED

'I RECKON THAT OUGHT to do it.' Leoni shoved her arm elbow-deep into the side pocket of our shared lady-sized trundle case to make room for one last shoe. I assumed the other one was already wedged in there somewhere. Standing at the door with my patience wearing thin, I scathingly reminded her that the cabbie waiting downstairs was already dangerously close to blowing a gasket and, no rush, but we've got a bloody plane to catch for Christ's sake. We slammed the front door closed behind us and rushed down the stairs to find Paul beckoning at us wildly through the taxi's open window. Well, we could hardly have left him behind all on his tod, could we? He had behaved like an injured puppy for twenty-four hours until we finally caved in and told him he could come along as the token male. But only on the firm understanding that he had to do what *we* wanted to do and no tittle-tattling to anyone when we got back.

'Get in, will you!' he urged crossly, virtually dragging Leoni into the cab by her coat sleeve and pulling the door shut with a loud bang. 'Airport, James!' he sang through the serving hatch. 'And don't spare the horses!' The taxi shot off before I had managed to seat myself properly, sending me flying into Paul's lap. The driver mumbled something from up front about his name being Mick, and people like us taking bloody liberties.

WE APPROACHED THE meeting point on the terminal concourse where Julia and Sara were waiting anxiously with an elegant woman in her mid-fifties wearing a snazzy white trouser suit to show off her amazingly well-preserved figure. She had magazine-perfect hair and a big red leather shoulder bag trailing gold buckles fashionably from one corner. Julia noticed my approach and we exchanged a high wave of recognition Leoni rushed forward enthusiastically, kissed Sara on both cheeks and preeningly allowed everyone to fuss over her new hair. As they finished their greeting, Sara glanced past me at Paul, who was standing just behind my shoulder excitedly grinning from ear to pierced ear.

'What the hell's that?' she pointed at him.

'Sara,' I introduced them, 'this is my friend and neighbour, Paul. He's staying with me for a few days so I invited him along. I do hope you don't mind.' Sara looked at me and frowned crossly.

'Hello!' enthused Paul, dropping his holdall to the floor and thrusting a friendly hand out.

'But he's a man!' Sara cried, ignoring his open palm. 'Are you blind? This is a hen weekend!'

'He's not a man,' I corrected her. 'He's a poof. Now hurry up or we'll miss that flight.'

Miss Joan Collins with the red shoulder bag approached Sara's side and cleared her throat loudly. Sara glanced at her apologetically, motioned her elbow towards the woman and addressed the three of us.

'Everyone,' she said reluctantly, 'this is my mum.'

Sara's mother smiled a serene Helena Rubenstein with perfect red lips and held one hand forwards. Not to shake, you understand, but to indicate the presence of her white-gloved greatness in our midst. Paul was clearly knocked out.

'Sophia,' Joan Collins purred in a deeply shingle-gravelled growl.

*

'SHE JUST TURNED up,' bleated Sara. 'There was absolutely nothing I could do to stop her. I got here with Julia this morning, and there she was, waiting for us at the check-in desk.' We had managed to give Sophia the slip temporarily by sending her on a tasteful-tie fact-finding mission around the duty free zone with Paul while we ducked into the nearest ladies' room.

Sara's voice was aghast. 'I never imagined for a moment she would even think about doing something like this, otherwise I wouldn't have mentioned it to her in the first place. I swear I don't know what's going on in her head at the moment, but she's behaving like a bloody teenager.' The sound of running water stopped. 'Dad reckons she went doolally when the menopause kicked in and she started taking hormone replacement horse pills. You wouldn't believe the size of those things.' The loo flushed and Sara emerged from trap three and began to wash her hands while we all looked on, speechless.

'You don't look much like each other,' observed Leoni.

'Not bloody surprising, she's had that much plastic surgery.' Sara touched up her lipgloss and addressed our reflections in the vanity mirror. 'She used to be called Sandra but decided it wasn't befitting after her big makeover.' She zipped her handbag shut and turned around to face us. 'Dad didn't even recognize her when he came to pick her up from the airport. She had given him some great cock and bull story about hiking to Machu Picchu to find herself, when she was actually planning to spend two months and most of their savings having her features rearranged in Palm Beach.' Leoni made a mental note to try and get a good look behind her ears to check for scarring.

Paul's head appeared around the door. 'We have to get to the boarding gate,' he said urgently. 'Like *now*.' And sure enough we all heard the last call for the British Airways flight to Schiphol.

THE CULTURAL VISIT to Holland that Julia had described to me a few days beforehand turned out to be something else entirely. Any misplaced notions about windmills and Rembrandts went right out of the window the minute we got to the hotel. Although it was unremarkable in itself, being the usual regurgitation of international blandness in hotels the world over, its situation was much less ordinary. The whole district appeared to be filled with wall-to-wall erotica outlets (live or pre-recorded in all formats), interspersed with the odd grocery store and an occasional hallucinogenic bong shop. We seemed to have been deposited slap bang in the middle of Sodom and Gomorrah.

'Ladies,' laughed Sara, 'welcome to Amsterdam.' We had gathered in reception after dumping our bags in the rooms. Me, Leoni and Paul bunked up in one, Julia, Sara and the Gorgon in the other.

'What shall we do first?' Paul clapped his hands excitedly then looked worried that he'd overstepped the mark by daring to make a suggestion and covered his mouth.

'Well I, for one,' rasped Sophia with a knowing glint in her eye, 'would like to find a decent cup of coffee.' Before we could respond, she was headed back out on the street and accosted the first passer-by with a cut-glass, 'Hey, you there! Excuse me,' then went off in the direction he pointed out to her.

'Oh, here we bloody well go,' said Sara. 'For God's sake someone put a piece of paper in her pocket with the name and address of the hotel on it. I don't want to go through *that* again.' And we all rushed off in hot pursuit of the rapidly disappearing red shoulder bag.

FORTY MINUTES LATER we finally gave up trying to find her and instead attempted to console a disgruntled Sara over a cold beer that it really didn't matter, and that Sophia was bound to be able to find her way back to the hotel, eventually. In fact, we insisted in our futile bid to cheer her up, it was actually great fun to have her mother come along on the trip. Mixing of the generations and all that. Sara wasn't convinced at all and moaned that she wouldn't be able to relax and really let her hair down with her girlfriends on the one night it actually held any significance for her. Whenever she said *girlfriends*, she would glance at Paul momentarily as if to explain the convenience of the mass collective. Paul was openly loving every minute of it and told Sara that she could call him whatever she liked.

'Mum always ruins everything,' Sara grumbled. 'She just has to be the centre of attention all the time. Tells everyone she was a model back in the sixties, even though she only got the one job advertising an eighteen-hour girdle and you couldn't see her face.' We all murmured sympathetic noises. 'Thinks she's bloody Raquel Welch. I expect Dad was glad to see the back of her for a couple of days.' Sara's mobile suddenly rang from her pocket.

'Hello?' We watched anxiously when she put a hand up for us all to keep quiet. 'Where the hell are you? We've been worried sick. Where? Hang on a minute, let me write that down.' We started searching around for a pen and paper, found one, but not the other, so Paul gallantly rolled up his sleeve and offered Sara his arm. She wrote down the details on his wrist while Paul bravely bit his lower lip through the stabbing pain of the needle-tipped biro, and together we launched our rescue bid.

*

'HOLY COW!' SHOUTED Julia as we shoved our way into the noisily crowded bar. 'Must be pay day.' We stood up on tiptoes to search the room for the tell-tale bouffant hair.

'There!' screeched Paul, and we edged our way to the far end of the bar, where Sophia was perched glamorously, holding court to four men of varying ages. Sara pushed her way to the front.

'Mother!' she yelled. 'What do you think you're doing?'

'Darling!' Sophia blew an air kiss in Sara's general direction. 'Come and meet Jens and Peter.' She paused when she got to the next chap.

'Animal,' he offered politely.

'Animal,' Sophia relayed, 'and Badger.'

'Beaver,' corrected the fourth man.

'I'm so sorry.' Sophia touched his arm. 'And Beaver.'

Sara covered her face with her hands, shook her head and peered at us through her fingers in exasperation. Paul was snapping his hips to the swinging music and shouted at Beaver, 'That's an interesting name. Why do they call you that?' The man called Beaver tilted his head back and opened his mouth to reveal the most enormous set of front gnashers.

'Thank God for that,' mumbled Sara. I can't imagine what she must have been thinking.

Sophia caught the attention of one of the staff behind the bar and tipped him a pre-arranged nod. A few minutes later, he returned amid much ado with a big cake on a stand, studded with crackling sparklers that shot out tiny white-hot stars.

'Congratulations, darling,' said Sophia, 'and if your Dudley turns out to be anything like your father, divorce the bastard.' She picked up one of the almost-spent fireworks and watched it fizzle out. 'Don't waste your fleeting years of beauty like I did. They'll be gone before you know it. Just you mark my words.'

'Don't be so horrible!' Sara retorted angrily. 'Dad loves you and he's always given you everything you ever wanted and put up with your ridiculous behaviour.'

'Ah yes,' said Sophia, 'but does he understand me?' She began cutting the cake into generous wedges and smiled to herself. 'I'm a complicated woman, darling. And your father is a simple man.'

'He's a fucking saint, mother.'

'Language, dear.' Sophia nibbled at her piece delicately and offered the plate around. 'Dudley won't want to marry a guttersnipe now, will he?'

The cake was delicious. We were hungrier than anyone realized, not having had dinner yet and with the flight being little more than a hop and a skip with no recognizable food on offer. The whole thing was gone before we knew it, and was inexplicably moreish with an unusual hint of something I couldn't quite identify. Must be a regional speciality.

'Wonderful cake.' I congratulated Sophia on her marvellous idea. She threw her head back and let out an alarmingly maniacal cackle then sat bolt upright and squinted into my eyes.

'Excuse my mother,' Sara said to Animal, 'she's self-medicating.'

FRIDAY NIGHT IN Amsterdam is much like any other Friday night in any other Western European city, full of people kicking back and filling the bars, full of the same noises but strangely different smells drifting in from the restaurants and canals. It's a relaxed kind of a place, and the Dutch are a friendly and hospitable lot from what I could tell. Happy to chat, keen to assist, putting us to shame with their commonly artful command of the English language. We're a lazy race.

If Sara had been tense earlier, she soon seemed to relax, and before long we were all laughing, drinking icy draft beer and butting into each other's conversations then forgetting what we were saying mid-sentence. I wondered if it was just me who was feeling abnormally light-headed. Perhaps it was the cake.

Leoni cupped her hands around her eyes like binoculars, shouting, 'Let's play "Last Man on Earth". Gary Rhodes or Wozza?' We all groaned at the chilling prospect. Even Paul.

By ten o'clock we were on a roll. Paul was flirting

madly with every man in the room, Julia, Sara, Leoni and I were laughing our heads off at the Tom and Jerry cartoons playing silently on the video screen above the bar, and Sophia's hair had parted company with itself in the middle of her chignon so that half of it was hanging slightly forwards like a flapping cloth cap. It wobbled dangerously as she left her growing audience and staggered over to our table.

'Right,' she announced in her forthright manner. 'There's a fabulous nightclub about three minutes' walk that way,' she pointed a thumb behind her shoulder in a non-specific direction. Then she was off.

Watching her disappear through the door, Sara said, 'Did anyone put that piece of paper in Mum's pocket?' We all looked at each other, then simultaneously sprang from the table and dashed after her, grabbing dancing queen Paul by his outrageously flirty shirt-tails on the way out.

THE SHOP FRONTS and video signs flashed a spectacular kaleidoscope of neon colours to our left and right and the voices from the passers-by rang out every word in a menagerie of foreign tongues. Leoni trotted to my side, held on to my arm far too tightly and told me that she loved me. Paul had skipped on ahead to keep up with the Tasmanian devil, while we took a more leisurely pace bringing up the rear. Rushing back towards us through the meandering crowds, he called out excitedly, 'It's a cabaret club!' then started shimmying his shoulders with jazz hands and singing a medley of show tunes in his best Liza with a zee.

God knows how much it cost to get in, but it cleaned us out. Julia offered the huge leather-clad goth on the desk her American Excess, to which he chewed on his gum noisily and said they only took the real thing. 'How quaint,' responded Julia before emptying the contents of her purse onto the counter and turning to the rest of us. 'Does anyone have any euros?' she asked.

'Yes,' announced Leoni, then looked confused and shook her head. 'But I don't understand them.'

SOMEBODY ON THE plane had mentioned that the reason the Dutch were so accommodating towards the English was something to do with the Second World War. Maybe we helped them hide the good pottery. In any case, next time a friendly European nation is under threat, I suggest we drop a couple of cross-dressing Dutch singers on the enemy country and wait for an early surrender. Not that they didn't try, and even the truly awful ones gave it their heart and soul and left the stage weeping tears of joy to a drunken standing ovation.

We had crowded around a small oval table, covered in empty bottles and lipstick-stained plastic glasses with an overflowing ashtray stuck in the middle (and I mean stuck. It was glued down, as Leoni discovered when she tried to steal it). The 'waitresses' were all six-foot-plussers in full character drag – Marilyn Monroe, Jane Russell, Mae West – none of them specifically recognizable, so you had to ask them who they were then say, 'Oh *yes*! We thought so. Brilliant likeness.' These were big girls, you see, so you wouldn't want to start a ruck with any of them.

One was particularly interested in Sophia, and batted away any customers trying to order a drink while s/he chatted to her for ages. Their conversation came to an abrupt halt when Sophia shouted, 'Bitch!', and stormed off to the ladies' room. Zsa Zsa Gabor came around to our side of the table and apologized for upsetting Sara's mother.

'I just assumed she was one of us,' he said.

WHEN THE LAST of the wailers finally stopped, we thought we had had our lot for the night and started to gather our things together. All of a sudden the lights went down, sinking the grimy venue into a gloomy semi-lit haze under a crepuscular red glow. A strict disciplinarian dungeon mistress appeared, standing on the bar beneath a thin blue spotlight.

'And now ladeez and gennelmen.' She cracked her bullwhip high above our heads and howled into the microphone. 'The moment you've all been waiting for.' Long drum roll. 'It's show time!'

Air horns went off and the whole place went bananas with people screaming, yelling and cat-calling. The club was momentarily plunged into complete darkness, then a shaft of light hit the stage and the rousing theme music to *2001: A Space Odyssey* blared through the distorted speakers, heightening the crackling tension of the baited audience below. The sequinned curtains went back, sending speckles of coloured light dancing around the room, and there in glorious Technicolor stood a breathtaking Adonis of a man, standing ten feet tall on a gilded Romanesque pedestal, wrapped in a floor-length golden lamé cape with an enormous bishop's mitre crowning the top of his waist-length hair. As the music and the crowd reached its deafening crescendo, he threw the cape wide open, arms stretched back to create a glittering backdrop to his more-than-Michelangelo masterpiece. We girls were rendered speechless.

Paul screamed, 'Oh – my – GOD!'

LEONI WAS WORKING on her second room-service club sandwich (I'd helped her out with the first one and Paul had eaten most of the fries, so we went back in with a double order) when Julia tapped on the door.

'I've got to sleep in here with you,' she said, crashing

onto my bed. 'Crazy woman in there's only gone and bought herself a family-sized bag of weed and is determined to smoke all of it before we go home tomorrow.' Leoni's ears pricked up. She dropped a big handful of chips into her hotel dressing-gown pocket and quietly slipped out of the door.

The smell of food reached Julia's nostrils and she reached out for one of the sandwiches. I thought about it and decided that now seemed as good a time as any.

'Julia,' I started, 'exactly how well do you know Dudley?'

'Why?' She picked out the slices of tomato and put them on the side of the plate.

'Leoni and I spotted him the other night when we were out with Paul and Sally.'

'Oh yes?' said Paul through a mouthful of chips. 'You didn't tell me. Which one was he? What did he look like?' I told him to hush and he bucked his head away sniffily as I returned to my conversation with Julia.

'What would you say if I told you he was paying a great deal of attention to a woman in a dimly lit corner who may or may not have been – ' how to put this delicately? – 'well, genuine.'

Julia stopped chewing. 'Our Dudley with a tranny? Are you absolutely sure?'

'Well, no. I mean, I didn't look up his skirt or anything. And they weren't exactly going at it hammer and tongs.' Oh, me and my big mouth. 'But I definitely saw them kiss and the she-man was touching his chest a lot.'

'Kiss? You saw him kissing a bloody transvestite? I don't believe it.' The unshockable Julia appeared well and truly scandalized. 'Have you said anything to Sara?'

'I thought best not to.'

'I should bloody well think so,' said Julia. 'Now someone get on the phone and order me four more of these. I don't know what's the matter with me today, but I could eat a horse.'

I NEED NOT HAVE concerned myself about us being so late down to breakfast. The whole hotel must have had a heavy night judging by the steady stream of jaded stragglers slowly creeping into the dining room. My head felt as though there was a little man inside it trying to poke my eyes out, and I had eaten so much before falling into a heavy slumber the night before that I doubted I would need so much as a vol-au-vent for at least a week. Coffee, on the other hand, and plenty of it, was essential to my survival strategy for the rest of the day.

Leoni was sitting by herself at a large table, struggling with a glass of freshly squeezed orange juice and hiding her bloodshot eyes behind a big pair of sunglasses.

'Sara and Sophia not up yet?' Julia asked as we joined her.

Leoni looked sheepish. 'They've gone.'

We frowned at each other.

'Gone where?' I said. Julia asked the waiter to bring coffee.

'Home, I think.'

We all sat down and tried to withstand the dazzling glare of the white tablecloth without wincing. Leoni gave us her worried look.

'I think I may have done something really bad,' she said quietly.

'Oh no.' Julia focused on her cup. 'Let's have it then.'

Leoni pulled in a deep breath before speaking. 'We were sitting around on the bed and Sophia was teaching me how to smoke.' We frowned at her disapprovingly. 'I don't know what came over me but I went and told her that we'd seen Dudley when we were out together the other night.' I slapped my hand onto my numb forehead and closed my eyes. 'Then I tried to back-pedal and it all went horribly wrong and,' she paused, 'then I think I lost consciousness.' She looked at me. 'And when I woke up, they were gone.'

Paul reached out for the little basket in the middle of the table and waved it through the tension. 'Apricot Danish, anyone?'

Chapter Eleven

SIX QUID FOR A PINT OF MILK

Marcus isn't such a bad chap. I know Leoni goes on about him like he's the devil incarnate, but it's really not his fault. Like so many white-collar husbands, his heart's in the right place; he's just a bit dense when it comes to noticing when his wife is teetering on the edge of a nervous breakdown. Stiff upper lip, women and children first while I have a large brandy and watch the ship go down, and six of the best never did me any harm. She doesn't help matters, mind you. The age-old preferred female method of slamming pots and pans around behind a tight-lipped kitchen door isn't a particularly effective way of communicating your inner needs.

Watching him now, bent down uncomfortably onto one creaking knee in front of an unusually coquettish Leoni, single red rose in hand (yes, a bit naff I know, but the bloke's *really* trying here, okay?), how could she have turned him down? Sally had found him sitting miserably on the doorstep when he got back from depositing his grieving family at the airport, and brought him up for a coffee, knowing from our earlier call from baggage reclaim that we couldn't have been too far behind.

'Salvatore told me everything.' Marcus spoke to her softly. Leoni hoped that this wasn't entirely the case as she looked down upon his thinning hair and wondered if he was moving towards a comb-over phase. 'I love you, darling – ' he reached up to give her the rose and took her palm – 'and I'm truly sorry for everything. I've been a complete prat, and I promise I'll make it up to you.' Marcus kissed Leoni's hand and for one horrible moment I thought he was going to start snivelling. We had all made to leave the room almost the second Sally knocked on the door with his sorry waif in tow, but Marcus had insisted that we stay and witness his heartfelt declaration of apology. He cleared his throat and pulled himself together for his final plea. 'Please come home. It's just not right without you.'

Leoni dropped to her knees and threw her arms around Marcus's neck. It was an excruciating moment for the rest of us, skilfully side-kicked with Paul's joyful announcement that this called for a glass of something special, followed by our hasty en-masse scuttling exit to the kitchen. We noisily assembled a tray of glasses and talked in raised voices to muffle the emotional sounds bleeding in from the sitting room. Paul rolled his eyes at us and we followed him back into the operating theatre with the drinks.

I caught Leoni's eye. 'Want a hand getting your stuff together?' She nodded with a tired but altogether satisfied smile and followed me through to her room. Somehow, Leoni had managed to accumulate about three times the volume of detritus she had originally arrived with, so I rummaged around in the wardrobe drawers for a few nice carrier bags (the shopping trophy sort) and helped her gather everything up. I folded up her dressing gown and laid it neatly beside the pile of clothes on the bed.

'Are you sure you're okay with all this?' I asked her. 'You know you're welcome to stay as long as you like.' I procrastinated with the packing, mindful that both she and Paul were about to leave, knowing how much I would miss having the constant company.

'It'll be all right,' she said softly as she zipped up her bulging case then came to my side to hold my hand. 'The men in Marcus's family have a history of dying young.'

'JUST A BIT FURTHER. Keep your eyes closed.' Upon reaching their house after patching up their differences, Marcus had led Leoni into their freshly redecorated dining room. All remnants of the dark-brown pebble-dashing courtesy of Leoni's boeuf mortar bomb had been magically erased and the broken furniture replaced. The newly arrived children, oblivious to the recent high drama in Parentland, were under threat of instant death if they so much as thought about exchanging a single bickering word, but they still squealed excitedly as their dad tenderly guided their blindfolded mum in through the front door towards his big reveal. 'Ready?' he said. Leoni nodded warily with a nervous smile, hoped he had kept the receipt, and Marcus pulled the loosely tied scarf from her eyes.

Standing in front of her was a hefty woman in her late fifties wearing a yellow nylon Age Concern dress set off with a gaudy string of blue plastic beads around her flaccid turkey-wattle throat.

'Leoni,' announced Marcus proudly. 'This is Pat. She's the children's new nanny.'

'Oh, thank God!' Leoni blurted, and before she

could stop herself, she had launched her upper body at the poor unsuspecting woman and started sobbing uncontrollably. The children burst in from the kitchen and rushed towards their mother. Josh stopped dead in his tracks and glared at his dad accusingly.

'Why is Mummy crying?'

'Because she's happy,' said Marcus with a knowing smile.

Finally, he felt like he was starting to get the hang of it.

RICK'S TAN WAS deeper than the sea. He keeps it topped up at every frying opportunity with the result that his dermis looks like it would come in jolly handy for a sturdy pair of hiking boots should the need ever arise. I had seen that the house was perfect for his return, shopping all freshly done and put away in its rightful places, party wreckage neatly repaired, and flowers sent to all half-dozen of his current favourites. Where he gets his energy from I don't know, although I suspect there is far less sex involved than he would have his pals believe. I have yet to stumble upon a hidden wood nymph in the bathroom on any given morning.

I took the bag from his hand as he lurched in red-faced through the doorway and waited for him to stop panting before attempting any communication.

'The flight from Rome was packed with Japanese tourists.' He cursed angrily, pulling off his jacket and fumbling around in the pockets for a cigar. 'I feel like I've been stuck in a cage full of fucking budgerigars for the last three hours.' He dropped the jacket on the black zed chair by the sitting room door and headed towards the tantalus on the side table. 'Any messages?'

'Thousands.' I smiled efficiently. 'Your first ex-wife wants more maintenance, the car's fixed and ready for collection, Toby Williams says he never wants to do business with you again, and,' I got to the one I was really looking forward to delivering, 'a lad called Ryan something-or-other rang to say that he thinks he's your love child.' I pretended all normality as I rearranged the little pile of yellow slips in my hand.

'Not him again.' Rick poured himself a Scotch. 'The mother's off her rocker, you know.'

'You don't say.' My determination to be non-judgemental sounded more sarcastic than I had intended. Rick didn't seem to notice, settled in the big chair behind his desk and flicked through the other pile of low-priority messages before pulling his diary out of his soft brown leather briefcase.

'Hell?' he started, looking at the pages. 'I need you to come to a function with me tomorrow night. It's one of those boring evenings with drinks and speeches, but you'll get to put on a posh frock and I promise there won't be a boat in sight.'

'Take one of your floozies,' I told him as I tidied the flowers on the coffee table, 'and I do wish you wouldn't call me that.'

'Can't,' he said. 'It needs to be someone respectable.'

'Well, I can't either,' I said firmly. 'I don't have a thing to wear.'

IT WAS A SHEER stroke of genius. Because his ex-wives have been ripping him off blind for years, Rick thinks that everything costs an absolute fortune. Not just shoes and dresses and school fees, but milk and bread and Mister Sheen, judging by the staggering amount of so-called housekeeping money that they got through. The wedge he gave me to resolve my wardrobe crisis would have kept Imelda Marcos happy for oh, let's see, at least an hour. I did the only thing any sensible woman would do, and headed straight for Selfridges.

'I'm looking for something that I can wear to a formal black tie evening do and a wedding,' I briefed the worryingly ordinary-looking personal shopper. She sized me up and down and appeared instantly bored.

'So that's two outfits,' she said without passion, writing some notes on a pad.

'No,' I told her. 'Just the one.' I was hoping to trouser a bit of change from Rick's largesse for the crippling council tax bill. What we get for it I don't know. Bins half-emptied once in a blue moon and a direct hotline number through to pest control when the local rat population start coming out on Harley-Davidsons.

After searching rail after rail and trying on dozens of depressing fashion-victim candidates, we finally discovered an exquisite pearl-grey silk two-piece ensemble with a floor-length skirt, set off by a single long strand of curling needleworked ivy in pale silver stitching. Perfect for Rick's evening of dowager respectability, it would be instantly transformed for Sara's wedding on Saturday with the addition of a feathered *My Fair Lady* Ascot hat that was so voluminous I might as well have chosen to wear the reception marquee. There was no hat box in the world big enough to contain its drama, so I escorted it home proudly in a taxi and kept it on its stand in my bedroom. Impractical, irresistible and, I thought, *un peu dangereux*.

When Rick came to pick me up the next evening at seven, he found me immobilized by a still-tacky top coat. Like an idiot, I had gone and painted my nails before I had properly finished dressing and didn't dare risk trying to struggle the little jacket on until they had completely dried. You only do that once. And nail varnish doesn't come off, no matter what anyone says.

'You'll have to come up for a minute,' I called into the intercom, pressing the buzzer. 'I'm not quite ready. First floor.' I left the front door ajar and went back to the bedroom to give my hands another blast with the hairdryer. Terrible for the old cuticles, I know, but desperate times call for desperate measures. 'Help yourself to a drink if you want it,' I shouted through to him.

Ten minutes later I was done to a crisp and went to show Rick the fruits of his hardly earned cash. He was quietly looking at the photographs on the mantelpiece and turned to greet me with an uncharacteristically gracious bow.

'What do you think?' I gave him a twirl.

'You'll do, Hell.' He smiled.

A MAN DRIPPING IN gold braid, who had apparently wandered straight off the set of an ITV *Mutiny on the Bounty* extravaganza, whispered into the ears of the overdressed guests as they arrived, then yelled their names pointlessly into the cavernous Guildhall as each couple stepped into the grand banqueting space. The whole thing was very impressive. I imagined 'Miss Helen Robbins' echoing around my ears and the room turning to admire the elegant mystery woman with whispers of 'Who is *that*?' gasping above their upturned heads. Not that anyone was listening, by the looks of it.

'Mr and Mrs Richard Wilton,' called the man with the tricorn. You what? I turned questioningly to Rick. He remained staunchly facing front, smile fixed on his face, my arm firmly gripped in the tuck of his elbow. Leading me stiffly into the crowded room, he leaned towards me and said through the side of his mouth, 'Just smile and make like a wife.' A liveried waiter sailed past with a tray of charged champagne glasses held high. Rick lifted two off as he floated by and handed one to me. 'Hold on to this for a minute,' he said, and then quickly downed the contents of the other before taking the fresh one from my hand and replacing it with his empty.

'So what's all this in aid of?' I whispered as I looked around.

'Dunno,' he said uninterestedly. 'We're here to meet someone.' He was scanning the room in search of a recognizable face but was beaten to it when a pair of matching penguin suits arrived by his side.

'Rick,' said the one on the left.

Rick turned and shook his hand. 'Chris. Good of you to join us.'

'And this must be . . .' The man called Chris was looking me up and down with a smile.

'Mrs Wilton to you, mate.' Rick was watching my face carefully as he made the introductions. 'The wife hates these things and likes to keep it formal.' I decided to play the part and adopted a snooty air,

offering nothing other than a small, hopefully enig-
matic smile. Chris was unperturbed and grinningly
tapped on the arm of his companion and nodded him
towards us.

'Rick, this is the chap I told you about. If you want
to take a punt with that Middle Eastern deal, he's your
man.' Chris looked pleased with himself and waited to
be heaped with praise. Rick rudely ignored him and
stared at the newcomer with interest.

'Julian Gartree,' the man introduced himself, confidently sticking his hand into Rick's Olympian grip.

Rick watched me for a moment then shook the
man's hand hard and looked into his face. It was an
alarming, intense gesture. Intimidating in a squaring-
up, football hooligan way. Still, what do I know? Maybe
this is how big business is done. 'Heard a lot about
you,' Rick said finally. 'In fact, I was wondering if you
might be able to help me with something else I'm
putting together,' and he slung an arm around the
stranger's shoulders and discreetly led him away to a
corner, talking quietly into the side of his head, leaving
me standing there awkwardly with Chris Whatsisname.
The human trolley rolled past us again and I helped
myself to a glass of bubbly while admiring the gathering flock of beautiful people dressed in their best.

Barely two sips later, Rick reappeared with a broad
smile, arm still casually draped around the now pale-
faced and silent Julian. 'Headache still giving you gyp,

darlin'?' he asked. I do wish he'd stop putting me on the spot like this. What's the right answer? Yes? No? Oh go on, Rick, give us a clue.

'Yes,' I said, quickly followed with, 'but I can manage with it.' That covers most exits.

'Don't be daft, love; let's get you home.' Rick took my unfinished drink and handed it to a passing waiter, saying to him, 'Get that man a brandy, would you?' He nodded towards the still mute Julian, stuffed a fifty-pound note into the waiter's top pocket and winked at me, saying, 'Looks like he could use it,' before leading me out of there.

'Is THAT IT?' I asked Rick as he looked up and down the deserted road in search of an orange taxi light.

'That's it,' he confirmed, spotting one at the far end of the street and sticking his fingers in his mouth. The shrieking whistle that flew from his lips almost shattered my eyeballs. I wish I could do that.

'But we were only there for fifteen minutes,' I mumbled. I suppose I felt a bit disappointed, all dressed up with no place to go. I'd even been to the hairdresser. When Rick had asked me to accompany him, I'd envisaged something a little more, well, lengthy. This evening might as well have been a red carpet visit to the nearest revolving door. The thought of sitting around at home on my own with a spam sandwich and an Elnett hairdo heralded a new low ebb.

'That's all right, isn't it?' he said. 'You didn't even want to come in the first place.' The taxi pulled up in front of us.

'I know,' I said. 'I just thought that it would probably include a dinner or something like that.'

Rick suddenly looked highly amused. 'Dinner, eh? Well, if you wanted me to take you out to dinner, all you had to do was ask.' He opened the door of the cab. 'Hop in.'

'You know I didn't mean that.' I felt my face reddening. 'I just got the wrong end of the stick. That's all.'

'Nope,' he said. 'You've said it now and you can't change your mind, so dinner it is.'

'But I don't want to!' I protested.

'Will you just get in the cab and stop arguing?' And with that he virtually pushed me through the open door and jumped in himself, shouting the name of a two-month-long-queue restaurant and its exclusive street through the glass to the driver. The cab rolled off and Rick started laughing.

'What's so funny?' I clipped indignantly.

'You,' he said.

IF I HAD BEEN disappointed not to have turned any heads during my grand entrance to the Guildhall, that soon changed as Rick helped me out of the taxi and led me in through the gleaming art nouveau glazed doors of the restaurant. The maitre d' greeted Rick as though he were President Chirac himself, then, catching sight of me next to him, dramatically took two small steps backwards and gasped, with one hand to his breast, murmuring appreciative approval of his regular's dining partner.

'Got a nice little table for two you could squeeze us onto, Tony?' asked Rick, shrugging off his silk scarf and handing it to the hat-check girl with a ten-pound note.

'For you – ' Tony bowed – 'I have your favourite place ready.' And he ushered us through the chattering classes and settled the pair of us at an unusually generous round table, set with softly glowing silver cutlery and sparkling crystal on a rigidly starched, pristine white-linen cloth. 'Would you like an aperitif?' Tony expertly dressed my lap with a single flap of the napkin and knocked away a non-existent fleck of dust from beside my knife with a long, tapered finger. I was so bowled over by my surroundings that I scarcely trusted myself to open my mouth. It was a dining room by which all others could be measured, an opulent scene from the Restoration. Enormous mirrors, tinged with the gilded crackle of time beneath their fading silvering, reflected the rich diners within their deeply carved mahogany features. This was one of those places where there is no such thing as overdressed, and I could detect that most of the women wished they had tried a bit harder when I wafted by in my shimmering floor-length silk.

'A glass of your finest champagne for the lady,' said Rick, 'and I'll have a Chivas on the rocks.' I smiled up at Tony, who nodded his approval at Rick's stunningly good choice. Tony slid away.

'This is very nice,' I understated, leaning towards Rick. 'I can't believe you just walked in and got a table like that.' I tried not to look ridiculously impressed.

'Easy,' said Rick. 'Only plebs try to book in advance. They keep most of them back for the likes of Madonna and Puff Duvet.'

'Really?' I was suitably amazed.

'Well, who would you rather have in your restaurant? A load of special occasion morons who've saved up for six months then bussed in from the suburbs?'

Tony arrived with the drinks and set them down on the table, then opened out and handed to each of us a heavy leather-backed turtle of a menu. 'I'll leave the wine list here,' he murmured discreetly, expertly leaving it there.

The dishes listed on the enormously varied pages all looked so delicious that I hadn't a clue where to begin.

I tried to gauge the likely capacity of the waistband on my skirt while eyeing the gourmet descriptions drizzled with butter and finished with cream.

'Try the lobster,' Rick suggested. 'They'll take you over to the tank to choose one, if you like.' But there was something else plaguing my mind, and I'm such a coward when it comes to making outright demands that I chewed my lower lip and suffered in silence for a while. Steeling myself for a moment, I decided to throw caution to the wind and grab the bull by the horns.

'Are we having a starter?' I asked in a small voice. Rick looked up from his menu, saw the poorly disguised discomfiture on my face and tried not to laugh.

'You go ahead and order whatever you want.' He smiled.

'Are you sure you don't mind? I feel really bad for having made a fuss like that. You didn't need to go to all this trouble. I'm sure you've got—'

'Drink your champagne,' he chided. 'A man's got to eat, hasn't he? And I can think of far worse people I could be having dinner with tonight.'

'Well, it's very kind of you.' I took a sip from my glass. To my complete surprise, the mouthful of cheerful bubbles I was expecting was instead the merest whisper of effervescent mousse. A bit like the old-fashioned R. White's cream soda we used to have on high days and holidays as children. It was indescribably delicious. I held the glass in front of my face with curiosity and noticed how the froth clung to the sides like beer.

'Good, isn't it?' I nodded back at Rick, still savouring the grapes on my tongue. 'If you're gonna drink champers,' he said, 'make it a good 'un or don't bother.'

'Quite,' I agreed, realizing there and then that I had obviously never tasted a *good 'un* before in my life.

'Right,' he said, finishing his Scotch. 'I know what I want. How about you?'

It occurred to me that I have never really known what I want. I could sit there for days and still not be sure. Maybe I should have been born a man. That way I might have stood more of a chance.

'Erm.' I looked at the menu again and started to panic. What if my choice were to prove a disappointment? What if I went for the duck then wished I'd had the lamb? 'I'll have the, er, oh no, wait, maybe I'll have the, er, um.'

Rick shook his head. 'That's settled then. I'll order for both of us or we could be here all night.' He raised his hand towards Tony, who somehow managed to float to Rick's side without apparently moving.

'You are decided?' Tony asked, producing a little pad from his top pocket.

'Yep,' said Rick. 'Bring us some of that stuff I had on Saturday to kick off with.' Tony cast his eyes upwardly to the right, pen to his lips, as though trying to summon the memory of what one particular diner had eaten five days earlier. Rick described it with his fingers. 'You know, that little fishcake thing with the bits of chilli in it.' Tony nodded his instant recognition with a mumble of excellent, very good, perfect. 'Then we want you to slaughter the two biggest sea monsters in the tank and cremate them with a thermidor sauce.' Tony is swept away by Rick's ingenuity, shakes his head gently and seemingly wipes away a tear of admiration. 'That should do it.' Rick winked at me, then back at Tony. 'And a bottle of number forty-seven,' he added, handing back the wine list without looking up. Tony almost fainted.

No wonder they had given us such a big table. Having satisfactorily demolished the first course in a matter of minutes, the biblical scale of Rick's main supper order unveiled itself. That thing was huge. How the waiter managed to bring it over without taking somebody's eye out was a miracle. He set the lumbering great crustacean down in front of me then came back with another one for Rick, who was already brandishing his knife and fork before the plate had made contact with the table. He was about to dive in with both feet when he saw me hesitating.

'Something wrong?' he asked with concern.

'It's looking at me.'

Rick sighed patiently, reached forwards and pulled

off both the bongers with the eyes attached, put them down beside his own plate and covered them up with his napkin.

'Better?' he asked. I nodded.

'Tuck in,' he said encouragingly, pointing at my plate with his knife, and watched until I had taken a first mouthful. It was meltingly delicious, and I gave in to the temptation of the rich sauce under the approving glances of my accidental companion. As a bacchanalian who quite apparently loves his food, Rick was soon moaning with pleasure and pulling appreciative faces at me through a full mouth. I felt compelled to join in by licking my fingers and squinting my eyes at him in agreement. We didn't talk much after that. Upon finishing our trawlerman's treat, Rick excused himself to the rest room and I nodded my thanks and compliments to the waiter, who cleared away our devoured plates. Tony wafted to my side.

'It was good?' he asked unnecessarily, eyeing the empty shells as they were carted away.

'Excellent,' I replied, dabbing at my lips. He nodded with a smile.

'You know Mr Wilton a long time?' he ventured, while replacing our used napkins with fresh ones. He gallantly ignored the stemmed eyeballs rolled up in Rick's and swept them out of sight.

'A little while,' I replied politely.

'It's nice for us to see him having dinner with a lady

179

friend. We were beginning to give up on him.' Tony removed the empty wine bottle from the ice bucket and wrapped the dripping bottom of it with one of the used cloths. 'Mr Wilton has been coming here for many years. Since I was that high.' He gestured a hand down towards his knee. 'He jokes with us that he prefers to eat alone, but every man would rather be in the company of a charming woman.' His eyes met mine briefly. 'He looks very happy this evening. I think it's a good thing that he has found someone. We all approve very much.'

I was about to explain to Tony that this wasn't what it looked like, what with me being nothing more than an overdressed minion with a free meal ticket, when Rick returned to the table and settled back into his chair with a smile. Tony stood behind him and raised a conspiratorial finger to his lips at me with a twinkle.

'That's better,' Rick announced. 'I reckon I could manage another bottle of that,' he said, pointing to the empty in Tony's hand.

'You'll be drinking it on your own,' I replied. 'Some of us have got to work in the morning.'

'Oh, go on, Hell! Keep a fat old git company for a while longer.' He hung a little-boy-lost expression. 'Tell you what, you can take the day off. Make a long weekend of it.' I smiled in submission and Tony announced he would find something even better in their cellar.

The fat-busting chocolate torte that found its way onto my plate ten minutes later was not one of my better ideas. Eyes far bigger than my poorly assessed waistband, I felt the zip give way the moment I tried to stifle a sneeze: that soft, ripping yarn sensation when you know you've overdone it and burst out of your container. Rick noticed the sudden drop in my face.

'You all right, Hell?' He put his hand on mine with concern, withdrawing it almost immediately as though having touched a rattlesnake in the lucky dip.

'Yes! Fine!' I shrilled with a plastic smile. 'Fantastic!' There was nothing for it but to hope that my jacket was long enough. Either that or die of shame at the thought of the diners behind me being flashed a horrific rear view of my smooth-line pearlized apple gatherers. Rick gave me a cheerful twitch and resumed his all-out assault on the European-sized cheeseboard.

Sidling off to the ladies' room with my clutch bag held conspicuously behind me, I found the hat-check girl standing by the door with a needle and thread at the ready.

'THIS TIME IT's serious!'
'Well, I can't see anything.'
'Look! There!'
We were standing in front of the searchlights in my bathroom, Julia's face not more than two inches away

from the illuminated mirror, and me peering at the reflection to see what it was that had caused her to get flashed not once, but twice, while speeding down the Westway on her way to see me over the crisis for which she had cancelled all her afternoon meetings. Thanks to Rick's generosity I was home anyway, still trying to digest last night's lobster in the manner of an anaconda dealing with a recently swallowed goat.

'There!' Julia pulled the skin taut just beneath her eyebrow and suddenly, glinting in the halogen light, was a two-millimetre white hair.

'Oh, for God's sake, Julia. It's completely undetectable unless you train an electron microscope onto it. And it's one of the ones you pull out anyway.'

'So? It's a bloody grey fuse wire in my eyebrow!' she shouted. 'It's started! The beginning of the end!'

I decided not to collude with Julia's ageing angst any longer and went back to the Caesar salad I was preparing for lunch while she continued to search her arched brows for any signs of further turncoats. She emerged a couple of minutes later, sulking her way onto a stool in the kitchen.

'Found yourself a new assistant yet?' I sat beside her and shared out the cutlery. Julia reached across me for the mayo, loaded her plate with two uncharacteristically large spoonfuls, and pulled a big piece of bread off the end of the French stick.

'Don't,' she complained. 'I'm gutted. Mind you,

Sara's yet to pluck up the courage to actually resign, which rather surprises me. She's probably biding her time until she catches me in a good mood. All I can say is she'll have a bloody long wait.' She dipped a chunk of bread into the mayonnaise and filled her mouth, chewing silently for a little while then adding, 'I don't think I can muster the energy to deal with all that again.' Julia shook her head. 'The thought of spending another year training someone else to do the job, only to have them up and leave just when things are ticking along nicely.' She took another bite, worrying the lettuce leaves around her plate with a fork. 'I just don't have the stamina I used to.' What she didn't say was how much she would miss Sara. I guess she felt she didn't need to. It just wasn't her style.

'Don't write her off just yet,' I mused. 'I wouldn't be surprised if she doesn't go and call the whole thing off after Leoni opened her big mouth.'

'You've got to be joking,' Julia said. 'Wild horses couldn't keep Sara from dragging Dudley down the aisle. She said she wouldn't care if Leoni had seen him dressed up as Papa Smurf with a bunch of daffodils stuck up his arse. Right now, she's just one question away from becoming a millionaire's wife and she doesn't need to phone a friend.'

We finished our lunch in virtual silence, save the predictable platitudes I offered to try to cheer her up. Clearing the plates away afterwards, I told her that things could be a lot worse. At least she had a husband – a good one too – one that she loved, who loved her right back. That, to my mind, was surely worth more than all the tea in China.

I waved her off from the balcony.

'See you tomorrow,' she called up.

Ah yes. The big day.

Chapter Twelve

DING, *DONG*!

IT WAS ONE of those glorious English summer mornings when the sun shines brightly and the swallows fly high in a sky far bluer than Butch Cassidy's eyes. Tiny white clouds tried their best to stay aloft but melted away and disappeared within a few minutes, unable to hold their own against such a confident day. My hair flew in the hot jet stream from the dryer and my thoughts were consumed by Sara on this, the morning of her wedding. Classic FM floated the summertime strings of Vivaldi through my neat and tidy flat, winding their high notes around the eerily empty rooms, reaching out and touching the cornices, settling their elegant Venetian score around my naked shoulders.

I moisturized my whole body, gently massaging my calves and noticing the way the skin crinkled and puckered ever so slightly as my long strokes reached the delicate crevices behind each knee. Sod the wrinkles. It was therapeutic, reaffirming, in a silent, familiar way. I remarked to myself that I should take the time to do it more often. The pearl-grey suit lay waiting for me on the bed, spread out expectantly, and I suppose in my mind I pretended that it was I who was readying myself as a bride that day. I knew this, deep down. I wanted to feel those feelings again, the excitement, the trepidation, the uncontrollable rush before the monumental step I was about to take. The thought of today becoming the wife of the man I adored enough to want to be with for the rest of my life. Somebody who would love me and take care of me. Cherish and comfort me. Let me feel it. Even if just for a little while.

Today, I looked like a woman (not that I usually look like a man, you understand). Stretching as tall as my moderate frame would allow, I considered my reflection in the full-length mirror and felt proud. Proud that I'd made it. Proud to still be here, in one piece, despite everything. The hands on the clock neared two, so I finished dressing and carefully lifted the sumptuous hat from its stand on top the little chest of drawers. A tiny flurry of dust fell from the enormous fringe, sparkling like playtime glitter as it dispersed through the rays of sunlight streaming in through the open windows. Mmm. A dusty hat. That would never do.

By the time I realized what a stupid *stupid* exercise it was that I had embarked on (and that's what I get for spending the entire morning wrapped up in some far-fetched romantic daydream), the entire ostrich-feather trim on my beautiful new Audrey Hepburn number had shot up the end of the Hoover like a rat up a drainpipe, whizzing around saying hello to the rest of the week's carpet scrapings. It all happened so quickly that there was nothing I could do to stop it. Why I didn't just give it a little shake out on the balcony I shall never know. Why didn't I just tip it upside down and administer a sharp tap inside the crown to knock the dust off? Why did I have to go and get the sodding vacuum cleaner, for God's sake? Why, oh why, oh why?

NATURALLY, I WAS LATE. By the time I scrambled in through the gothic doors, panting like a fugitive on the run, the organist was already in full swing, giving it his all and rolling his shoulders wildly from side to side, gown sleeves flying, as he let everyone have it with both barrels. Some of the trickier passages got the better of him, but he ran up and down the finger-breaking toccata with such blind confidence anyway that nobody seemed to mind. The church was respectably full. Everyone was smiling, dressed up to the nines, and chattering irreverently in an ungodly manner that suggested most had gone for a quick livener or three in the pub around the corner first. Leoni spotted me and stood up, waving her pink-gloved arm in a huge beckon and pointing urgently at the vacant slot between her and Marcus. I scurried in beside them, apologizing to the confused old tortoise couple I had to clamber over unceremoniously on the way through.

'Love the hat!' whispered Leoni.

'You should have seen it before,' I said sadly.

As luck would have it, though, the hat actually looked significantly better without the feather muppet trim. Still dramatic with plenty of brim to hide behind, but far less frightening for the uninitiated.

I scanned the pews. 'Where's Julia?'

'Up there.' She pointed. 'Second row. Behind crazy woman.'

I sat up straight and looked dead ahead. Front pew, on the aisle, was a museum-piece scarlet headpiece with a pair of quarter-scale white doves perched precariously on one side. Directly behind it was Julia's dark, shiny hair. At that instant she turned and saw me. We exchanged a wave and a smile. She pointed at her head then to mine and gave me an approving thumbs up, then pointed at Sara's mother's insane headdress and did a small winding loony gesture by her temple with her eyes crossed.

The organist pulled out all the stops and bellowed the opening notes of the Trumpet Voluntary. Holding a deafening chord until our brains began to rattle, he turned and nodded at the congregation to stand up. Amid much scraping and rustling from the highly strung assembly, the groom rose from his seat and stepped out to take his place in front of the aisle before the smiling priest, followed moments later by his best man. Dudley looked innocent enough, so I put the memory of his public peccadillo out of my mind. Everyone deserves a second chance, a clean slate, at least once. It was no doubt just an insane one-off, a final venting before his wings were clipped. Either that or Sara was about to get spliced to a closet woofter. Everyone shuffled noisily to attention, clearing their throats with a couple of last-minute harrumphs and good-measure coughs. As the sweet music rose to fill the flower-strewn church, Sara emerged into view and took our collective breath away with a celestial sigh.

She was lovely. Just lovely. Like a breath of fresh air on a summer's day. To my great surprise, she had chosen the very simplest of gowns, free from artifice or adornment, cut from layer after layer of softly flowing duchess silk that moved in slow motion behind her. I would imagine Lady Guinevere might have demanded where she had got it from and ordered a couple for herself. Handfuls of pale, waxen flowers were scattered through her softly tumbling hair, and a delicate set of daisy chains took the place of the usual heavy jewellery around her neck and wrists. My heart leapt for her and my eyes spontaneously filled with tears as I remembered. And there it was – The Feeling. The calm outside the church as my sister and best friend fussed around me perfecting the folds of my dress, adjusting the veil that whispered in front of my face, lacing my outlook behind a clouded, sugared lens. The wide smiles on the people who watched me walk down the aisle on my father's arm. The way I had felt so grown up, and so very special.

I turned to look at Dudley, wanting to catch a glimpse of his expression at the very moment he first set eyes on his bride. What I saw instead caught me completely off-guard. There, standing beside him, was the most beautiful man I had ever seen. And he was staring straight at me.

GLANCING AT MY watch for the thousandth time I wondered if anyone would miss me if I just slipped quietly away. I could always send them a text message later saying I had a headache and needed to go.

Twenty-five minutes I'd been sitting there in the powder room, trying to collect my self-pitying thoughts. Having taken as long as possible over a one-ounce wee that I didn't really need, protractedly washing my hands, fixing make-up that didn't need fixing, reading the labels on the little bottles of this and that (it was a very nice powder room, in a very nice hotel), I finally sat down quietly on one of the comfortably upholstered lady chairs and tried to fade into the wallpaper as other women came in, did their thing, and rushed out again.

It's not often I feel like a gooseberry, but going to a wedding on your own (albeit 'on your own with a small group of becoupled friends') is a dead cert for any single woman of a certain age who wants to look and feel like a small, round, hairy grape. Weddings make married people feel all in-love again, unless they can't stand the sight of each other, in which case they're on the phone to their lovers and lawyers from the nearest lavvy within two minutes of the conjugal kiss. Leoni and Marcus were being demonstrably aren't-we-stronger-than-ever-darling with each other, while Julia and David had settled into a quiet serenity with deep, meaningful glances passing between them every now and then. Sara was busily performing to the gathered lenses, taking to the flashing paparazzi like a duck to water, working her dress like a movie star, and I'd just hung around holding on to a rapidly warming champagne glass and smiling inanely like a vicar at an Ann Summers party.

IT HAD BEEN a glorious service, filled with hundreds of uplifted voices singing 'All Things Bright and Beautiful' and rounded off with a tearful burst of spontaneous applause. But I felt like crying so badly that my eyes hurt with the effort of keeping their contents at bay. After all, it wasn't that I'd had a problem with being married, it was just that I'd had a problem with being married to Robert. I liked the idea of its permanence. Being able to tick the 'get married' box off the list of life's To Dos. It was everything I had ever wanted. Tenderness, stability, playing house. Trouble was, in my world it had turned out not to be quite the same thing in practice. More a case of emptiness, hostility and playing Hitler. Seeing Sara brought it all rushing back. Deep in my heart I wished her all the luck in the world as I helped myself to another handful of tissues and poked at a stray salty droplet in the corner of my eye.

I decided to have a stern word with myself. You can't go back in there like this. Now pull your bloody socks up and go and find the others. I opened my handbag, checked for my keys, dropped a few coins into the tip jar and took out a ten-pound note ready for the short taxi ride home.

'Don't tell me you're leaving already?' He was waiting for me outside the ladies' room, leaning casually against the dado rail on the opposite wall, smoking a cigarette, his other hand hanging loosely in the tuck of his trouser pocket. To begin with, I didn't realize it was him, and was already crouching my way towards the more discreet side entrance in the hope of avoiding the other guests. It was only when he took a couple of steps into my direct path that I looked up into the face I had met for that burning instant as Sara floated down the aisle.

'You'll miss my speech,' he said. I smiled up at him apologetically, the cab fare and keys a smoking gun in my hand. After a moment's pause, he added thoughtfully, 'It's really rather good.' Perhaps he noticed my sadness, perhaps he thought me shy, but either way he was gentle and soothing in his manner. He smiled some more and jerked his head towards the reception. 'Shall we?' he asked. I nodded back, squeaked a small okay and accepted his arm.

Judging by the rising volume as we walked in through the double doors, the welcoming champagne had all been efficiently polished off. Everyone had already found their seats, busily making new friends and pulling distance-greeting faces at old ones around the room. Spotting me from a table by the wall, Leoni got to her feet and rushed over, slicing her way through the seated guests. 'Where the bloody hell did you get to?' she hissed. 'We all thought you'd been . . .' then she noticed the figure standing next to me and stopped talking, her eyes fixed on his face.

'She's been having a moment,' he explained with a charming smile.

'Oh. Okay.' Leoni shot me a questioning furrow then started making her way back to her seat. I followed behind, mouthing a thank you to the stranger. He flashed his eyes at me. 'I'll be watching you,' he said with a playful wag of his finger.

I took my place next to Leoni and Marcus. David and Julia were seated at the same table on the other side, together with two couples we weren't acquainted with. Introductions were hastily made and instantly forgotten through a blur of table decorations. The shrill-voiced wife with the strange bread-roll felt creation on her head (from the Philip Treacy bakery collection, I presume) helpfully suggested we use our place cards turned around the other way as on *University Challenge*. Julia glanced at David, discreetly removed theirs from the table and dropped them on the floor. Bread head quickly tired of trying to make conversation with the unsporting Julia so turned her attentions to the bemused chap with the handlebar moustache to her other side.

No expense had been spared with the wedding breakfast. Napkins were waved into laps and a small army of waiters teemed into the room from behind the painted screens in front of the kitchen doors. A steady stream of fresh crab, foie gras and other haute couture delicacies arrived in front of me and left again virtually intact with mumbled apologies to the waiter's raised eyebrows. My previously ravenous appetite, deliberately saved for the sumptuous banquet, had mysteriously shrivelled away and I found I couldn't manage so much as a mouthful. My heart thumped so violently that I convinced myself the whole table would hear it thundering away in my chest.

'What's the matter with you?' asked Julia as she watched another untouched plate being removed by the waiter. 'Cat got your tongue?'

'She's feeling a bit emotional,' explained Leoni without looking up, as she hammered on an unyielding claw with the fat end of the pepper grinder.

Julia tossed a little ball of crumpled streamer paper into my plate to raise my attention. 'Look at Sophia,' she mouthed at me, nodding her head towards the wedding party. 'She looks like she's having a nervous breakdown.' I glanced over towards the top table and saw Sophia reaching into her handbag, sneaking something out and slipping it in her mouth. Whatever it was, she swallowed it without water, swiftly followed by a generous wine chaser.

'Do you think we should book her an ambulance?' I whispered back behind my hand.

Julia laughed and shook her head. 'I'll tell you all about it later.'

After an hour of missed heartbeats, the tinkling sound of teaspoon against glass silenced the inebriated guests towards the now upstanding father of the bride. Sara looked up at him adoringly and clapped enthusiastically along with the rest of us. I did my best to keep my eyes fixed on the piece of paper he was holding unsteadily, but found them wandering to the tablecloth, then along its length to the end of the trestle, then up and into the direct gaze of the smiling Mr Fabulous. He picked up his glass and tipped it ever so slightly towards me, took a sip and returned his eyes to Sara's tearful dad, who was midway through spluttering something about putting too many esses in his speech.

'CONGRATULATIONS.' I KISSED DUDLEY on the cheek as we shared a few words. 'I hope you'll have a long and happy life together,' I told him sincerely. 'She's a wonderful girl.' The guests had reached that point in the proceedings where most of them should have left half an hour ago, if only to sleep it off for a while, and the once fairytale venue had been thoroughly decimated. Dudley was doing the rounds to say his goodbyes, his already slow progress being severely hampered by several small groups of drunken friends who were determined to get him to extend the occasion by announcing an all-night free bar.

'Thanks, Helen.' He squeezed my arm tenderly. 'I would have asked you first, but I know you would have been far too sensible to accept me.'

I laughed at the lovely thought. 'If I hear one more person refer to me as sensible,' I scolded him, 'I'll chop off their head with an axe.' A ripple of alarm flashed across Dudley's face, then his expression became earnest.

'You're a remarkable woman, Helen. Truly you are. I hope you find your soul mate one day.' He leaned in and whispered to me. 'He'd have to be one special man.' I nodded my silent agreement and accepted his warm hug with a weary smile.

'Oi! You muscling in on my date?!' Sara swept her dress dramatically beside us, hands on slender white silk hips, beaming from ear to ear, and with that it was well and truly time for us to go. Julia had her coat on and was standing near the door waiting for me, and I took one last fruitless glance around the room in the hope of seeing the hot prospect who had somehow disappeared while I wasn't looking. I could have asked Dudley about him I suppose, but every time I tried to form the sentence I lost my nerve. I kicked myself hard as I dejectedly went to join Julia. All I'd had to say was, 'Who is that nice chap, the best man?' or, 'I'd love an introduction to—' but no, instead I chose to remain silent on the subject for the entire event rather than risk sounding like I was actively shopping for a husband of my own. All those articles in all those magazines about assertiveness and the modern woman, and I couldn't even get past the first measly hello. I saw my friends into their shared cab and waved them off as they disappeared into the cheerful evening traffic.

'Taxi, madam?' offered the claret-collared doorman. I indulged myself in one last longing gaze behind me then nodded and stepped forward towards the open door of my waiting pumpkin.

STANDING DESPONDENTLY ON the pavement outside my empty home, rummaging around in my bag for my now invisible house keys, I barely noticed the black cab pulling up at the kerb close beside me.

'Have lunch with me?' called the voice.

I looked up and there he was, smiling at me from the lowered window. I felt my face light up and my cheeks begin to glow. What is going *on*? This is just ridiculous!

'Sorry to run out on you like that,' he said, leaning his arm on the glass. 'Got caught up with a couple of ancient great aunts who'd been at the sherry and needed taking back to their room,' he explained. 'They held me captive for an hour, but I've always wanted to shout "follow that cab".' We both laughed.

His taxi driver had a broad grin on his face. 'Go on, love! Say yes!' he shouted. 'I've just been through two red lights!'

'HE'S BAD NEWS,' said Leoni as I helped her put the washing out on the line. 'I don't care how memorable you think he is, I got the whole nine yards from the bloke with the fruit-bat moustache hanging on his face.' She reached into the plastic washing basket and started untangling a duvet cover that had knotted itself into a deadly Chinese laundry ball with three pillow cases. 'He was at Cambridge with Dudley years ago. Used to be in business together until his taste for fast cars and Bolivian marching powder got completely out of hand.' Leoni threw the cover over the line and stabbed the remaining two dolly pegs at either end. Millie had drawn little faces on them with coloured felt tip pens and had even finished a few off with a little mop of string hair.

'So how come he's good enough to be playing the role of Dudley's best man, then?' I picked up the empty basket and returned it to the kitchen table.

Leoni followed, filled the kettle without answering the question and gave me one of her finely honed lecturing glares.

'As a matter of fact,' I started defensively, 'he's already told me all about that.' And indeed he had.

WE HAD MET for lunch the next day in a little restaurant by Primrose Hill that's been there for ever. I took the bus, even though it meant changing once or twice, just so as I could savour the journey for that much longer and share the air of anticipation with my fellow passengers as we trundled along sporadically at a snail's pace. Daringly jumping off the bus's rear platform at a red traffic light and walking the last little way, I detoured into the park to climb the hill and noticed that the leaves were starting to turn, just a little, with tiny tinges of rust appearing around their lacy edges. There was the smallest hint of seasonal change in the air, that faint scent of something that isn't quite summer, even though the ambient temperature still feels about the same.

My face was glowing when I reached the miniature bistro and found him waiting for me at a little table in the corner by the open window. The breathlessness wasn't down to the flush of exercise either. I had felt like that all morning, lying in the bath singing along to Steve Wright's Sunday Love Songs, changing my clothes three times, each outfit progressively shouting 'trying too hard' just a bit louder until I finally reverted to Plan A and put my trusty jeans back on.

Upon seeing me he stood up and broke into a broad grin.

'Helen.' He leaned over to kiss my cheek. 'I was wondering whether you'd have second thoughts and think the better of breaking bread with a total stranger today.'

'You know my name? That's not fair!' Silly as this may sound, our conversation through the taxi window the day before hadn't got as far as that. The name of the restaurant and its location, yes. The names of the diners, well, no. For a moment it occurred to me that women have disappeared like this, seduced by their own loneliness then dragged off and dismembered by the shark who'd spotted their injured fish distress signal. They do say that it's always the person you least suspect.

'I know a lot about you, Helen Robbins,' he teased. A little warning bell went off inside my head. It must have registered on my face because he immediately laughed and said, 'Don't look so worried! You're perfectly safe. I asked Dudley about you and he said that you were far too good for me and told me to stay well away.'

'You men are scoundrels,' I chastised him good-humouredly. 'Swapping notes behind a girl's back.

How could I possibly feel anything other than totally disadvantaged?' I made myself comfortable in the seat opposite him and tried to sneak a quick-check peep at my reflection in the window.

'We'll soon fix that,' he said, and called to the waiter, setting the memorable lunch in motion with two marvellously invigorating Bloody Marys and a basket of freshly baked bread. He raised his celeried glass towards me. 'Sebastien Charles,' he said. 'How do you do?'

I raised my glass against his. 'Very well, thank you. Cheers.'

'So,' he began, dunking a chunk of bread into the little dish of olive oil. 'What caused you to try and do a Cinderella yesterday? And don't pretend that you weren't attempting to escape.' He put the piece of roll into his mouth and challenged me with expectant eyebrows while he chewed.

'Ah, that,' I said, toying with my fork. Right. Might as well start the way I mean to go on. 'I was married once. I suppose it brought back a lot of memories.'

I immediately thought better of screening the director's cut version and decided to leave it at that. He nodded and finished dealing with his mouthful. 'You?' I asked.

Sebastien took a long slug from his glass before answering. 'Always the best man. Never the groom.' I smiled at his honesty. 'I suppose I have what you might call a textbook colourful history.' He started dipping another piece of bread. 'I used to hang out with a pretty rum crowd. Got into some bad habits.' He looked up at me. 'Expensive bad habits, if you get my meaning.' I wasn't sure that I did, and it must have been apparent. 'The trouble with coke is that you lose all sense of what's normal.' I tried to look as though I understood. 'Especially when everyone's doing it. But that was all a long time ago.'

'How long?'

'Two, three years.' Not long enough to be a dark and distant memory then, I thought to myself. In fact, wasn't this all a bit heavy, man? I felt compelled to adopt a serious expression with a sincere furrow. Not my best look.

'What made you stop?'

'The people at the Priory, mainly. And the friend who took me there.'

My tummy rumbled noisily. 'Sorry,' I said. 'Haven't had any breakfast and I think the tabasco in that Bloody Mary has set me off.' Sebastien raised his hand for the waiter and we ordered the same thing. Or rather, I asked what he was having, then announced that it was exactly what I'd been thinking of. I wanted us to have something in common early on, regardless of whether or not it came with polenta.

'Dudley said that your husband had passed away.' I nodded a small admission. 'Do you want to talk about it?' His hand crept towards mine on the table but stopped short of my fingers.

'Not particularly,' I said. What I really wanted to know was how come a bloke like that didn't have a girlfriend. Maybe he did. Not an easy question to ask, so I smiled instead.

'I can't imagine what it must be like to lose your spouse like that.' He shook his head into his drink. No, you can't, I thought. It's bloody fantastic, mate. Recommend it to anyone.

'I don't suppose you can,' I said with a gentle smile. 'Being as you've never been married. How have you managed to avoid that one?'

'More fool me.' He finished his Bloody Mary. 'I was so busy playing the big I Am and sticking gear up my nose that I forgot I'd already met The One. It wasn't that I didn't want to. It's just that it was the furthest thing from my mind. I never got around to asking.' He wiped the celery stick around the bottom of the glass and munched on the end. 'I suppose I just assumed, but then she got fed up with waiting and went off with somebody else. I didn't realize what I'd got until it was long, long gone.'

BY FOUR THIRTY, as we reluctantly prepared to leave the now almost empty restaurant under the encouraging glare of the exhausted staff, I felt as though I had known him for ever. We walked up to the top of Primrose Hill in a bid to counteract the effects of the profiteroles and stopped for a while on the highest bench to look down at the city skyline, dominated by the ugly phallus of what used to be the Post Office Tower. There was a revolving restaurant up there years ago. If our postal service is anything to go by, God only knows what the food was like. Sebastien held my hand for some of the way when we walked back down again, sending my adrenal glands racing, and reluctantly saw me to the bus stop.

'Let me take you home,' he repeated. 'I'd never forgive myself if something happened to you on the way.'

'I'm fine, really. I like taking the bus.'

'Let me come with you then.'

'No!' Funnily enough, I really did feel the need to be on my own for a little while, to ponder what had just happened and try to regain some sense of proportion. He looked at me mischievously.

'I already know where you live. You can run, but you can't hide.'

LEONI RAPPED HER knuckles sharply on the table in front of me. 'Are you listening to a word I'm saying?' she demanded. 'Bloody hell, Helen. You've got that distant look in your eyes and I'm not sure that I like it.' She ran a bread knife through the wrapper and split the biscuit packet in half, spilling a pile of dark chocolate digestives on the wooden surface next to the empty laundry basket, picked one up herself and pushed three towards me. I smiled and slid them around a while then turned my attention back to Leoni. Her air was serious as she lowered her voice. 'You don't think you're in love with him or anything stupid like that, do you?' she asked semi-mockingly.

'You know what, Leoni?' I snapped one of the biscuits in half. 'I think I might just be.'

Chapter Thirteen

LET'S DO IT

I WATCHED THE FULL moon rising into the night sky through the undraped window. It moves faster than you may think. Pick a spot, like a leaf on a tree or a chimney pot silhouetted against its brightness and it will pass it by in just a few minutes. You can feel it circling us in space if you concentrate. As it climbed higher in the neighbouring heavens, it shook off its yellow veil and shone the pearly silver white of which love songs are made. Waves of happiness washed over me as I stared out at the stars with a smile on my face, my feet toastily tucked into a big pair of fluffy oatmeal socks.

The startling intrusion of the telephone snapped me

back to reality with a jolt. Wasn't it a bit late to be waking the dead? Nevertheless, I rushed to answer it anyway, clumsily knocking over a vase of freesias in the process, then forced myself to wait a full three agonizing rings before picking up.

'Hello?' I hesitated expectantly, desperate to hear Sebastien's luscious Midnight Caller voice, and felt instantly guilty for my pang of disappointment as Julia's familiar tones reached my ear.

'Next time you decide to go out spying,' she started, 'can I suggest you either get your eyes tested or check your facts before jumping to conclusions?'

'What on earth are you talking about?' With my thoughts now solely occupied with one thing and one thing only, nothing else made any sense.

'I've found out who that transvestite limpet was that you saw attached to Saint Dudley the other week.'

'You're kidding me.' Julia's efficiency never failed to surprise me, not that I cared any more.

'That's not the half of it,' she whispered. I took the phone back to the sofa, pulled the soft lilac throw up around my knees and settled in for a cosy gossip. 'I'm afraid I decided to take it upon myself to have a word with Sophia about her soon-to-be son-in-law at that bizarre family and friends dinner at Scalini's the night before the wedding.'

'That was a good idea,' I said, then added 'not' to the end of the sentence.

'Don't,' she winced. 'I can hardly bear the thought of it. Why David didn't stop me I don't know, but I think the thought of losing Sara to some philandering bastard who was about to ruin my life, never mind hers, all became a bit too much for me.' She paused to take a sip of whatever it was that she was drinking. 'I mentioned that Leoni wasn't the only one who had seen Dudley out at that place – what's it called again?'

'Salsaville.'

'That's the one.' She started laughing. 'She went white as a sheet then dragged me off to the ladies' room and begged me not to say anything. For a moment I couldn't understand why she had reacted so badly, then it dawned on me.' She stopped talking and took a long slurp.

'What?' I almost shouted at her.

'It was *her*.' Deafening silence for dramatic effect from Julia, and sharp intake of breath from me.

'No way.' I flicked off the television with the remote. This deserved my undivided attention.

'Way. That's why she and Sara rushed off like that in Amsterdam. She thought Leoni had recognized her and was about to turn crown witness for the prosecution. The poor woman was a complete nervous wreck. No wonder she avoided us all like the plague at the wedding.'

'So are you telling me that Dudley's been playing the bloody generation game with Sara and her mother?

I wouldn't have thought he had it in him. That's *completely* outrageous!'

'Not a chance,' she said. Shame, just when we were about to indulge ourselves in some seriously wild speculation. 'She insisted they should get to know each other better, seeing as they were about to become related, so she made him take her out on the town. Threw herself at him all night according to Dudley after I told him the cat was well and truly out of the bag. He was very sweet about it and said that she had been a bit overwrought during the day and probably swallowed a few too many lithiums before dinner.'

'Thank God for that,' I said.

'Mmm. Well, not entirely. She's also got it into her head that everyone thinks she looks like a man in drag, so now she's on her way back to Palm Springs to sue the ventricles off her plastic surgeon.'

'Well, at least it will keep her out of poor Sara's hair for a while.'

'I doubt that very much,' Julia giggled. 'She's expecting poor old Dudley to do the suing.'

RICK TOLD ME I could take the week off and I greeted the news like an asylum seeker who had just been granted full refugee status. Said he had some business to attend to abroad (yeah, right), no doubt involving a hostile takeover bid for the ripest cleavage on the beach or a paternity case in Rio. I don't know why he bothers to keep up the pretence that it's work. He's always chasing after something or other, never settling for long enough to get comfortable. It seems like a very complicated way to run an otherwise cushty life. I told him – if he's not careful, he's going to keel over and have a heart attack one of these days. He reassured me that he could dodge bullets, and slapped his ample belly a couple of times to prove it.

I would like to have taken a little holiday somewhere myself, but I still wasn't out of the woods from a Visa point of view, so instead I stood and gazed longingly at the special offers penned on the dayglo cards pinned up in the window of the travel agents. For a fleeting moment I was tempted to be reckless and march right in to buy a first-class ticket to Hawaii on the next available flight, but instead I just stood there and congratulated myself emptily for being good and, I admit, sensible. I even walked home.

THE LITTLE RED light on the answerphone was glinting when I dropped my handbag onto the coffee table. I did my lemon impersonation and stared at it for ages, torturing myself that it was a Dear Helen You're Dumped/Sacked/A Rubbish Person, then pressed the button and listened to the message with my heart (and knuckles) chokingly in my mouth.

'Helen? It's Sebastien. Just wondering what you're doing.' Pause. 'Anyway, whatever it is, maybe you'd like some company doing it.' Another pause. 'Or maybe you're standing there listening to me waffle on and you'll pick up.' He hummed tunelessly for a minute. 'Okay, I sound stupid now, I'll hang up. Call me.' I played it about a gazillion times. Who needs Hawaii?

WE MET FOR lunch the next day. And a sandwich in the park two days after that. By Thursday, I was so head over heels in love that I cried myself to sleep. This isn't the way it's supposed to be, I sobbed to myself in the bathtub with a third glass of wine. I'm a grown woman. I'm not supposed to feel like this, as though I've been slung head first into a rough-cut log toboggan and thrown down the bleeding Cresta run. But that was exactly as I felt, without a scrap of self control. There was absolutely nothing I could do about it. I had lost all sense of normality with no reliable point of reference to turn to. Couldn't sleep, couldn't eat, couldn't think of anything else except that man. It was kind of fun at first. I even invited the madness along with hugely complicated visions of my future. It was exciting for a while. Exhilarating even. But now, as I lay there with a cellulite-busting nobble glove bobbing in the soapy water, it was just bloody exhausting.

'You've got to play it cool,' advised Sally as I paced up and down their sitting room the following morning, wearing a trench into the spotless carpet while he tried to hand me a nice cup of calming herbal tea. It's his own blend, and so effective that it makes you wonder what he puts in it.

'But we both know what's happening here,' I pressed him.

'So the man wants to cook dinner for you tonight and you're worried about what's on the menu for dessert.' He sat down on the sofa and watched me sigh and groan as I marched around. 'If you don't want to go just ring him and say so. If he's such a great guy he won't mind, and if he does, well.' Sally made his point with an exaggerated sip from his Andy Warhol mug.

I stopped and turned to face him. 'It's not that,' I said. 'It's just that I, well, it's not as though, if you think about it,' I started pacing again. 'Oh, you know what I mean!' I finished with a flourish of my hands. 'Just by knocking on the door I'm saying yes. And what will that make me look like?'

Sally put his tea down and pointed at me with both index fingers. 'I think it will make you look like a normal, red-blooded woman who knows a good thing when she sees it.' He paused for thought. 'Or then again it could make you look like the whore of Babylon.'

His face was deadpan for a second, nodding gravely, then he broke into a wide smile of perfect flashing teeth.

I couldn't help but laugh.

'Seriously, Helen. Just go there and whatever happens, happens, yes?' Sally stood up, squared his shoulders and clapped his hands. 'Now, on to more important things. Have you decided what you are going to wear?'

IF EVER A VIEW had been created simply to impress, this was surely it. Standing out on the widescreen terrace beyond the enormous sliding glass doors, a million lights reflected on the Thames from the brightly illuminated landmark of Tower Bridge. Cars passed silently in the distance, criss-crossing the river, leaving streaks of white headlamps and red tail-lights as they passed each other in the night.

'Have you been living here long?' I called over the soft music into the big, sparsely furnished space.

'Ages,' he yelled back from the relative darkness of a far corner where he was fiddling with the lighting level. 'I got it before everyone caught on to the old docklands warehouse trick. Bought the whole building with a couple of partners and split it up. Kept the best three flats for ourselves and sold the others to pay for them.' He strolled to the fridge, reached inside the door for a bottle of wine and brought it over to me, lazily striding the enormous expanse of dark wood between us in his bare feet. 'I rent it out when I'm moving around. Haven't been here for the past year and it's good to be back.' He stepped out to join me on the decking and watched the traffic on the bridge. 'I guess I've never been comfortable staying in one place for too long.'

Refilling both our glasses, he lifted his and softly chinked it against mine. For a moment I thought he was going to kiss me. In a bird-flapping panic I quickly looked away towards the river and asked him about the few boats I had seen casually tethered below us, rocking on the low tide. It's not that we haven't kissed before. We have, a couple of times. But only at the end of the evening, and they were restrained exchanges that signified the finish of something (as in, the conclusion to the date), not the beginning (as in, we're about to have turbulent sex). He smiled and told me he had absolutely no idea whose boats they were, but that if I didn't like them, he would arrange to have them removed immediately. Everything suddenly felt suffocatingly intense: I shouldn't be here; I shouldn't be doing this. And I was perilously close to the kind of nervous hysteria that could get a grown woman sectioned.

'What are we eating?' I nimbly slid past him and retreated far too obviously towards the safety of the kitchen, a big open-plan affair taking up about a quarter of the enormous living space. Perhaps I could cleverly distract him with a spatula or hide for a while behind pot-stirring duty with extra steaminess. Alas, and somewhat to my surprise, there was nothing to stir. The hob gave me the cold shoulder and I nervously rearranged the shop-fresh tea-towel slung casually to its crumbless side. A quick glance below to the glass oven doors told a similar story. Spotlessly clean and thoroughly unused, without so much as a cormorant goujon in sight. I started to feel nervous and more than a tad uncomfortable. No food. And this was supposed to be dinner. It was starting to feel suspiciously like I'd been had, or was about to be.

In those few nerve-racking moments, he had crept up silently behind me, and whispered quietly into my startled ear, 'Try the fridge.'

I gingerly opened the heavy door and found the shelves heaving with generously loaded dishes of tapas and colourful salads, seafood of every description, and enough chocolate and wine to sink a battleship. He brushed past me gently with a playful bump on my hip and started unloading the food. 'Well, don't just stand there, wench! Make yourself useful.'

We went daringly informal and laid out the shame-lessly epicurean picnic on the rug, took all the cushions from the sofas, lay among the feast and slowly grazed upon the never-ending courses for several hours while watching Holly Golightly cry over a silly cat and Cary Grant clamber around Mount Rushmore to save a damson in distress without so much as scuffing his brogues. Eventually, even the relentless city drone dimmed into the growing night-time silence. Sebastien rolled over on his side to face me, head propped up on one hand, and reached over to touch my nose. 'Now,' he said mischievously. 'Where were we?'

Chapter Fourteen

AFTERGLOW

IT'S A GOOD JOB I don't have a silly cat to cry over. It would certainly either have died of starvation or hanged itself from acute loneliness by the time I rattled home with shamelessly wild-child hair late on Sunday night. And I wouldn't have cared a bit, either. Get home, slam the door, put on some music, drop cat in bin. I felt terrific.

The whole weekend I had spent ninety per cent of my time in bed, engaged in various highly enjoyable activities – eating, sleeping, sharing newspapers, etcetera. I had had no need whatsoever for my clothes, because the only ones I wore after discarding my own five hours into my visit, were his. Nice big cotton shirts.

Soft socks. Outsize sweaters with the sleeves rolled up for me.

The twinkling red light on the answer machine went unnoticed and I decanted myself into my own bed, wishing that it smelled the same as his rather than of freshly tumbled Lenor. I lay there for a while, tossing and turning, then got up to retrieve the T-shirt I had worn home from Sebastien's pad and dragged it back under the covers with me. I had already made a mental note to buy a pint of his aftershave tomorrow (I had a quick shufti in his bathroom cabinet to make a note of the name) and spritz it liberally on everything I owned as a constant reminder.

Sleep came easily, but I don't remember what I dreamed of.

'BEEN AWAY? YOU look like you've had a bit of sun.' Rick glanced up from the desk in his study. He appeared to have spent the last week on a rotisserie.

'You must be confusing me with someone else.' I smiled cheerfully. 'I can't afford a holiday so I've been catching up on my housework and slipping in some well-earned beauty sleep.'

'You should've said!' He stretched his arms out as if to burst into song. 'I could have done with a bit of grown-up company.'

'And what makes you think I don't have grown-up

company of my own?' My sharp retort took him aback. Me too, for that matter.

'Well, whatever you've been doing – ' his smile faded – 'it suits you.' I felt really dreadful for having snubbed his generous humour.

Taking a seat opposite him, I opened the household folder. 'Could you stick a moniker on these for me please?' I put a small pile of cheques on the desk and reminded him that I needed to pop out shortly to pick up his new shirts. He orders them six at a time, every two months, always the same colours. Two white, two blue, two pink. You wouldn't catch a woman doing that. She'd consider it an infringement of her basic human rights.

'Thanks, Hell,' he said as he signed away. 'You've made a big difference, you know. I really appreciate having you around to take care of all these things.' He motioned at the wall briefly, snapped the lid back onto his pen and looked up at me. 'How are things going with you? Heard any more about Lomax the low-life?'

I so wished I hadn't mentioned anything. To me it could only be water under the heartbreaking Bridge of Sighs, and it hadn't escaped my notice that Rick had been treating me differently since I laid my soul bare. He now thought I was a bit tragic, which didn't feel great, so I made more of an effort with my Brave Face and hoped he had forgotten the conversation.

While I'd like to say that I had gotten over it, there's

just no getting over something like that. The only way I could deal with it was not to think about it. Pretend that it never happened. Convince myself that the money was never there in the first place. Focus on the positive and be grateful for what you have, I told myself sternly every time I found my spirits flagging. After all, I had much to be thankful for. I had learned to stand on my own two feet and walk my path in this unforgiving newfangled fast-paced world. And of course, I had met Sebastien, although as Leoni had pragmatically pointed out, I would have met him anyway, so he didn't count as a silver lining.

'I'm afraid there's more chance of me being struck by lightning than ever tracking him down.' I took the folder back and held it guardedly against my chest. 'But I've never been happier, so it doesn't matter.' My smile was genuine, even if the sentiments behind it were not.

Rick shook his head incredulously and looked back down to the newspaper on his desk. 'Mother Teresa's got nothing on you,' he quipped.

'REMIND ME NEVER *ever* to take a family holiday again.' Leoni dropped herself into the vacant seat between Julia and me, and waved at the waiter to fast-up with a drink. 'Trying to fit five bodies into two cramped rooms of sheer purgatory and attempting to control the bombshell they manage to create within ten seconds of arrival.' She took the bread from my plate and pulled a lump of crust off. 'And Marcus getting himself into a state looking at all the nubile topless girls adorning the beach, then expecting some kind of pornographic redcoat entertainment the minute I've managed to slip the kids a Mogadon.' Her vodka tonic arrived. 'It's like pain,' she said, taking a two-inch sip. 'You forget about pain, then you find yourself giving birth all over again and reaching for a machete.'

'At least you didn't find yourself locked out on the balcony naked again for five hours in the blistering sun,' said Julia.

'And as for the hotel.' Leoni dipped her crust in the oil. 'Cockroaches the size of your shoes.' She shuddered at the thought. 'It rained for four days out of the seven and every disease-ridden arthropod in Spain headed for our balcony to take cover.'

'Kids back at school?' I thought they had to be because the shops were now relatively free of screaming banshees being dragged along the carpet by their shredded mothers.

'Thank God,' she said. 'By the first week of September I'm barely holding on to my sanity. The delirium kicks in after the school drop-off when you realize you've actually got shot of them for a few hours. I can't understand these people who want to educate their children at home. Must be complete masochists.'

Julia sat back to make room for the plate of antipasti she had ordered for us to share. 'Well, at least you've got a nanny now.'

'I know.' Leoni pulled a grimace and picked up a slice of bresaola with her fingers. 'And don't think me ungrateful or anything, but I swear there's something seriously wrong with that woman.'

'Things not working out?' I asked her.

'I'll have to get back to you on that,' she said. 'Let's face it, she's hardly Maria von sodding Trapp. Marcus and I went out for dinner the other night. We weren't back late or anything, about half ten, and Pat was collapsed on the sofa, spark out, snoring like a tran- quillized rhino. All the lights and televisions were on and I found Millie crashed out fully clothed on her bedroom floor and the boys watching stripping Italian housewives on Sky.'

'That doesn't sound good,' I said.

'Oh, they thought it was brilliant.' She munched noisily on a beefed-up crust.

Julia tipped a small pool of dressing on the edge of the plate and Leoni dunked her remaining bread into it. 'She means the comatose nanny.'

'Mmm. I suppose it is a bit worrying,' conceded Leoni, 'but I don't have to pick the kids up from school this afternoon.' She started laughing and helped her- self to a glass of wine from the bottle cooling on the stand beside us. 'So who gives a toss? Besides, I want to hear all about your fabulous new lover. Marcus is doing his best to recapture the flush of our early years, but it feels like I'm being stalked by my dad.'

Julia stopped eating. 'Oh yes? What's all this about then?'

Pardon me? Did I not specifically mention to Leoni to keep this all under her hat? Probably, in fact definitely come to think of it, but, on the off-chance you haven't noticed, discretion has never been her strongest suit. Julia had that look on her face, the one that she reserves for anyone who has dared to keep her in the dark on a hot topic. I felt my cheeks redden.

'It's nothing,' I tried hopelessly, my face casting Leoni a withering thanks a bunch motormouth, now look what you've gone and done.

Leoni pulled a face. 'Sorry. I've done it again, haven't I?'

'It doesn't matter,' I said. 'I just wanted to keep it to myself for a bit longer. You know, until I know whether or not it's going anywhere.'

Julia noticed that I was deliberately avoiding her gaze. 'Hellooo?' she said, moving her head around until her eyes found mine. 'Is what going where, and with whom, may I ask? Or am I no longer privy to such information?'

Leoni leapt in to rescue my blushes in her typically subtle shotgun style. 'She's been doing the hokey-cokey with Sebastien bloody Charles,' she said. Julia sat there agape and said nothing, staring first at Leoni, then at me. If I didn't know better, I'd say that she looked a little shaken. It's the Big Sister Syndrome. Overprotective, with an element of having her nose put out of joint by her second-fiddle sibling having taken up with a surprisingly good catch.

Mario appeared with our main courses and clocked the awkwardly silent expressions on our faces. 'Ahh!' he said knowingly, tapping the side of his nose and closing one eye. 'I see I have caught you talking about me again!' We smiled up at him, thankful for the ice-breaker. 'Women talk about me all the time!' he cried, waving his pepper grinder above his head. 'They cannot 'elp it. I make them go craaa-zy!' He sang a little bit of something Italian. 'My wife, she say I make her go crazy every single day for thirty-four years!' Proudly raising his voice to its full glass-shattering volume, he finished the aria and took a bow to a very respectable round of applause.

Julia poked at her veal and kept her thoughts to herself for a moment, then sighed. 'Helen. Do you have any idea what Sebastien Charles is really—'

I interrupted her. 'Yes, I do. I know all the things that you think I either don't know or should know, and I know them because he told me himself.'

'Oh really?' she said dryly. 'You do surprise me.'

'Why?' I snapped at her. 'Just because he's made a couple of mistakes in the past. I don't see what the big deal is. First Leoni, then you.' They both saw my hackles rising, which is saying a lot for me, and Julia smiled apologetically and put her hand on mine. 'Anyone would think that I'm past it. Why shouldn't I have a boyfriend?'

'I'm sorry,' she said. 'It's just that I worry about you and I wouldn't want to see you get hurt again.'

'Well, you don't need to concern yourself on my account,' I told her. 'I'm a big girl now and I can take care of myself, thank you.' I turned my attention to my lemon sole, not that I wanted it any more. My stomach was churning. What business was it of theirs anyway? Besides, nothing to report so far this week. No call. No flowers. Nothing.

The conversation thereafter became stilted, poisoned as it was with unfinished business and an argument that no one wanted to start, but was probably long overdue. Quarrels between sisters can escalate disastrously without warning. I've seen that syndrome at first hand. A few choice wrong words at the wrong time and before you know it, you've stopped speaking to each other altogether. It can go on for years, believe me. And it's never worth it. The love between sisters is like no other. Perhaps the bond is almost too close, too intimate, and that's what renders it so fragile.

'You eating that?' Leoni pointed her fork at my fish. I shook my head. Without warning she picked up my plate, swapped it for her own in one deft move and tucked in.

'WADDYA RECKON, HELL?' Rick leaned back in his chair and relit the soggy cigar butt, disappearing behind a heavy curtain of thick blue smoke and avoiding the questioning gaze of the terrified interior designer cowering behind the set of drawings he held up for closer inspection. Although Celebrity Craig had come highly recommended, he had a peculiar look about him and a curious rodentine manner. Marsupialman, Rick called him when he wasn't there. I looked at the artist's impression of a caber-tossing, tartan-clad cabin with rope handles dangling from the hidden storage solution.

'It's nice,' I said, not wanting to rock the boat.

'Nice?' Rick wrenched the cigar from his mouth. 'Didn't you hear what he said? This is supposed to be the ultimate masculine marine interior,' he quoted, picking up one of the visuals. 'The sort of toy that your mates see and want to buy off you there and then for ten times what you paid for it.' He spun the picture around to face me. 'What don't you like about it?'

'I didn't say that I didn't like it,' I replied diplomatically. Craig looked as though he was about to add something with a half raised finger, then thought better of it.

'Yes you did. You said it was *nice*.' He took a swig of coffee. 'And when you say something's nice, what you really mean is that it's crap. I know that look. It's what you said about my car.' He nodded at me. 'So come on, speak up. That's what you're here for, isn't it?'

'Well.' I really didn't want to get into this, especially not in front of the child. 'Don't you think it's a bit, erm,' I struggled to find a suitable adjective, 'Highland fling?' Rick laughed like a drain.

Skippy bristled and was compelled to speak. 'I can assure you,' he started defensively, 'this is the very last word in current cruising style.' He could say that again. Opening the book of fabric swatches and urging Rick to feel the quality of the weave, he tried a different tack. 'Ralph Lauren has this very same material for all the soft furnishings on his.'

'Really?' I gushed, suddenly impressed and reassessing the patterns in front of me. I turned the swatches up the other way and tilted my head. Perhaps they would look better on.

'So is it a yes or a no?' Rick demanded. Clearly, he had come to the end of his micro-attention span and was fidgeting irritably with a paper clip. 'Look,' he said. 'I don't want *nice*, and I don't want something that's gonna make me wanna puke the moment I go below deck.' The now harassed Craig started pointing out the creative genius behind his gaspingly expensive designs while Rick's shutters came down. I sensed that the show was over so stood up and cleared the cups from the desk. Rick took the hint. 'Tell you what, mate. Why don't you leave everything here and I'll get back to you when I've thought about it.' I was already handing him his coat.

After seeing Craig to the door with his crayons, I went back to the study to retrieve the used coffee tray. 'It's fucking horrible, isn't it?' Rick said, flicking through the designs again and shaking his head. 'So what does that say about me?' He stubbed the cigar out in the ashtray and looked up. 'Bloody pouch-face spends two whole days with me, at vast expense I might add, then tells me he knows exactly what would suit my successful personality. And what does he come up with? A fucking floating Hogmanay.'

I put the tray down on the coffee table. 'It's not that bad,' I said. 'Just a bit OTT.' I sat down in the chair on the other side of the desk and spread the pictures out in front of him. 'Look. He's got all the basics right.' I pointed out the good bits. 'So if you tone down the sporrans, I think you'll be halfway there.' The ring of my mobile phone broke my concentration. I stopped talking and sprang to attention.

'Do you want to get that?' Rick asked impatiently.

'Sorry,' I mumbled as I rushed to the bag I'd left by the front door. 'I must have forgotten to switch it off.' Truth was I'd been checking it every few seconds for days. As soon as I saw Sebastien's name on the caller display, I wished I had turned it off. This was hardly the time or the place to be having a lustful conversation.

'Hello,' I answered officially, knowing that Rick was probably eavesdropping.

'Missed me?' he demanded with confidence.

'Yes, but I can't talk right now,' I whispered. 'I'm at work.'

'No you're not,' he laughed mischievously. 'You're coming out with me.'

'I'll call you back later,' I smiled.

'Wrong again,' he said. 'I'm coming to pick you up right now. Should be there in about twenty.' From the tone of his voice, he was deadly serious, and dangerously playful.

'I can't do that,' I hissed, quietly pressing myself into the coats.

'Yes, you can. Tell him you're sick. Tell him you've got a dentist's appointment. Tell him whatever you like because if you're not outside that door in nineteen minutes, I'm coming in to get you.'

'Please don't do that.' My heart was pounding with excitement.

Sebastien lowered his voice. 'If you don't want me to drag you out, you know what you have to do.' And in that instant I made my decision.

'All right then,' I whispered, 'but not here. I'll meet you on the corner.' I heard him laugh again just before he hung up.

'Everything okay?' asked Rick, appearing in the doorway with a ridge of concern on his forehead.

'Yes, fine,' I lied. 'I've gone and forgotten that I had a dentist's appointment today. That was the reception-ist at the surgery calling to remind me.'

'Oh,' said Rick. 'Thank God for that. I thought you were plotting to have me assassinated.' He watched me shove my mobile back into my bag guiltily. 'I'm the kind of bloke that's congenitally wary of hushed voices.'

'Do you mind if I skip off early?' I could feel my face reddening.

'Aw, Hell!' he moaned. 'We were going to do the boat today! Can't you ring them back and rearrange it?'

'Sorry, Rick.' I put my hand to the side of my jaw. 'I really have to go.'

SLOPING AWAY LIKE a burglar and hiding in the doorway of the block of flats around the corner, I prayed that Rick wouldn't appear and catch me bunk-ing off to meet my mid-morning lover. A quarter of an hour later, a big silver car slid up to the kerb. Sebastien stepped out of the passenger side and looked up and down the road before spotting me emerging from the shadows.

'Very cloak and dagger,' he commented as he opened the back door for me. 'Jump in.' There were two other men in the car and, judging by the sickly sweet smell when they said hello, at least one of them had had a vodka breakfast. Sebastien asked the bloke on the back seat to swap places, so he got out and went around to the front while I budged up to make room.

'Where are we going?' I asked, feeling more than a little uncomfortable in the company of these strangers.

'To the races,' Sebastien replied with a smile. 'It'll be fun.'

I HAVE NEVER BEEN so bored in all my life. The sport of kings it may be, but watching a bunch of horses running about and listening to wandering prides of ill-mannered, moneyed men guffawing at their mounting losses in between smoked salmon sandwiches washed down with overpriced champagne, turned out to be quite far removed from my idea of a good time. I'd not been to the races before, and had always imagined it to be quite an elegant business. Instead I was inextricably caught up in a chilly open-air dullsville somewhere in the Home Counties without any form of escape pod.

Sebastien was far more interested in his friends, both the two and four-legged varieties, than in me, and seemed completely unaware of my predicament. He came to my side briefly but frequently to say, 'Okay?' and 'Enjoying yourself?' before returning to his form. I was thoroughly ashamed of myself for having abandoned my post that morning. I could have been having a perfectly enjoyable day, up to my armpits in samples, talking damp-resistant trimmings with my boss and his creepy interior designer. What on earth had I been thinking of? That Sebastien was going to turn up on a white charger and whisk me away to Hollywood? Oh, do grow up, woman. And for pity's sake try to do it quickly. On Sebastien's next rapid pass, I gave a little tug on his arm.

'Do you think we'll be going soon?' I asked with an innocent smile.

'Not for a good while hopefully,' he said distractedly. 'The big one's on at three o'clock, then we normally meet up with a couple of the trainers, depending on who's here. I expect the boys will be wanting to go on somewhere afterwards. I'll get them to drop us off at my place later, shall I?'

'Oh.' I tried not to sound completely crushed. 'I didn't realize it was an all-dayer.'

Sebastien came to his own conclusions and whispered in my ear. 'Are you trying to tempt me home early?' I smiled as attractively as my boredom would allow. He put his arm around me. 'Why don't you have a flutter?' he suggested, reluctantly pulling his wallet out of his inside pocket.

'I'd rather not.' I backed away from the out-held notes. 'I wouldn't be comfortable gambling. It's not really my thing.' He looked taken aback, then a little exasperated. I smiled uneasily. 'It's okay, you go ahead.'

'Well, if you didn't want to come you should have said,' he sniped tetchily.

Well, excuse me. 'Yes,' I felt my cheeks flush. 'But I didn't know where we were going, did I?'

It was an uncomfortable moment, and I wasn't sure how to handle it. Giving in is so much easier than making a stand. 'I didn't mean to complain,' I apologized. 'It was lovely of you to bring me.'

'Hey, Sebastien!' called one of the jackals. 'Come on! They'll be off in a minute!'

HAVE YOU EVER stood in a customer queue for just that bit too long, then thought sod this and left? That's kind of what happened. My original intention had been to go for a wander to see if I could find something vaguely interesting to occupy myself with. Then I realized that I really would rather be most anywhere else than there. A friendly policeman standing near the empty winner's enclosure noticed my loitering with intent.

'Can I help you, madam?' he asked helpfully.

This was going to sound pretty stupid however I put it, so I came straight to the point. 'I wonder if you would be so kind as to tell me where this place is, please,' I said. He looked perplexed. 'I came in a car as a guest,' I explained, 'and now I have to make my own way home and I have no idea where I am. Perhaps there's a station nearby you could point me towards?'

'I see,' he said, rocking on his heels. 'Well, you're in Ascot at the moment. There is a station, but it's quite a long way from here.'

'I don't mind,' I said. And he pointed out the way to me and told me to be careful. You're not kidding, I thought.

IT TOOK ME bloody ages to get home, what with one thing and another. I sent Sebastien a feeble text message from the train apologizing that I had had to leave like that (with something along the lines of *didn't want to spoil the fun*), then popped into the Marks & Spencer by the station to pick up a saucy little meal for one. Well, might as well try to salvage something of the day, even if it's only a beef olive and a bag of chocolate raisins. The marathon walk to the station had left me plum tuckered and starving. I stuck the oven on, soaked the abortive mission away in a hot bath, crept into bed with a loaded supper tray and wondered if Janet Street-Porter ever had days like this. I suspected not. She'd be far more likely to hammer matches down the offending man's fingernails and string him up by the bush oysters.

Sebastien's message beeped from the phone on the bedside table. Maybe I should just leave it. So I opened it. It read, *Are you still speaking to me?* I felt a sudden head rush. *No*, I responded. Minutes seemed to pass. Beep-beep. *That's a shame.* I thought so too, but asked the question *Why?* anyway. The next one was a bit of a shocker. *I'm downstairs.*

You have never seen me move so fast. Linford Christie wouldn't have stood a chance. I was off the bed in a split nanosecond, hurling the half-eaten in-flight meal back on the tray, skidding into the kitchen and flinging everything, packets and all, in the dishwasher then slamming it shut. Scrambling back to the bedroom to open the windows for some much-needed post-gravy fresh air, I gave the duvet a flap to dissipate the crumbs and quick-changed my weary cotton pyjamas for the unworn silk kimono Paul and Sally had given me as a spookily prescient post-moving-in gift. Not bad for a fifteen-second dash, although the overall instant-goddess effect was slightly marred by the unsightly sock scars left around my ankles. Another message landed with a beep. *Let me in. You know you want to.*

I went to the intercom, pressed the buzzer, and unlatched my internal door.

Chapter Fifteen

INCONCEIVABLE

I DECIDED TO TAKE the plunge.

After running through various mortifying scenes in my head as I envisaged telling my ancient and crusty old GP that I was in need of some regular anti-baby artillery and imagining his shocked response, I wound up at a faceless family planning clinic in Soho. I could just breeze in any time between ten and twelve without an appointment (I'd already done a dry run and got as far as the sign on the front door), and enjoy complete anonymity while demanding they fix me up with five kilos of high-grade progesterone tabs.

The nurse commented that my blood pressure was up a bit and gave me a lecture about salt-induced suicide and killer chip fat. Knee-high to a grass-hopper, she must have weighed seventeen stone. I was finally dispensed a prescription for six months' worth of unfertilized sex. Sitting on a park bench and swal-lowing the first of the pills with a mouthful of water from my Boots meal-deal lunch, I have to say that I felt quite liberated. Like those flower-haired hippie girls in the sixties with their louche hats and floppy morals.

I walked all the way home from the park in a pleasant daze. On impulse, instead of letting myself in at the first floor, I carried on up the next flight of stairs and knocked on my neighbour's door. To my delighted surprise for the time of day, Paul answered it with a tomato-stained tea towel tucked into the top of his jeans. The smell of freshly chopped basil filled the air.

'Hello stranger!' he cried before calling over his shoulder. 'Hey, Sally. Guess who's decided to put in an appearance?' Then back to me as he reached for my arm. 'You come right on in here and don't even *think* about not staying for dinner. We're having a sort of New England clambake thing followed by homemade pasta.' He ushered me in, pulled my jacket off roughly and shooed me into the sitting room. Sally started hauling himself out from under a pile of coffee-table sized picture books on the sofa.

'Don't get up,' I protested. 'I feel like I haven't seen

you for ages and just wanted to pop in to say hello.'
Sally smiled and continued to unfurl himself, pushing
the volumes out of the way as he stood up and
stretched in my direction for a hug.

'What do we say, Sally?' asked Paul. They looked at
each other and sang out together, 'Two's company,
three's a goddam party!'

I love those impromptu evenings that magic themselves out of the blue. The ones where you think it's
going to be a perfectly ordinary day, and instead you
end up having a brilliant time with good food, great
company and enough wine to satisfy your soul but
keep your head. We talked about all kinds of things,
listened to some really interesting music that Sally had
ordered on import, and caught up with all the gossip.
Well, most of it. I was suddenly too coy to share mine.

'Oh! I know!' I remembered that I had something
else entertaining to throw to the baying Colosseum.
'You'll never guess who I met. You know that designer
bloke off the telly? The pint-sized one with the
pudding-bowl haircut.'

'Looks like a wallaby?' volunteered Paul.

'That's the one! Well, he's doing a job for my boss at
the moment and I sat and had a coffee with him while
he showed Rick his designs.' Paul responded with a
long *oooh* and they exchanged an impressed nod. 'He
had some of the fabric that Ralph Lauren used all over
his yacht.'

Paul nudged Sally's knee with his foot. 'He's got a certain reputation, hasn't he, Sal?'

'You could say that.' Sally smiled. 'He wanted a column on the magazine once. Turned out he was so thick he couldn't even string a proper sentence together. Vague Craig. That's what they called him.'

'Well, I never.' You just can't tell with some people, can you?

'Don't believe a word he says,' Sally warned me. 'The only reason he's on TV is because his old man owns half the production company.'

Paul was nodding furiously and slapping his knees. 'We like to take the piss out of his shoes!'

I laughed along with the pair of them, but couldn't help feeling a bit of a twit. If there's one bad penny that keeps rearing its ugly head, it's my ridiculous naivety. I tried my best to block out the way I had gushingly lifted his swatches to my cheeks.

Chapter Sixteen

REBEL WITHOUT
A CLOUSEAU

I LIKE WATCHING PEOPLE in public places. Restaurants, shops, cafés. I like looking at what they're wearing. Imagining them trying it on in the shop and picturing them at their point of decision. That split second when, looking in the mirror, they made up their mind and said, yes, I like that; I'll get it. Especially if they're wearing something really gross. Maybe they bought it without trying it on first. (Risky, and usually indicative of deep depression or other serious condition.) Perhaps they just have really bad taste. It happens. Then there's the barnet. The woman sitting opposite me on the bus this morning looked as though she ought to be on her way to Offhair, or whatever the styling ombudsman calls itself. The burning question in my mind: did she really want it to look like that? Did she really say, 'Mmm, lovely, thanks,' when the mirror was brandished behind her vandalized head?

Arriving at Rick's house, I found the Russian cleaner leaning up against the closed door of his study, ear pressed to the wood. She put her finger in front of her lips as soon as she saw me stepping in through the front door, waving the other hand towards me to come and listen in, although I could hear the shouting perfectly well from where I stood. The door opened. Rick looked unsurprised to see Mrs Kremlin standing petrified in front of him, and she quickly scurried off sideways, flicking her duster robustly at the picture frames en route.

'Helen. You're late,' huffed Rick. 'Come in here for a minute, would you?' I quickly hung my coat on the stand, mumbling a weak excuse about the buses being full. (Truth was I'd overslept, and looked like it.) The disgruntled designer was sitting in a chair, lips pursed tightly, veins throbbing at his pounding temples. 'I've made a decision about the boat,' Rick said firmly. He opened the walnut cigar box on his desk, took one out and pointed it at me. 'You do it.' I looked at him, open-mouthed. 'You pick out all the stuff. Make sure that Craig here doesn't get carried away.' Was I hearing this right? Me, decorate a yacht? Is my name Ivana Trump? 'No offence.' He looked at the humiliated artist in residence. 'But I'm not about to become a guinea pig to your big ideas and Helen knows what I want.' *Do I?* 'So, what about it?' he finished.

Returning to my first principle of staying employed, I answered efficiently, 'I'm sure I can manage that.' I should probably mention here that I was about to explode with excitement.

Rick got up from his desk. 'Good,' he announced, then to Vague Craig, 'and I don't want to see so much as a Scots porridge oat in there, right? Now, you two put your differences behind you and don't fuck it up.'

'Leoni?' She sounded like she was in a submarine. Maybe she'd thrown her scramble switch. 'Where are you?'

'I'm in the cupboard under the stairs,' she whispered loudly. Well, ask a silly question.

'Any particular reason for that?' I probably didn't want to know, but what else could I say?

'I'm waiting for Pat to get back with the children. She thinks I've gone out for the afternoon. My car's hidden in the garage and she's got no idea that I'm here.' She sniggered.

'Okaaay,' I said slowly.

'I don't trust her and I want to see exactly what she gets up to behind my back. This is going to be *really* interesting.'

'So why don't you get one of those secret video recorders you hide around the house? A kettle-cam or whatever they're called. Unless you're planning to spring out on her and unleash that all-important element of surprise.'

'Have you seen the bloody price of those things?' she bellowed. 'No thanks, I'll just wait here and watch her through the crack of the door. I'm sure she's been helping herself to all sorts of stuff and God knows what she's been feeding the kids. She's not used a single vegetable since she's been here. I should know; I count them every morning.'

'Don't you think you're being a bit paranoid?' I suggested.

She chortled menacingly. 'I've got food and everything.' I heard rustling as she inventoried her supplies. 'Jaffa Cakes. A chicken deli banjo with sesame seeds. And a couple of those ready-mixed Gordon's gin and tonics in a can.' The ring pull clicked and hissed, followed by a small slurping sound. 'Mmm. Not bad.' She made little tasting noises. 'Could do with ice and a slice.'

'Sounds like you're digging in for the duration,' I said. She interrupted me with some heavy scuffling sounds.

'Shit, they're back. Gotta go.' And she hung up.

As usual, I had managed to have another conversation where I had clean forgotten to say what I had called about. But that's the way things tend to go with Leoni. My plan when I picked up the phone had been to tell her that she and I had landed ourselves a plum job. The only required skills were advanced magazine-flicking, extreme window-shopping and obsessive list writing. There was no one alive who was better qualified. We had merely to pick out everything necessary to fix up one medium-sized yacht and make sure that nobody stuck the wallpaper on upside down. For our troubles, Rick was picking up the tab for an all expenses sojourn in the putrid Portsmouth Holiday Inn while we oversaw the final fit-out, and had promised me a hefty bonus, which I would offer to split with her.

THE INSTANT HE tasked me with the job, I'd panicked, then immediately remembered how Leoni had steered me through the mystifying process when I'd had the flat decorated in just over a week to great acclaim. All those years swotting over the glossies had left her with a curatorial knowledge of cutting-edge magazine interiors. As she watched her own low-budget attempts at home-improvements being destroyed by a succession of unbelievably destructive child-transmitted mishaps, she dreamed of her perfect home (given another existence) and even kept a scrapbook of her wish-list items. In the heat of the moment, I may even have described her to Rick as an 'accessories consultant', to which he'd said, 'Whatever', and Craig had sniffed huffily.

My good news would have to wait. I thought about Leoni, hunched like a trapdoor spider in the cupboard under her stairs, surrounded by household equipment, armed with generous rations, and ready to light up her face with a torch like that bit in *The Blair Witch Project*. Sometimes I think she's got too much time on her hands.

SEBASTIEN PUT HIS arm around my waist, munching the carrot he was chewing loudly against my ear.

'I like your place,' he said. 'Maybe I should move in with you.' I turned in alarm, butter dish still in my hands. 'Only kidding.' He poked my tummy harder than was comfortable. 'We'd never agree on the furniture.'

I'm not sure what it is, but why can't I feel the same level of relaxation in Sebastien's company as I can with someone I'm not having sex with? Men, I mean, with the exception of Sally, although I don't think he really counts. I'm always just that little bit on edge with Sebastien. Worried that I'm going to go and say something stupid and reveal my vastly inferior intellect. And going to all that trouble with my appearance, even when I want to look like I haven't made any effort at all. Do men behave that way when they're in love with a woman? I doubt it. I suppose that I wanted him to need me a little, and I wasn't convinced that my raw material was up to it.

Sitting at the dining table together with a simple feast of roast chicken and salad, he looked relaxed and comfortable. 'So, Helen.' He began carving the chicken. 'Am I a leg or breast man?' I smiled, watching him expertly cut through the thigh joint.

'Leg,' I answered confidently.

'See?' he said. 'You already know me better than my own mother.' He placed a few slices on my plate and passed the salad bowl to me. 'She'd have liked you a lot.'

'I'm sorry.' I looked at him sympathetically. 'I didn't realize.'

'Oh, she's not dead or anything like that,' he said matter of factly. 'Poor old girl lost her marbles. She's in a nursing home now. Just sits in a chair all day and looks out at the sea.'

'How awful,' I said. 'Do you visit her often?'

He spoke through a mouthful of chicken and reached for the pepper grinder. 'Don't see the point really, but I phone the nurses now and again to check how she is. They stopped moaning at me about her not having visitors ages ago, so I expect she doesn't recognize anyone.' He refilled his glass. 'I don't suppose she'll last much longer.' I pictured the lonely old figure, wrapped in a shawl and sitting in a winged armchair, looking out at the bleak coastline with empty eyes. Sebastien caught my gaze and smiled broadly. 'More wine?' he asked cheerfully.

Don't get me wrong, but his whole demeanour seemed alarmingly cold-blooded for a devoted son. I realize that men find it a lot easier to detach themselves emotionally than women do. Less guilt, I guess, but you would have thought he could at least have attempted to look a little less pleased about his poor mother's imminent demise. I felt so bad about it that I was momentarily tempted to volunteer to visit her myself.

'I HAVE NEVER FELT so humiliated in my life.' Julia and I were helpless with laughter and fought to keep hold of ourselves while Leoni described how she had finally been released after four and a half hours locked in the cleaning cupboard. 'She came blundering in, snatched Millie's coat from the kitchen table – that much I *did* see – then she shoved my door shut, threw the bolt and went straight back out again.'

'Why didn't you call out to her?' Julia managed through her tears.

'And say what exactly? "Oi, let me out; I'm hiding in the cupboard spying on you"?'

'No!' Julia spluttered. 'She didn't know how long you'd been in there, did she? You could have said, "Hang on a minute, I'm just in here getting something."'

'Well, I didn't bloody well think of that, did I? Besides, what about all the food?'

Julia was bent double again, so I took up the pinata stick. 'Why didn't you ring one of us or Marcus and tell us to come and let you out?'

'What is this?' she snapped back. 'Twenty bloody questions?' We apologized and Julia pulled herself upright and draped her arms around Leoni's sunken shoulders. 'I was stuck in there for hours,' she said. 'It was like a challenge. Wondering how I was going to get through this. How long my oxygen would last. Making plans about who was going to raise my kids. Looking for something to scratch a last message onto the wall with.'

'How did Marcus find you?'

Leoni looked gutted. 'He just opened the door to put his coat away, and there I was, sitting among the empty packets, stinking of gin and desperate for a pee.' Julia let out such a belly laugh that even Leoni cracked a little smile. 'He looked really shocked. Then a bit scared. You know, I think he thought I'd finally gone over the edge.'

'What on earth did you say to him?' I asked her.

Leoni acted the scene for us, trotting out her best Vincent Price impersonation with curled fingers. 'Then I looked right into his face and said, "Don't you say a fucking word."'

Chapter Seventeen

WHERE YOU STICK IT'S IMMATERIAL

IT'S RARE THAT I have Rick's place all to myself. He does everything humanly possible to avoid early starts and is usually merrily shouting at some broken underling on the telephone when I arrive at nine thirty. That morning the house was like the *Marie Celeste*. I checked the rooms for bodies, found myself alone, and decided to swing the lead. I was having one of those days when you suffer a huge attack of inertia the minute you wake up and can't be bothered to do anything constructive before nightfall. Biorhythms, the

Chinese call them. It's nice for one's laziness to be clinically recognized. Rick has a whopping great plasma TV impaled on the sitting room wall. Its dominating black screen boomed at me invitingly. I took a few props through in case I got rumbled (empty notepad, decoy file), kept half an ear out for the door, and switched it on. The doorbell rang almost immediately. Typical.

'Rick about?' The stocky little man at the front door craned to see over my shoulder.

'Not at the moment,' I responded. 'Can I help you?'

'Yes,' he said. 'Can you make sure he gets this?' He handed me a large padded envelope.

'Certainly,' I said, looking at it. There was nothing written on the outside. Danger Mouse flashed briefly across my internal plasma screen. What if it was something illegal? Worse still, what if it were something legal, like a court summons? 'Actually,' I said, 'maybe you should come back later.' I tried to hand the envelope back to him, but he pushed it towards me.

'Don't mind me asking,' he asked anyway. 'But you're Helen, aren't you?' I didn't answer, except to go red. He smiled at me. 'Tell him it's from Spud. He'll know what it is.' He had quite a nice face for a man named after a tuber. A quick nod and a wave and he was gone. I took the packet into Rick's study, wrote *From Spud* on the front, left it on his desk and snuck back to the sitting room. The big screen burst into life at the touch of a button. There was a crummy American made-for-TV film on Channel Five. Perfect.

'WHEN ARE YOU off to Plymouth?' Sebastien called to me as I finished clearing up in the kitchen, on my own, again. He seemed to have cottoned on to my habit of having dinner around seven and was rapidly eating me out of house and home.

'Portsmouth,' I corrected him. 'Next week sometime, I think.' I finished drying my hands on the towel and went to join him on the sofa. I felt a certain satisfaction seeing him looking so at ease here. It made me feel like a job well done. 'Why?' I dropped into the seat next to him. 'Are you going to miss me?'

'Actually,' he started, walking his fingers up my shirt buttons, 'I was going to ask you a favour.'

'Oh yes?' How intriguing. 'And what kind of favour could you possibly want from a girl like me?' I asked modestly.

Sebastien sat up a little and engaged his most charming smile. 'I'm having a bit of work done on the flat,' he said. 'Those old buildings need constant maintenance and I've been having a few problems with the underfloor heating. It's going to make a bugger of a mess, and I was wondering if I could come and crash at your place while they sort it out.'

Well, that was unexpected. To say the very least.

Him being here with me around was one thing, but leaving him unattended in my space when I'd be a couple of hundred miles away? I wasn't sure how I felt about that. What if he went rummaging around in my stuff? What if he thought all my CDs were crap? It had to be a no. Ages I sat there, processing the information and formulating my refusal while he waited for a gilt-edged invitation. Go on, Helen. Say no. You can do it. Think *Grange Hill* – Zammo or whatever that kid's name was with the drugs problem – and just say no.

'I don't know what to say,' I said politely while I tried to think how best to put it.

He leaned towards me and pulled me in for a kiss. 'Thanks,' he murmured. 'I knew I could count on you.'

WITH AN UNLIMITED magazine budget courtesy of Rick's petty cash tin, Leoni had cleared the shelves of WH Smith and had thrown herself wholeheartedly into the World of Interiors. She stuck pictures on big pieces of card and called them 'mood boards', constructed enormously detailed lists, and told all the neighbours that she was now officially a high-flying designer to the stars.

A thousand tattered sheets later, Leoni and I were really looking forward to inspecting our joint handi-work taking shape down at the docks. Not that either of us had actually had to raise a hand. There was a small swarm of worker ants doing all that under the watchful eye of curmudgeonly Craig, who was now barely speaking to either of us. Leoni had high-handedly branded his designs 'an unworkable concoction of everything repugnant that ever existed in the history of vile taste', and demanded that we all wear nothing but white during our creative meetings lest we should confuse our eyes. She was in her element, or, as she liked to say, 'exploiting her natural dimension'.

LET ME TELL you something about Leoni. She's not dense by any stretch of the imagination. Mad, yes. Thick, no. She once got 'interlocutor' in the *Observer* Really Hard Crossword. It was a stinker of a clue. Put people like that in the right environment and they shine like diamonds on the beach. A mere two weeks after taking the project on we were ready to inspect. Upon reaching *Sundowner* at midday, we found a thoroughly agreeable hive of activity in full swing. Leoni introduced us loudly to the uninterested workmen and piped herself aboard.

'I can't wait to see this,' she beamed up at me as she backed herself down the steps confidently. I followed closely behind her, brimming with excitement.

What lay in wait for us defied description.

Somehow, Craig's mutated sense of visual aesthetics had taken the basic elements of Leoni's very specific instructions and transposed them into what could only be described as *Midnight Express* prison ship. Everything was white, but that awful public-service white with greying streaks in a semi-gloss finish. The fitted furniture didn't fit at all. Laser-beam lighting, strong enough to burn your retinas out, bounced off the surfaces, highlighting every shoddy detail. It was like standing in the middle of someone else's conspiracy dream. Craig stood in front of us proudly, cashmered arms folded in arrogant stance, waiting for our reaction.

Mortified, Leoni leaned to the wall for support and immediately began to hyperventilate, then took a gulping inward breath. 'What on earth have you *done*?' she screamed. 'You cretinous, grotesque little man.' She recovered herself sufficiently to lunge at the shocked and confused Craig, who clutched his Blackberry protectively to his chest and tried to step out of her way. She was having none of it. 'Who the hell told you to paint everything *white*?' She pulled at her hair. 'Can't you read? Are you blind? It's hideous! You complete and utter *moron*.'

'You said neutral!' he shouted back at her. 'I've got it written down. Look!' He started tearing through the pages of his black leather pad with shaking hands. 'There! It says *neutral*.'

'Oh, for God's sake! What are you? Some kind of

design amoeba, you brainless half-wit?' Leoni put her face in her hands. 'This is totally *not* what we talked about.' She lifted her head, looked around and tried to take it all in. 'And where's all the material that's supposed to be on the walls?'

Craig quietened instantly. 'Walls?' he said. 'You never said anything about the walls.'

'Craig.' Leoni locked her eyes with his. 'We sent you ten grand's worth of Liberty print, which you were supposed to use on all the walls. Where is it?' He refused to answer and scowled back at her. Leoni ran at the now wide-eyed Craig and kicked the cupboard door beside him with a violent bang. '*I said* where is it?' she screeched right in front of his ashen face. Bloody hell. I don't think I've ever seen Leoni lose her temper before. I've seen her get pretty close sometimes, like when someone tries to help themselves to one of her chips, but nothing like this.

Craig burst into tears. 'Nobody said anything about putting it on the walls!' he howled. Then he stormed up the steps and started shouting at everyone to get out of his way.

Leoni rushed after him screaming like a banshee. 'You come back here, you little bastard! I haven't finished with you yet.' The workmen all started cheering. One of them yelled, 'Go on, love! Kick him in the nuts.'

Scrambling up the steps behind her, I emerged to

find Leoni now standing stock still, jaw dropped, staring upwards towards the sky. Following her gaze, I turned to see the new spinnaker being reeled into place, its enormous balloon wafting theatrically in the autumn breeze. And I have to say those big expensive prints look *really* impressive, given that kind of scale.

'DON'T WORRY ABOUT it,' I said to her.

Leoni was stretched out on the Holiday Inn army bed, surrounded by the contents of the minibar. She had gone through everything edible, and was now busily arranging the little bottles of assorted boozelets into geometric patterns on the bedspread. 'Your boss is going to go berserk,' she said. 'You are going to be *so* fired, and it's all my fault.'

'He won't,' I replied confidently. 'He's not like that. Knowing him, he'll probably think it's great.'

'What are we going to do?' She unscrewed the top of the minuscule Bailey's bottle and offered it to me. I shook my head: no thanks and don't know. 'It's a bloody disaster, that's for sure.' She put the bottle to her lips and tipped her head back. 'I feel completely sick when I think about what he did with that lot. Thank God we got it all down before it started raining.' She looked at the enormous heap of fabric piled in the corner of the room.

'Well, if we're going to sit here and unpick it,' I said wearily, 'I'd lay off the hooch until later.'

Leoni sighed and pulled herself up, passed me a pair of scissors from the emergency haberdashery shopping bag, and hauled the mound towards us. 'Which end do you want to start at?'

Soul-destroying is not the word. Had it not cost a grillion pounds a metre, we'd have binned the lot of it instead of wearing our little fingers red raw as we set about undoing yard after yard of rock-hard sailor stitching. The battle fatigue kicked in a couple of hours later when we gave up, hands cramped and deformed.

'Wait a minute,' Leoni said as she finished the Lilliputian bottle of Jack Daniel's. 'I think I've got an idea.' I looked at her with trepidation. 'There's a bloke I know who owes me one hell of a favour.'

I don't know why I didn't think of it myself.

'I CAN SEE WHY you called me,' whistled Sally as he surveyed the HMP hell tanker. Leoni stood with her hands on her hips, lips puckered into a teeth-sucking purse and nodding in agreement as Sally examined the surfaces with his hands. 'How many workmen have you got?'

'Five,' I said.

Leoni bit her lip and raised her hand timidly. 'I think you'll find it's three,' she mumbled. 'I fired two of them yesterday for laughing at me when I started crying over the sail.'

I tried to stifle my irritation. Having slept on it, I had decided that Leoni was probably right. There was a real possibility that I could be keel-hauled and made to walk the plank over all this. Craig had stormed off in high dudgeon yesterday, leaving us in charge of a small group of highly intimidating workmen who stared at our chests and made crude jokes the moment our backs were turned. The only reason that they hadn't walked off the job yesterday was because Leoni had given them a rocket and told them no one would be paid until it was finished. It had the desired effect, but nobody knew what they were supposed to be doing, so we sent them away for the rest of the day while we attempted to rescue some of the raw materials and formulate Plan B.

Sally looked at us sympathetically. 'Don't worry about it,' he told Leoni. 'It's not as bad as it looks. We'll manage.' He went up on deck to rally the depleted troops and told them to make a start on stripping out some of the damage. Then he suggested Leoni and I leave them to it and go get ourselves a coffee, saw us off the vessel and got straight onto his mobile phone. At the end of the jetty, I turned to give him a wave but saw that he was deep in conversation, leaning easily on the shining rails across the stern. As far as fashion accessories go, I have to say the old tub really suited him.

An all-day full English breakfast towards the end of a difficult morning has a wonderfully calming effect. Suddenly all your energies are sent in to deal with three thousand calories of fried bread, sausages and beans, washed down with eight slices of jammy toast and a bucket of char.

'That's better,' groaned Leoni, rubbing her tummy and looking like Jerry the mouse after a fridge raid.

We were wondering if we should go back and check on the crime scene, but soon concluded that the sight of all that terrible mess would only upset us again. Leoni kept looking at the laminated wine list in the middle of the table and checking the clock on the wall. As the big hand crept a little past midday, she announced that the sun was officially over the yardarm and said that she was ordering a bottle whether I wanted it or not. And that if I didn't, she had every intention of sitting there and drinking the whole thing all by herself.

'What else is there to do?' she said. 'I'm buggered if I'm going to spend the whole day worrying again, and I *really* need to relax.' She did a few half-hearted shoulder-rolling exercises and tilted her head this way and that to illustrate her sky-rocketing tension levels. The waitress brought our bill.

'We won't be needing that yet,' said Leoni without looking at her. 'Bring us a bottle of house red, please.' The waitress sighed at the inconvenience. 'And we'll be staying for lunch as well.'

THE SMILE ON Sally's face when he joined us a couple of hours later was enormously reassuring. He pulled a pad out of his trendy man-bag and passed us a series of little sketches that he'd knocked up. He didn't say anything, just smiled at us and sipped at his wine while we cooed and gasped. The glum waitress beamed when she noticed him and visibly melted under the spell of his soft vocals while taking his order.

After lunch, Sally was adamant that there was nothing more Leoni or I could do to help, and said that we might as well go home and he'd stay on to take care of everything. Leoni's lower lip began to quiver. 'I don't want to go home,' she said. 'Please don't make me go home. I want to stay here with you.'

'But we can't all stay, Leoni,' I said. 'We've only got one room, for a start.' I was quite up for getting home a couple of days early myself. At least my temporary resident this time was somebody who came with various extras, and my lunar cycle was slap bang in the middle of its physical needs phase. Some planetary action would go down very nicely at the moment.

'Then you go,' she said. 'It's not as though Sally and

I are strangers to a bit of intimate contact.' She raised her eyebrows at Sally and gave him a suggestive pout. Sally laughed and tweaked the side of Leoni's hair with sufficient force to make her wince.

He read my mind. 'Yes, why not?' he said, looking around the diner. 'I like it by the coast, even if your English sea is freezing and everyone wears terrible clothes.' He picked up Leoni's hand and kissed it. 'My wife and I will spend our honeymoon here and we will fall in love all over again.' Leoni fluttered her eye-lashes.

IT WAS GETTING dark by the time I got home and let myself into the flat quietly, having stopped off on the way to pick up a few throw-it-together dinner essentials. Closing the door softly behind me, the delicious aromas wafting around the place announced that Sebastien had already beaten me to it. So he can cook, after all. He kept that pretty quiet. Slipping off my coat, I hung it up on the hat stand and crept in, spotting the dinner table dressed for two, candles still unlit, and stealing a sneaky peek in the saucepan simmering discreetly on the hob.

When I emerged from the kitchen, I found Sebastien standing silently by the door and staring down at the bag on the carpet. 'I wanted to surprise you!' I called out as I moved towards him with a hint of uncertainty nagging at the back of my mind. 'But I see you already knew I was coming.' He didn't say a word for a moment, then smiled quickly and kissed me hello.

'I rang the hotel and they said you'd checked out, so I guessed you were on your way home.'

Well, that's strange. Seeing as Leoni's still there and I never actually checked out. The orange-faced receptionist hadn't struck me as being that observant.

'I wasn't expecting you back just yet,' he said distractedly. 'In fact I was just on my way out to grab some wine.'

'There should be a couple of bottles in the fridge,' I told him brightly.

He started pulling on his jacket and slid his mobile into his pocket. 'No,' he said. 'I mean some proper wine. Back in a mo.' He flashed me an ad campaign smile and disappeared down the stairs. I sat on one of the kitchen stools, waited for him to get back, and set about convincing myself that he didn't look exactly thrilled to see me. Tired and hungry, I deduced this evening could go one of two ways. Either I'd find my Elvis CD and have 'Suspicious Minds' blasting at full volume on his return, or I'd stop being neurotic and take advantage of a home-cooked dinner and, with any luck, some fat-free afters. By the time Sebastien got back with the wine, which I have to say was an excessively expensive accompaniment to a mediocre bowl of spaghetti alle vongole, he had visibly recovered from the shock and suggested we work up an appetite.

SEBASTIEN CREPT AWAY early the next morning, taking a rain check on my sleepy offer of a lazy day due to some pressing engagement. I lay back against the pillows when the door clicked shut and closed my eyes, letting the pinking sounds of the waking central heating filter into my subconscious and cat-napping the next hour or so away.

Drifting peacefully, I tried to remember how life had been when I hadn't had to accommodate the job, or the man. Those days when I used to loll around fantasizing about the future, filling my time any way I wanted to. Deciding to take a long, leisurely stroll down Memory Lane, I went for full-blown slovenly in-home dress code (old jumpers with holes in), wrote a few long-overdue letters including one to my mother, and spent the rest of the day doing absolutely nothing.

'MORNING!' I SHOUTED OVER the banging as I let myself in.

Rick was in his kitchen, thumping the side of the Gaggia with his outsize fist, empty cup hanging in the other hand. 'What are you doing here?' he snapped grumpily. Being a full-blown caffeine and nicotine addict, he can be a bit tetchy if he doesn't top up his rations regularly. 'You're supposed to be in bloody Portsmouth.' I put my bag down on the kitchen table and went to relieve him from machine-destroying duty. Giving one of the steam jets a vicious upper cut with the metal milk jug, I reconfigured the coffee holder and gave it another go. Bingo. We had lift-off.

'It's all under control,' I said proudly, presenting him with a steaming mug. Sally had called me late yesterday evening with a glowing progress report. He and Leoni had befriended the workmen over a couple of dozen pints in the King's Head, poured oil over troubled waters, and everything was running like clockwork. Rumour had it that the chief whip of the on-board decorating squad was Arthur by day and Martha by night, and that he rather fancied the cut of Sally's jib.

Rick took the coffee and cheered up instantly. 'Ace,' he said, downing it in one. For a moment, I thought we were going to spiral into another of his spontaneous conversations from the expectant look on his face when he handed me his cup, hanging around in front of me for no apparent reason. Mercifully, we were saved by the vulgar blare of his mobile, swiftly followed by a shout of, 'Yep, gotcha. I'm there in five.' I passed him his briefcase and waved him off as he barged out of the door. Save the absence of a quick, meaningless peck on the cheek, for that moment we must have looked like a long-married couple.

MY MENIAL TASK for the day was to sit and wait for the plumber. The downstairs loo had been making worrying noises that, in the last two days, had amplified to a deafening groan lumbering through all the pipes on every flush. It sounded like the house was going to fall down. Trying to find someone who's prepared to come out and sully his hands with your dodgy ballcock is no mean feat, either. You'd have more luck hiring a NASA astronaut for the afternoon. I got a flat 'You must be joking, love', or words to that effect from the first two plumbers I managed to raise, so I took a leaf out of Rick's book and offered the next random number extra money. Hey presto.

Rick's drained coffee cup was still warm in my hand, so I took that as a sign from Moses and made myself a double-sized, extra fatty latte. It was the Russky's day off, which was a bit of a shame actually. Her chillingly aggressive behaviour is simply her post-Soviet manner. Once you get over the initial shock, you kind of get used to it. Like watching video nasties back to back. You soon become desensitized.

I heard the post drop on the mat and went to pick it up. Before long, I'd caught myself reading all the envelopes as I stood there, not that there were that many today, and turning them over to see if I could tell who they were from. I'm not normally nosy by nature, but I expect you might have done the same under similar circumstances. Depositing them on Rick's desk in the study, I noticed the padded envelope I had taken in the other morning from the pleasant-looking potato. It was sitting on the coffee table. And it was open.

I pinched at the very edge of the package, pulled it up a little, bent down and took a peep inside. Disappointingly, there wasn't much in it. A folded-up note, couple of photographs. I shouldn't have done it, I know. This was clearly a confidential package. Whatever was in there was none of my business, but I tipped the pictures out anyway. They were pristinely glossy, and I immediately worried that Rick would know I had been tampering with his smalls if he saw so much as the slightest smudge. I picked up the empty envelope and held it open by the side of the table so that I could glide the contents back in without leaving any evidence. Using the folded-up note to gently shove the photographs along the surface and drop them in untouched, they fanned out on the glass surface, revealing themselves in part. At first I thought they were holiday snaps, palm trees and big cars swaying in the background. Then I recognized the face on the top picture. It was the man in the penguin suit to whom Rick had been so proudly introduced at the dinner we never ate. The one who looked like his dog had just died. I forget his name.

As the top photograph dropped off the edge of the coffee table back into the wide-jawed Jiffy bag, I caught a full-frontal view of the same man in the next frame. Only this time he was sitting at a table talking to someone else. Momentarily forgetting my concern about leaving marks on the shining finish, I snatched up the photograph and squinted closely at the faces. There was no mistaking it. The man he was talking to was none other than great Lord Lucan of suckers' savings plans. It was Lomax.

I WAS STILL TREMBLING when Julia came dashing in through the door, dropping her bag on the carpet and not even bothering to take her coat off before rushing to my side. Her face was flushed with the effort of getting here as quickly as she could. I had stashed the photographs exactly as I had found them, helped myself to an enormous slug of Rick's billion-year-old Armagnac straight from the decanter on the side table, then answered the door and told the Super Mario plumber to sling his jangling spurs. You should have seen the look on his face. Like Brad Pitt being dumped by Ann Widdecombe.

Home was all I could think of. I needed to get home. Now. I'd phoned Julia from the taxi, although

I don't really remember what I said to her. Whatever it was, she had literally shouted at me, 'I'm on my way.'

Julia sat close by on the sofa, put her arms around me then started rubbing my back. 'Jeepers,' she said softly. 'I think you might be in shock.' She took the throw from the back of the sofa and draped it around my shoulders. Gently pushing me backwards into the corner, she told me to lie down and eased my legs up beside me, softly pulling off my shoes and sliding a cushion under my feet. She took her coat off, laid it across my knees, and covered my legs. 'Shhhh,' she said, and pulled a tissue from her sleeve for my stray tears.

JULIA ANSWERED THE buzzer and left the door ajar, only for it to be thrown wide open a moment later with a call of 'What's up, chicks?'

Darling Sara. Same as ever. Only now in more expensive clothes. I was still welded to the sofa, being waited on hand, foot and finger by Julia. I was also slightly squiffy. A pot of hot, sweet tea had been quickly finished and replaced with an enormous snifter of brandy, twice replenished, and the afternoon had disappeared in a marshmallow blur. Julia was right. I was feeling much better. Still shell-shocked, but shrapnel removed from my acceptably impaired brain. I had instantly told Julia what I knew, which wasn't much, come to think of it, and she had shaken her head incredulously, perching on the arm of the sofa while she took it in. Then she had rung Sara.

Sara and Julia had come to an arrangement after Sara stumbled into Julia's office one lunchtime and found her boss sniffling quietly at her desk. Julia conceded defeat and let her barriers down for once, admitting her affection for the girl with a warm hug and a generous severance cheque. Sara had put her arm around Julia and laughed. 'You didn't think I was going to abandon you, did you? What did you think I was going to do? Settle down and start breeding? Yeuch.' But she did rewrite her ticket and Julia offered her a part-time gig with an assistant of her own. It was a perfect act of dedication. Or should that be delegation.

Sara was positively glowing, her polished skin shining a golden tan from the Bermudan holiday, its rich caramel hue enhanced by her vibrant dress. I'd not seen her at all since the wedding. Nor had anyone else for that matter. She'd been up to her eyeballs after the honeymoon, taking all the presents back to Horrids and exchanging them for credit notes that she could then spend on shoes. 'It's my contribution to recycling,' she justified.

'Sit down,' Julia said, nodding Sara towards the free sofa. Sara did as she was bid and we waited for her to finish settling her migraine-inducing chartreuse skirt.

'Sara,' she started, 'we've got one hell of a situation on our hands.'

It took her nearly forty minutes to relay all the information. Sara stood up and said coolly, 'I'll fire up Thunderbird One.'

AFTER WHAT COULD have been a fitful night were it not for the Mickey Finn that Julia slipped me, I woke up with the most God-awful headache. I somehow managed to haul my sorry arse out of bed and drag it towards the nearest source of fluids. As I shakily held a glass against the tap, Julia swept into the kitchen, wearing my silk kimono and looking sinfully glamorous for such an unearthly hour. The warm hug she gave me matched her smile. 'Feeling a bit rough?' she asked, taking the glass from my hand and putting it down on the drainer.

'You could say that.' I ruffled my painful hair and yawned. Julia waltzed to the fridge, opened the door and poured a large glass of juice, then handed it to me with a matching pair of paracetamols.

'What you need is a protein fix,' she said, turning to the cupboard. 'I'll make us some eggs. Scrambled or poached? I've got my swirling vortex knack down to a tee.' The clattering of the pan was unbearable, and I put both my arms across my face in protest, squeaking, 'No noise! No noise!' So she wrapped it in a tea towel, put it away and reached for the coffee pot instead.

'You're staying in bed today,' she smiled. 'And I'm bunking off with you.'

I leaned my head down and rested it in the crook of my folded arms on the work surface. 'My bloody brain hurts,' I grumbled from my sunken position. 'I am so confused I feel like my head's about to explode.' Lifting it much too quickly, it went into a sickening wall-of-death spin. God, those pills were strong. Pulling out from the nosedive, I tried to focus my eyes on my sister. 'I can't believe I didn't read the note,' I said. 'Of all the things I should have done before stuffing it all back.' I'd never make it at Smersh.

'Listen,' Julia said, 'I've spoken to Rick.'

'What?' I shrilled, hurting my own ears. 'What on earth did you go and do that for? I've got enough trouble to deal with.' This just didn't bear thinking about. 'Now he's going to know that I've been sneaking around the place while he's not there and prying into his—'

She held up her hand to stop me. 'It's nothing like that,' she soothed. 'I've told him that you're not very well and that you need a couple of days off. He's totally cool about it. Nice bloke actually,' she smiled. 'Sara's filling in for you.'

'Oh God, no.' I winced at the thought of Sara being unleashed on my boss and doubted he would survive longer than a day without running up a white flag.

'You just need to gather yourself for a while and think about what you're going to do.' The coffee bubbled loudly from the hob and she got up to move it off the heat with the zebra head oven-glove. Making mine just the way I liked it (extra milk, extra sugar, extra everything), Julia slid the cup silently along the surface towards me. 'It'll be all right, you know,' she said confidently.

I wished I could share her optimism. Seeing Lomax's face again had brought the sickening anxiety flooding right back with brass knobs on. And what the hell was Rick doing with a bunch of photographs of him anyway? From where I was sitting, it just didn't make any sense.

My shoulders automatically hunched upwards to my pounding ears in reflex to the serrated noise of the entrance buzzer. Julia wafted past me and picked up the intercom with a knee-weakening 'Hello?' She listened for a second, smiled quickly and leaned over to wave at me, huddled by the sink. 'Yes, lovely!' she purred. 'First floor!' and gave the button a swaying Mae West press while reaching to the floor for her bag. Ruffling around for a couple of pounds, she handed them out of the door with an Oscar-accepting thank you and pulled back holding a bundle of cellophane-wrapped, rose-laden heaven. My heart leapt and flew around the room. I hadn't seen Sebastien since he stole away the other morning, nor had I heard from him. He's a very busy person. Julia tore the card off the top and opened it with one hand. 'They're from Rick!' she laughed. 'Told you he wasn't cross!'

CONSIDERING THE CURRENT state of my tattered nerves, anyone would think that no one could give a flying monkey's about my plight of ruination and mental torment. Nobody seemed in the slightest bit bothered. In fact, I would go so far as to say they were all being unbearably cheerful. Maybe they'd held a high-security summit about it behind my back and decided that it was the safest way to handle a woman who may give way at any second with disastrous results. It's like 'don't mention the war'. Whenever I tried to bring it up, they would clumsily change the subject or avoid the question.

News had spread quickly via the jungle telegraph, flushing out a steady stream of first messages then visitors. Leoni leapt on shore as soon as she heard and got on the fastest train back from Portsmouth, but her head was so full of trimmings that she seemed to have clean forgotten that it was me who was floundering in the middle of a fast-track crisis.

She crashed in through the door later that afternoon

and waved a succession of images at us on the back of her digital camera, all of which were far too small to fathom in the split second for which they flashed across the little screen. 'It's *fantastic*,' she cried. Then calming herself for a moment with a sober, 'Or, at least it will be, when it's finished.'

Her capacious Mary Poppins carpet bag was packed with lumps of wood and scraps of oddments. 'This,' she said, holding up a fragment of something unidentifiable, 'is going on all the deck cushions.' She returned to her bag for a string of buttons. 'And these,' she held one up, 'are going here.' Leoni momentarily lunged the back of her camera at us again. 'And *this* . . .' Oh, for God's sake, woman, we get the picture, okay? Leoni pulled a little sample pot of varnish from her bag and started struggling pantingly with the lid. Suddenly it burst free, splashing the sticky contents across Leoni's face *and* my Corian sink.

'Oh, fuck. Sorry,' she said, and quickly covered the treacly puddle with my day-old David Mellor tea towel. I should have known better than to squander my minuscule weekly luxury allowance on such a vulnerable bauble, no matter how conspicuous I had felt on my millionth purchase-free browse. It was my penance for being inexplicably drawn to preposterously expensive kitchenalia shops.

Thankfully, Leoni had to go. And not a moment too soon, just for that day. You need to have a full complement of Duracells in place to survive Leoni's bucca-neering enthusiasm. She checked her watch then looked up at the kitchen clock for confirmation. 'If I get going now,' she surmised, 'I can be back in time for the school run.'

'That'll be nice,' Julia said wistfully. 'Millie and the boys will be so pleased to see you.'

Leoni frowned. 'I'm not picking them up. Pat is. I can be lying in wait a good ten minutes before she's due home. Don't worry,' she said. 'I've taken the bolt off the door.'

Chapter Eighteen

SING IT, FAT LADY

HEAVEN SAVE US from ourselves. And if you can't manage that, I'd settle for saving me from me. Just when I thought it was safe to go back in the water, here I am again, drowning for all to see. Not waving, as the troubled swimmer once famously said. I busied myself with any household task I could find.

Handling plants has a strangely grounding effect on me. Even if they're doomed to early death having been fatally plucked from their mother ship. I tended the roses Rick had sent (and wished for a short while that I still had a garden of my own before remembering the War of the Weeds). As I can no longer afford such floral luxuries, I was in no great rush to see their vermilion petals drop to the carpet. Snip a little bit off the bottoms each day, change the water and pop in an aspirin, and they'll thank you for a rewardingly long spell. I rearranged them in the vase and refilled it under the running water. Pulling the heavy vessel towards me, I cack-handedly caught the side of the lip against the mixer tap and it gave way with a splintering smash, crashing into the sink and sending the blooms flying. The sudden violence of the erupting glass froze me to the spot and rang around my ears. I stood there shakily and looked at the mess. A crimson droplet of blood fell by one of the flower heads and burst into a pretty pansy of the same colour.

Julia rushed into the kitchen, slipped on the wet floor and grabbed hold of the handle of the fridge to prevent herself descending into a neck-snapping triple salchow. 'Shit!' she gasped, panting like a trapped rabbit as she righted herself. 'What the hell happened?' I turned from the sink and looked at her tearfully, then held up my bloodied hand.

It wasn't as bad as it looked: a little blood mixed with a lot of water. Julia cleaned up the wound with some kitchen towel, and what we had feared was a mortal gash turned out to be nothing more than a nasty cut. She patched it up nicely with a Steristrip then planted a kiss on the big plaster she patiently fashioned around my knuckle, before wrapping an unnecessary white dressing around the whole thing the way you would for a sorrowful kid. 'You'll live,' she said.

Julia needed to go out for a while that morning, having come to the end of her same-clothes-wearing tolerance. We're not quite the same size, so there was only so much borrowing to be done. Picking up her bag from the side, she cursed irritably and looked at her watch. It transpired that she had arranged a sister-sitter, believing me too deranged to be left on my own for longer than five minutes. I protested initially, until she put her finger in front of her lips and said softly that it was someone I liked. I knew immediately that she had called Sebastien.

I HAD JUST FINISHED dressing, having found the relatively simple task severely handicapped by my throbbing left index finger, when the buzzer went. I was pleasantly impressed that Sebastien had done the decent thing rather than invading my borders unannounced with his borrowed key. It was still missing from its hook. I smilingly pressed the release button without speaking into the intercom, opened my front door and leaned against the corner of it appealingly.

The sight of another sizeable bunch of the Queen's best blooms puffing up the stairs broadened the smile on my face. Yet the heavy gait was all wrong, and

Sebastien turned out to be Rick, leaning his hand clumsily against the wall as he reached my door and gesturing with the flapping flowers that he needed to get his breath back for a minute. I stood aside and motioned him to come in, with a glance over his shoulder at the empty stairs in the hope that Sebastien was right behind him. No such luck.

'Ouch. That looks painful.' He noticed my hand. 'I'm not disturbing you, am I?' He shook the mac from his shoulders and looked around. I helped him with his coat as best I could and hung it on the stand.

'Not at all,' I said. 'I've just put some coffee on. Do you want one?' He followed me through to the kitchen. 'It's out of a normal espresso pot that doesn't drain the national grid, I'm afraid. Hope that's okay with you.' He laughed good-naturedly and sat on one of the stools, setting the bouquet down beside him.

'They're lovely,' I said cautiously, not knowing whether or not my cover had been blown and trying to assess his facial expressions. 'And the ones you sent yesterday. You really shouldn't have.' I struggled inwardly over whether to say anything about the envelope. The mass hysteria of an ambulance-chasing posse of fascinated friends with too many righteous opinions had no doubt clouded my judgement, so I decided to keep quiet. I cleared a space on the worktop and put out some fresh cups. Rick stood up.

'Here, why don't you let me do that?' he suggested.

'I am capable of making a cup of coffee, you know.' Really? Could have fooled me. 'You sit yourself down here.' Rick steered me towards his now vacant stool, so I did as I was told and left him to it. He clapped his hands together, said, 'Right', as though about to tear a telephone directory in half, then picked up the pot from the hob.

His sickening yelp of pain was immediate and intense. The steel percolator fell from his burning grip and bounced off the floor, splitting open at the middle join, spilling coffee and scalding mashed-up grounds everywhere. Enter unbelievable mess and serious injury number two for the day, and I'd not even had my elevenses.

My boss sank to the kitchen floor, clutching his barbecued hand and writhing in agony. I rushed to soak a tea towel under the cold tap, draped it over Rick's reddened palm, and pulled a tray of ice from the freezer. Squatting down next to him, I carefully placed some cubes in the cloth, trying to assess the severity of the burn. 'Shit, that hurts,' he complained, catching his breath through gritted teeth. He turned his hand around and watched me rearrange the make-shift ice pack, then looked at my own dressed injury. 'We're a right pair, aren't we?' He smiled bravely, and I put my arm around his shoulder and asked him if he wanted a lollipop.

Some small movement caught the corner of my eye.

I looked up, startled, and saw Sebastien standing there, staring coldly down at us from the door, key still in hand. My horror instantly transmitted itself to Rick and we immediately tried to scramble to our feet, both of us exclaiming, 'It's not what you think.' Rick lost his footing on a stray ice-cube before he'd even made it onto his knees and skidded back over into the murky puddle of mush, taking me down with him.

Now, I know that it's not particularly helpful to laugh at inappropriate moments. Like that uncontrollable desire to start cackling in the middle of the funeral of a good friend. I think it's attributable to shrivelled nerves. Or maybe it was the look on Rick's face as he flailed around beside me on the sodden floor, suit and shirt stained beyond salvation. I dissolved into peals of near-hysterical laughter, was completely unable to compose myself, and had to pull myself up, with my one good hand, by the kitchen drawer handles as though climbing a free-swinging tree ladder. Catching just enough air to attempt a sentence, I giggled at Sebastien and began a rib-tickling account of how Rick and I came to be entangled on the floor together like that and why my left hand was strapped up like an amputee. He just stood there, stony and uninterested.

'I wouldn't have thought he's your type.' Sebastien curled his lip sarcastically, taking a packet of cigarettes from his jacket pocket and souring the air with his consummate spite.

'Sebastien!' Shocked as I was, I didn't want to cause a scene, so I opted for British diversion tactics and tried making a polite introduction instead. 'This is my boss, Rick.'

Rick half-raised a damp hand towards my disgruntled suitor. 'All right?' he said.

'I'm not bothered who it is.' Sebastien lit the cigarette, knowing full well that I don't like smoking in the house. If you want one, go and stand out on the balcony. 'It's not as though we're exclusive, are we?' He filled his lungs with a long drag and slowly let the plume out, the acrid smoke hanging a big flat cobweb in the stillness. I could feel my face turning red, but my rictal smile stayed put while I failed to compute the information.

'Don't be so silly!' I laughed nervously. Pull yourself together, woman. 'Rick was just leaving.' I widened my eyes urgently towards Rick while he brushed himself down. 'You'd better have someone take a look at that hand,' I told him, wrapping the wet cloth around his icy clenched fist then quickly fetching his raincoat.

'Yeah,' he grimaced. 'I think you're probably right.' He nodded unsmilingly at Sebastien on the way out, but didn't say goodbye or attempt a handshake. Then Rick turned to me with some concern and nodded his head into the room beyond. 'You sure you're gonna be all right here on your own with that arsehole?' I scowled at him and shut the door.

SEBASTIEN WAS WAITING in the kitchen, leaning up against the sink with his smouldering cigarette and looking most unimpressed. He continued to stand there and watch me as I set about cleaning up the floor, but made no attempt to assist, even though he could see that it was a real chore with just one operational hand. Only when I had nearly finished did he say, 'I'll lift that,' then bent down to pick up the washing-up bowl and pour the dirty suds away before pulling me up to my feet.

'So,' he said, eyeing the fresh roses still lying on the worktop. 'Your boss make a habit of turning up here with flowers often, does he?' It didn't escape my notice that he had arrived empty-handed, as usual.

'It wasn't like that,' I answered testily. 'I've been a bit under the weather and he just dropped by to see if I was okay.'

'How thoughtful. And here was me thinking that you needed taking care of,' he observed wryly. 'Julia said something about your having had an unexpectedly nasty shock this week.'

'Oh, *that*. It was nothing, really.' I filled the kettle under the tap, although why I felt the need to create a third hazard with another couple of pints of boiling water is anyone's guess. 'It was nothing,' I mumbled. 'Really.' For whatever reason, I had never mentioned a word to Sebastien about my wireless high-rollin' investment bungee jump. Least said, soonest mended, my mother always used to say. It had been hard enough to cast it all from my mind, and he had provided a welcome distraction. I still felt pretty stupid about broadcasting it, anyway.

'Well, it didn't sound like nothing,' he said. The kettle gurgled as it came to the boil, and I supposed then that I owed Sebastien some kind of explanation. How can you expect to have a successful relationship with somebody without flashing them at least a glimpse of the skeletons rattling in your closet? Without prompting, I decided to set out my stall.

'I got taken to the cleaners by a man who turned out to be a bit of a shark,' I said. 'I used to be quite comfortably off. Which explains how come I live in a place like this.' I gestured up at the ceiling and shrugged with a half-hearted sigh. 'But then everything went pear-shaped.' I picked up the kettle as though dealing with a couple of pints of nitro-glycerine, and carefully poured enough of its contents to float the teabags in the pot.

Sebastien hardly reacted at all. No coo of sympathy. No string of logical questions. He simply stood there staring at the floor, an artificial smile creeping across his face. Nothing more was said while I took down the cups and fetched the milk from the fridge. He eventually broke the silence.

'There's something I've been meaning to tell you,' he said. I sat down on one of the stools and felt my heart lower its bar, bracing itself for the inevitable. 'I've been offered a job in Hong Kong.' This time it was my turn to look at the floor and smile. I nodded understandingly. 'It's beginning to get cold here, which I can't stand, and when the leaves start dropping off the trees, that's usually my cue to move on.'

'I see.' Suddenly I wished that the ground would open up and swallow me whole. The tension was palpable, a heavy awkwardness stifling the space and making everything look strangely new, as though I hadn't noticed any of it before. The coffee pot, new; the bread bin, new; the knife block, never seen it before in my life.

'Sounds like it could be a great opportunity for me.' He stretched his arms behind his head and effected a long, self-conscious yawn. 'If I can get an apartment high enough to see over the smog.'

The sound of my heart beating drowned out the legion of desperate pleas before they formed words in my mouth. Then I started to feel cross and more than a little humiliated. I fixed my expression and tried to sound interested in his plans, and mature in these matters. He studied the end of his burning cigarette in a stiff refusal to meet my injured glare.

'When are you going?' I asked politely, wondering how long he had known and how come he hadn't mentioned it before, chicken shit.

'Soon,' he said. 'In the next week or so I expect,' glancing at his watch. 'They'll email me.'

The tea was brewed. Six minutes, on the dot, optimum flavour. A fully fledged tea master had told me that. I picked the pot up by the handle and very deliberately poured the whole of the steaming, straw-coloured fountain straight into the sink while Sebastien watched. Turning to him with a tight smile, I held my good hand out towards him. 'I think the tea will have to wait until another time,' I said pointedly. 'Good luck, Sebastien.' He reached for my hand and pulled me into his shameful embrace. It took every ounce of my diminished self-control to prevent me grasping him firmly by the gonads and twisting them until they snapped clean off.

Chapter Nineteen

THERE'S ALWAYS SOMEONE WORSE OFF

WHY IS IT that one is always the last to know when it comes to the important things that affect us most? Like the first wife having no idea that her husband was playing Rick 'Two Dinners' Wilton for the last six months of their marriage while he sneakily set up home with his mistress and went gaga over their new baby. The first of several, he had told me that there is something totally irresistible about an attractive woman who breedingly confirms you have lead in your pencil.

'We did try to tell you,' said Julia when she came

back later that afternoon to the news that I had been unceremoniously dumped.

'I wish you'd tried a bit harder,' I moaned despondently. Sebastien's playing of his get-out-of-jail-free card had been excruciatingly embarrassing. Under different circumstances, I might have felt less red-faced about it, but to be dropped like a hot brick while smiling inanely from a coffee-mutilated lounging outfit set off with a bandaged hand was cruel in the extreme. It gave me no room whatsoever for theatrical manoeuvre or a sweeping exit of my own.

'I bloody well would have.' Sara spoke through a mouthful of blueberry muffin. She had stopped off at one of those ludicrously overpriced coffee bars on her way over and picked up a job lot of patisserie.

'But you weren't here, were you?' Julia reminded her.

'Why didn't anyone ring me?' Sara ignored Julia's acid drop and helped herself to a croissant from the big pink paper bag. Obviously back on solids, then. 'It's not as though you would have been interrupting anything. Dudley's actually a bit boring when you're stuck with him twenty-four hours a day.' She pictured her new husband obsessively flossing his teeth in bed, pulled the corner of the pastry off and dunked it in her paper cup. 'He's only got one mood. Never gets upset or heated about anything. He's so bloody polite it makes me want to scream.' Give it a couple of years,

Sara. 'I could have done with a bit of drama. You should have called me. Oh well, next time.'

'There won't be a next time,' I said firmly. 'Aged aunts at the sherry, indeed.' I shook my head. 'What kind of mug am I?'

'Aw, cheer up.' Sara sidled up to me and offered me a bite of her soggy, half-eaten croissant. 'You weren't to know, were you? And, technically speaking, they were strippers, not hookers, even if they did make an exception for the best man. Dudley said there was a very angry letter from the hotel manager waiting for him when we got back from our honeymoon. God knows what happened. He wouldn't let me read it and I couldn't find it when I ransacked his study.' She finished her coffee and burped. 'I hate that shredder. Jammed it with a lump of steak once but he just went out and bought a new one. Never even mentioned it. Don't you think that's weird?'

As if this weren't bad enough, Sara also declared that she had more than a sneaking suspicion that Sebastien had thought I was loaded. It seemed to have been his main motivator in most of his previous relationships. Julia nodded her agreement. 'I suspected as much,' she said, then surprised me by adding, 'you have that look about you.'

'Really?' I said, surprisingly encouraged.

*

ALL ALONG I HAD known that this day would come, just not quite so soon. Now that it had arrived and gone away to reveal a fresh new morning, I wasn't nearly as distressed as I had anticipated during one of my many mental rehearsals over the preceding weeks. In truth, my relationship with Sebastien had always been a whole lot more hard work than it was genuinely worth. I laughed dependably at his jokes, even though they were unimaginative, predictable and mostly unfunny. His friends, at least the two I had been subjected to, were frightful excuses for human beings. His table manners left an awful lot to be desired, and he had a nasty habit of talking with his mouth full and pointing at me with his cutlery. I could go on. It was nice to have been in love for a while, even though I knew it wasn't proper love, of the lasting, perfect rags-to-emotional-riches sort that you find in the pages of an unfeasible Barbara Cartland novel. No. This had been more of a *Fatal Attraction* scenario, only with a less psychotic woman. I suppose I could learn, given time.

Sentiments aside, the episode had left me feeling a little, well, high and dry. 'Oh, is that it, then?' sort of thing. Funny how even the most tenuous love affairs manage to feel strangely permanent until you're not in them any more. Then you instantly feel like it was never real in the first place. Shazam! A relational mirage. On the upside I wouldn't have to shave my legs every eight hours or remind myself to take an anti-sprog pill every day. I dropped the blistered packets into the bin and removed the cartoon bunny magnet from the fridge door before picking up my keys and heading off to work.

'THANK *GOD* YOU'RE here.' Rick wrenched his front door open before I could remove the key from the latch, almost tearing my hand off. 'It's Olga Korbut,' he growled. 'I can't understand a bloody word she's saying.' He pointed through to the kitchen. Helga was crumpled into one of the chairs, rocking steadily backwards and forwards, howling a tearful stream of Russian expletives (she had taught me a few during our morning coffee breaks together, so I'm probably not the right person to get tangled up with at Ukrainian Customs). I went to her side and crouched down on my haunches, putting a hand out to comfort her knee. There was a damp, mangled letter in her fist, which she pushed into my face. I took it from her, peeled it open, scanned the text, then looked up at Rick.

'It's from the immigration department,' I said. Helga looked up.

'Yah,' she shouted angrily. 'Wanghar immiglatzon fark.' Well, I could hardly have accepted her tuition without giving something back, could I? I held the letter out to Rick. He took a defensive step backwards.

'What are you giving it to me for?' he said. 'I don't bloody well want it!'

I gave him one of my ex-wife laser death-ray stares. 'Maybe you should have thought about that before you hired an illegal immigrant and started paying her cash.' Helga continued to weep and wail.

'She's a bloody cleaner!' he said. 'How am I supposed to know she's a fucking alien?'

'Yah.' Helga snorted and nodded. 'Faark schron-yohit gronski.' Rick and I looked at her warily and realized that she might as well be from Mars for all the good it would do us. She really was terribly upset, so I got her a tot of brandy (European-measure) from Rick's study and pressed the glass into her hand. 'Nostrovia!' she shouted angrily, then threw it back in one.

'You can't just ignore her,' I pleaded to Rick. 'She's been clearing up your grotty mess and picking up your pants for years, and now you're going to stand by and watch her get thrown into prison or deported? I can't believe you'd be that heartless.' I passed sentence on him with folded arms and an upturned nose.

Rick remained motionless for a couple of moments, then leaned forwards and snatched the letter from the table. 'Oh, give it here, for Christ's sake,' he said, pulling his mobile out of his pocket and scrolling down the numbers. He lifted it to his ear.

'Mike?' Protracted pause. 'Yeah, mate, never mind

that. Listen, I've got a bit of a problem with one of my domestic staff.' He hung on for a second and his eyes rose to meet mine. 'No, not her.' He pressed the phone to his ear a while longer, started laughing, then put it facedown to his chest. 'Mike says did you manage to wash the ink off your fingertips and you still owe him twenty quid.' Was there nothing this man couldn't fix?

'IT'S FINISHED,' ANNOUNCED Sally as I let him in.

'I know,' I replied sagely, walking back into the flat and shaking my head as he followed me in. 'I feel like a prize wally.' Thank heavens I hadn't allowed Sebastien to take those compromising pictures he'd suggested that day. I never thought I'd feel a certain empathy towards that poor girl with all the hotels nestling in the bank. I reached for the kettle then noticed Paul scampering in behind Sally with a bottle in his hand. Sally looked at me blankly. I blushingly realized my mistake. 'You mean the boat, don't you?'

'It's a triumph!' squealed Paul, waving his hands in the air and making all hail gestures in front of his boyfriend. 'Sally's brought pictures and we're going to have Show and Tell with champagne cocktails Colombian-style!' Paul broke into song and wafted around the kitchen, taking down glasses and peeling the foil from the cork, before firing it across the square through the open balcony door with a Grand Prix

299

winner's flourish. Filling three flutes, he handed one to each of us then raised his own in preparation for his toast. With our full attention, he shouted, 'Any port in a storm!' then nodded at Sally. 'Especially hers.'

I took a celebratory sip, and decided to make an announcement of my own. I raised my glass, and they looked at me expectantly. 'I've been chucked.' A spontaneous cheer went up from all three of us.

Chapter Twenty

SUFFERING SUCCOTASH

RICK WAS IN an unbearably good mood. Must have made another heap of money overnight. He had adopted a new mood-signaller today – singing excerpts of ancient Rod Stewart numbers and giving it a bit of pelvis-jutting thrust. The sight of his bathrobe-clad 'Do Ya Think I'm Sexy' on his way upstairs from the kitchen to get dressed was enough to put me right off my biscotti. Helga was on her hands and knees in the corner, scrubbing merrily at the skirting board and cheerfully mimicking the lyrics like a cleaning linguaphone set. Rick returned a few minutes later, physique mercifully hidden beneath a tracksuit that made him look anything but athletic, and nodded me through to his study.

Sitting at the desk, he reached for a cigar and I automatically picked up the box of extra-long matches and struck one for him. Puffing with vigour to get his stogie going, he wafted away the jungle of smoke that had gathered between us with a giant wave of his arm. 'I wanna have a party,' he said. I took out my pad and made a mental note to ask Dudley where they had booked the stag-night strippers from.

'What, when, where and how many?' I quizzed him efficiently, having now got this kind of thing down to a fine art.

'You,' he replied. 'And that decorator friend of yours, whassname, and everyone else who helped with the job.'

'Oh!' I said. 'That's nice.'

When are you going to say something and put a stop to this endless dithering? You can see the man's in a good mood, so just out with it and ask him. Julia's advice was still fresh in my ears. She had made me swear not to tackle Rick about the contents of his classified package, saying that she felt quite certain that everything would come out in the wash. More importantly, I was in no position to jeopardize my livelihood and the gas bill had already gone up twenty per cent. I put the question to the back of my mind and returned Rick's smile with a well-rehearsed counterfeit. The moment passed, and the unsayable remained unsaid.

'Yeah, well, I'm feeling pretty good about myself today.' He leaned back in his chair and rubbed his hands over his corporation. 'Old Mrs Gorbachev in there thinks I'm the best thing since sliced cabbage now.' He looked pleased. 'You can invite her along too.' His expression darkened for a moment. 'And I suppose you'd better ask that boyfriend of yours while you're at it.'

'That won't be necessary,' I mumbled shyly.

IF THERE'S ONE thing I do know, it's how to make complicated arrangements. Were there a degree in the subject, I could walk away with a double first without even unzipping my pencil case. With the weather turning and the boat far too small to accommodate the bulging guest list, Rick had armed me with an open chequebook and pointed me in the direction of the picture-windowed restaurant he had taken me to just before our first seafaring adventure. Leoni went wild with excitement and insisted on designing the invitations herself. When they came back from the printers, I noticed that she had added a line to the bottom, accrediting herself as *marine creative consultant*. Available for weddings and bar mitzvahs too, no doubt.

WE WERE LUCKY with the weather that day, which was just as well given the brutal, coastal venue. Rick waited for me to pull in the folds of my skirt, pushed the car door shut, walked around and slid in behind the steering wheel. 'I haven't been on a nice long drive for ages,' I commented, settling my handbag in the footwell and pulling my seatbelt across my lap. I had arranged a minibus boozer-cruiser for all of us, but Rick had said that he fancied taking the car for a run, and I agreed that the autumn leaves at this time of year certainly do make for a fine backdrop. He jokingly suggested I come along for the ride and, much to his surprise, I delightedly jumped at the chance.

Winding our way out of London and humming south along the unusually clear roads, I gazed out at the English countryside's burnished colours as it wound itself down in spectacular fashion in preparation for the coming winter. I would have enjoyed it a whole lot more were it not for Rick's incessant incoming telephone calls. To my relief, he finally said, 'Enough, already,' and switched the blasted thing off.

'Want to stop for something to eat?' he asked as we passed a big blue sign with a knife and fork on it among other iconic motorway heraldry. I pictured the pair of us sitting in a Happy Eater.

'No thanks,' I said.

'Sure?' he persisted. 'I'm feeling a bit peckish.'

I twisted towards him. 'You've had two Danish pastries and a pork pie this morning. How can you possibly be hungry?' He huffed a mumbled answer and went all defensive. 'Think about something else,' I told him. 'Like your expanding waistline.'

'I've got big bones.' He sulked quietly.

SLOWING INTO A HEAVY traffic jam, we reached the last few miles of our journey and the sky began to fade. Rick leaned forward and switched off the radio, opened the window a couple of inches and peered at the besuited man in the old banger next to us who was busily picking his nose. 'Charming,' said Rick. I pretended not to have seen.

Suddenly Rick took a deep breath and exhaled loudly. 'It's been nice having you around,' he said, which seemed a bit of an odd remark. I automatically returned the compliment, opting for the safest bet.

'And it's been nice for me to be around you, too.'

'If things should change between us,' he rolled the window back up, 'I just wanted you to know that it's meant a lot to me.' For a moment he looked a bit sad. Not sad pathetic, but sad unhappy. Oh God, I thought. What have I done now? This is where I find out he's the one who's installed micro-cams around the house, and my sleuthing has been caught on CCTV. I'm history. He's just using me to orchestrate one last social gathering so that he can shoot me in front of a hundred goading onlookers. It was at that moment that another potential answer dawned on me. He's got another woman. He's finally buckled under the pressure of being lonely and treated himself to a mail-order bride from Bangkok. My days are numbered, soon to be replaced by a new, ring-toting wife with a red-hot wok.

'Why should anything need to change?' I asked him, feeling a hot flush rise. Early menopause hinted at the back of my mind. That would be all I needed right now, to begin my final descent into wizened huskery.

He switched the radio back on. 'Don't mind me,' he flashed half jokingly. 'I'm just being maudlin.' Strange man.

RICK'S CAR ROLLED to a halt at the end of the marina. We made our way down the jetty to inspect the all-new *Sundowner*, watching Leoni, already on deck, billowing fabulously in the autumn breeze like Jason's *Argonaut*'s heavily bosomed figurehead. She looked like the fashion centre-spread from *Vogue*'s 1974 September special. Trails of colourful silk streaming behind her, she was wearing her purple kaftan, scarf and super-shades set, with a scarlet wide-brimmed hat flopping deliciously over her eyes, and a couple of hundred yards of Arabian muslin shoulder drape going on.

Pointing her out to Rick, I said, 'That's Leoni.'

'Blimey,' Rick responded. 'She's not gonna get run over today, is she?'

Hearing the distinctive slap of our shoes hitting the gangway, Leoni turned her head then swished her way over to greet us. She shone a beaming smile directly at Rick, shaking her enthusiastic hello and cementing it with a kiss on his cheek. Rick laughed and said, 'Steady on!' Clearly, he was smitten.

Leoni squeezed my hands and flashed me an inquisitive twitch. Leaning in to kiss me, she pressed her mouth against my ear. 'He's lovely!' she whispered. Saints alive, we must all be setting our sights a lot lower these days. First it's me and Paxman. Now Leoni and Rick. Whatever is our world coming to?

Greetings over, we moved towards the cabin doors. Rick looked around the deck area and let out a low whistle. 'Bloody hell. Amazing what a lick of paint can do, isn't it?' *A lick of paint?* Have you any idea how close you could be to dying today if Leoni hears you say that? She appeared not to have heard and waited by the little doors, bouncing on her heels with glee.

'You are *so* going to love this!' She clapped her hands rapidly. 'I've not been able to sleep, I've been so excited about seeing it.'

Rick looked delighted, winked at me and took the cigar out of his mouth. 'Then don't you think you'd better lead the way?' he suggested to Leoni.

She rubbed her hands to warm them in the chilly evening air. 'Okay!' she beamed, without moving. We all stood there for a minute, smiling at each other pointlessly.

'Well, go on then!' urged Rick impatiently.

Leoni smiled vacantly at him, then at me. 'Key?' she asked.

IT WAS FAR too nippy to stand around indefinitely, squabbling about whose fault it was, and we reluctantly turned down Leoni's offer to smash the door in with the on-board jet ski. Our sneak preview would just have to wait until a key could be found.

The welcome we received from the restaurant manager was warm and effusive (I should jolly well think so given the extortionate cover charge he had levied on every shrunken head), and the big open bar space had quickly filled up with the fifty or so guests. It was fun introducing Rick to my curious little menagerie. He greeted Julia like an old friend, making mention of how nice it was to put a face to the voice on the phone. She returned his cheek kiss and squeezed his hand in a way she usually keeps only for insiders with maximum security clearance, which surprised me somewhat. He did bristle a bit when I presented him to my neighbours, and made masculine noises with a deep-throated thanks and a firm handshake when I explained Sally's crucial role in the finished master-piece.

'How do you like it?' drawled Sally.

'Dunno, mate. Haven't fucking seen it.' He looked Sally up and down uncomfortably. 'Keyless entry hasn't made it as far as nautical technology yet.'

Sally took a sip of his cocktail and thought for a moment. 'I think I know how to solve your problem,' he said with a smile, then pulled his phone out of his pocket and went outside to make a call. Rick leaned in to my side as he watched Sally glide to the door.

'Is he one of those poofs?' he asked me. I gave him a withering stare.

A LOUDLY MUFFLED pad-padding on the microphone beckoned the attention of the guests. Rick was standing, one hand in his pocket, mike (the thing you speak into, not the lawyer) in the other. 'If I could just have your attention for a couple of minutes,' he said, at which a few of his friends started heckling, 'I'd like to say a few words.' Everyone quietened down. 'I know I haven't seen some of you for a while.' He nodded at a couple of specific faces in the crowd. 'So thanks for coming.' The audience gave an appreciative murmur. 'We're hoping that someone's going to turn up with a key any minute so that I can show off what I dragged you all down here for.' Everyone laughed while Rick rolled his eyes. 'But in the meantime, I'd like to say a big thank you to the people who worked so hard on the renovations.' He looked around the room then spotted me hiding behind David. 'Helen? If you'd like to come up here for a minute. You too, Leoni.' Leoni looked thrilled and positively sprinted through the gathering. I went out and joined her amid a lovely round of applause.

Rick leaned towards me uncomfortably and shielded the open mike with his hand. 'What's the name of your poofy – sorry – gay friend again?'

'Salvatore,' I said patiently. 'Sally to his friends.'

Rick turned back to the audience and found Sally's face in the crowd. 'I'd invite you up here too, Sal,' he said in his gruffest voice, 'but I've only got two bunches of flowers, mate.'

'Send them to me, darling,' oozed Sally provocatively. 'And make sure you write something sweet on the card.' Rick blushed violently and everyone started laughing.

Standing there on the little stage, grinning self-consciously, he thanked us some more in front of everybody and handed each of us a bouquet and a garish coloured envelope of the sort that trumpets a vulgar greetings card inside. Leoni went to tear hers open, but Rick stopped her and suggested she pop it in her bag for later. 'You too,' he said to me. He then looked up. 'Right, you lot,' he announced. 'That's enough Mister Nice Guy. Now let's all get pissed.' A loud cheer went up from the crowd.

The dreadlocked DJ saw that as his moment to let rip, and set his steel wheels in motion with a thudding noise that someone younger than me might have wanted to dance to. Leoni remained at my side smiling excitedly. 'Isn't this great?' Then she noticed a waiter with a loaded canapé dish walking past, lifted the entire plate from his hands, tossed one into her mouth and held another towards my face questioningly. The waiter looked at his empty palm and turned back towards the kitchen doors.

Rick was engrossed in conversation with some of his guests and pointed out of the window in the general direction of his inaccessible trophy. I was discreetly searching around for somewhere to discard the revolting little paté disaster I had foolishly tried despite my better judgement, and surreptitiously dropped it into an ice bucket when no one was looking. Quickly glancing around to check I hadn't been caught, I noticed Rick smiling at me.

At that moment I was distracted by some commotion at the main entrance and went to see what all the fuss was about, as was my duty as the organizer of tonight's hoolie. Paul emerged from the scrum. 'There's some bloke at the door demanding to see Sally, dressed like the biker from the Village People. The manager won't let him in. Said he doesn't want his sort in here.' Paul's eyes flashed excitedly, his voice changing to a high-pitched squeal. 'I think there's going to be a brawl!'

'Not if I can help it.' I marched up to the doors and there on the step, bike chains dangling from his leather chaps, was the chief whip from our boat renovating crew. Sally was standing outside with him, saw me, and pointed towards the snivelling biker.

'He's got the key!' Sally mouthed at me, then put his arm around the builder's shoulders and offered him a hankie. I stepped out to join them, hushing the over-wrought restaurant manager and telling everyone else to go back inside.

I took the key from Sally's hand. 'You're a bloody genius,' I said. He nodded at me to take it back inside so I made haste and left Sally standing there awkwardly trying to comfort his inconsolable fan, who was painfully sobbing. 'You never told me you had a boy-friend!'

EVERYONE WAITED ON the quayside under my small-voiced direction while Leoni and Sally led Rick on board and prepared the way for the grand unveiling. At the flick of a switch, the deck and masts lit up like a Christmas tree with hundreds of white lights twinkling up and down the rigging. The mirror-smooth paint-work gleamed and we all watched on as quietly as an excitable half-cut crowd could manage. The cabin doors were opened and Rick disappeared momentarily from our view. Seconds later there was a howl of,

'Fucking hell!' closely followed by Rick's head rising from the steps. He leaned his arms on either side of the wooden doors and smiled, cigar hanging between his teeth. 'You have got to see this!' he shouted at us, then went back below. Moments later, music blared from the hidden speakers, jolting the crowd into a disco-powered bunfight, all clamouring at once to get on board. Sally pushed his way towards me and took my outstretched hand, leading me gently through the mêlée and walking me past the scrum towards the bow.

'I've left a hatch open.' He winked. 'I'll drop you through it.' I took off my shoes and Sally lowered me through the small aperture into the silent chamber below. I waited for him to follow.

'What about you?' I called up.

'Too big.' He smiled down at me. 'Take a look around before the rats move in. The light switch is over there.' He pointed. I found the lights and turned them on. The grotty space I remembered from just a week or so ago had undergone the most spectacular makeover. Burr walnut panels faced all the cupboards; the deeply coloured Liberty fabric now sumptuously cushioned the walls. The tiny bathroom, mirrored and marbled, might well have been shipped down from Claridge's. It was utterly fantastic. Had I not already had a pretty fancy place of my own, I would have wanted to buy this one and cast myself adrift there and then.

The noise behind the closed bedroom door was gathering pace. Rick pulled it open from the other side and momentarily froze when he saw me standing behind it. His immediate silence fell across the gathered guests. 'Just hang on there a minute you lot,' he said to them, then stepped inside the cosy cabin and shut the door behind him.

'I came in through the window,' I explained without really needing to.

'I'm speechless,' he said.

I twiddled my fingers nervously. 'Are you sure you like it?'

'I like it so much,' he confessed with sincerity, 'that I wish I hadn't asked this bunch of reprobates down here to trample around it.' Rick's expression was tender. 'It feels really—' He thought for a minute, then settled on 'special'.

From the hefty sounds pounding in from beyond the door, the peasants were starting to revolt.

SEVEN O'CLOCK THE next morning, I was sitting at the breakfast bar in the kitchen with a cold cup of tea languishing in front of me, the open card from Rick sitting upright beside it, and the buckled cheque still in my hand. The telephone shrilled on the wall beside me, and I reached up and snatched it to my ear. I had

Leoni on ringback. She takes the phone off the hook every night and replaces it when she gets up for her morning wazz. Don't ask me why.

'It's me,' I said quickly.

She yawned loudly and smacked her lips. 'I was having an erotic dream about Thierry Henry,' she mumbled. 'Got me into a bit of a state, actually. Then I woke up next to bloody Godzilla. I was just on my way to take a cold shower.'

'Have you opened your card from Rick?'

'Yep,' she said sleepily.

'Was there anything in it?'

'Oh yes,' she laughed, suddenly awake. 'A cheque for two thousand smackeroonies.' I heard her kiss the ends of her fingers. 'I feel whole again.'

'Oh,' I said.

'Why? Was yours empty?'

I looked at the slip in my hand. 'No. Not exactly.' I stood up from my seat. 'Look, I'll call you back later.'

STANDING OUTSIDE RICK'S house on a Sunday felt a bit out of context. It didn't seem right to use my key, so I pressed on the doorbell and hoped that he was home. After two rings I was ready to give up, when the door opened. The moment Rick saw me, he nodded, unsurprised, and waved me in. 'I wondered if it was going to be you,' he said. 'Excuse the state of me. Didn't get to bed till after four.' I followed him in and closed the door softly behind me.

He tried to make a beeline for the kitchen, but I called him to a halt there and then, taking the folded scrap out of my bag and holding it open in front of me. 'Rick?' I questioned him. 'What's this?' He stopped, dropped his shoulders, and turned to face me knowing full well what was in my hand.

'It's yours,' he said, then continued away from me. 'I know it's not all of it, but it's about all Lomax had left. Spud did offer to cut his nadgers off to make up the difference. Fancy a coffee?' I followed him into the kitchen. 'Or maybe you could do with something stronger.'

Dropping myself into the same chair that Helga had collapsed into, I put the cheque down on the table and stared at it. He came and sat beside me while the kettle boiled, confirming my suspicion that the only person in the house who knew how to get a drop of anything drinkable out of the silver beast was me. 'Put it back in your bag. Better still, put the fucking thing in the bank before someone else tries to nick it off you.'

'I don't understand,' I said.

'Course you do. You don't have to be a rocket scientist to figure it out.' He laughed. 'What did you think I've been doing this last month? Working? Don't be soft.' Tears pricked at my eyes, mercifully didn't fall out, and I nodded a humble thank you very much I don't know what to say. Rick looked at the floor. 'It really got to me when I saw you so upset that day,' he said. 'So I thought to myself, right, do something useful for a change. Help the girl out.'

I was so deeply touched that I was lost for words. Well, almost. 'How did you find him?' I asked. 'Even the police said I didn't stand a chance.'

'Well, they would, wouldn't they?' Rick smiled. 'That's the trouble with being a law-abiding citizen, Hell. People like you turn to the great, lumbering plod when what you really need is a few dodgy friends in low places.' He winked at me and got up from his chair. 'You just need to know which rocks to look under.'

He opened the cupboard and pulled down a jar of instant. 'He's a right slimy bastard that Lomax,' he said, as if I didn't already know. 'But we got him *real* good.' Rick came back to the table with two mugs, put them down and left the room, returning a few moments later with a decanter. Topping up the drinks with a generous ration of firewater, he picked his up and held it towards me. 'Cheers,' he said, and whacked his mug against mine with a clunk.

SOME WEEKS BEFORE in an expensive beach restaurant somewhere in the sun-drenched Caymans,

Richard Lomax had been paid a visit by one of his old muckers from the trading-floor days. He hadn't seen Julian Gartree since they pulled that stunt off together during the dizzying heights of the dot com frenzy. The shareholders' investments had neatly disappeared down an untraceable online hole before any of them could say split derivative, and the two partners had pocketed the proceeds and moved on to the next bunch of gullible punters in search of a new investment craze.

With all that money idling around doing nothing in his offshore accounts, Lomax had fancied setting himself up as a bit of a showbiz Svengali. He'd seen at close hand the pulling power of the media moguls he attempted to rub shoulders with in the well-heeled watering holes serving the millionaires' hideaways. Admiring the receding scabs around his slowly healing hair plugs in the bathroom mirror, he'd been looking forward to hearing more about his old friend's vertical career shift into bankrolling blockbuster movies. The lucky bastard was making a fortune, and had even complained that an investigative journalist working on the *Sunday Times* Rich List was onto him. Lomax grudgingly sent a driver to pick up Julian and his new business partner from the airport and made his own way to the restaurant, the mounting jealousy eating him alive on the way.

Lomax enviously eyed the fat bloke with deep-fried

skin puffing on a cigar, swapping a discreet word in Julian's shell-like while the three of them lunched together. He doesn't look much like a media mover and shaker, he thought, with increasing resentment.

'You ain't got enough money, mate,' the man had eventually proclaimed loudly, finishing his burger in three bites and wiping his stuffed mouth with a ketchup-stained napkin. 'Come on, Ju. We're wasting our time here. I thought you said this bloke was a serious player.' Then, looking at Lomax, 'No offence, mate. But we're talking telephone numbers. Of the international variety.' Lomax was mortified, and hastily glanced around the restaurant, terrified that the tendon-slicing putdown had been overheard. Rick stood up. 'Who do I have to shag round here to get the bill?'

Lomax jumped to his feet, yapping sharply, 'I want a slice of the action! How much will it take?'

Rick turned to him with a smile, stuck the cigar back in his mouth and hitched his yellow floral Bermuda shorts up a notch or two. 'How much have you got?'

The promise of a six hundred per cent guaranteed return after four months blinded Lomax into handing over a staggering amount of money. Rick and Julian gave him the whole nine yards, including a visit to the Playboy mansion and a subsequent spell at a private clinic in Arizona for a spot of dialysis. Spud had acted as a sort of go-between, exerting just enough starch to make sure that Lomax made the payments and didn't ask too many questions before the funds had cleared. All in all, Rick had managed to extract more than a million quid from the stone that had previously refused to bleed.

'I, I, I DON'T KNOW WHAT to say,' I stuttered.

'Save it.' Rick patted my hand. 'It was fun. While it lasted.'

In true Brit style, Rick turned out to be one of those men who doesn't know what to do when faced with a woman when her waterworks breach. I couldn't help myself. It was like the weight of the world had been lifted from my shoulders, and the relief was too much to bear. As I covered my face with my hands and started howling, he started off with a pleading, 'Oh, come on, Hell! Don't do that! I thought you'd be pleased!' He shuffled around uncomfortably, clearing his throat and looking for something absorbent, then offered to drop me home. We drove without conversation, me sniffling happily into a sodden tissue, him mumbling occasional comments about Ken Livingstone's loose screw.

Slowing to a halt in the leafy square, Rick turned the rumbling engine off, got out of the car and came around to open my door. I accepted his helping hand with a whimpering thank you.

'I suppose this is it, then.' Rick walked me to my

door. 'You've been great, Hell. I'll miss you.' He looked at the wet leaves stuck to his shoes. 'Try and stay out of trouble, right?'

I managed a red-nosed smile. 'I'll do my best.'

'And I don't want to hear about you doing anything stupid with the money, either. There's a lot of very nasty people out there,' he cautioned me sternly.

'Don't worry.' I nodded with a swallow. 'I know.'

He hung around for a bit, checking my face for signs of temporary madness, then parked a clumsy kiss on my cheek. For a moment, he looked as though he was about to say something important. He put his hands behind his head, then let out a big sigh. 'Keep in touch,' was all he said, then got back in his car and drove away.

I BARRICADED MYSELF IN and sat on the sofa, hugging my knees and breathing too deeply. Then I got up and paced around the room for a good half hour. The turn around the tidy kitchen provided little distraction. I didn't want anything to eat. Didn't want tea. I kicked the question around all afternoon.

I'm a simple soul who stopped seeking answers that don't exist a long time ago. I now accept that sometimes things happen in life with no rhyme or reason. You can waste an awful lot of time pondering on the whys and wherefores. It serves no purpose in the end and, I've decided, is a rather pointless occupation. Spend enough hours suspended in this vacant mind-lock and life will pass you by. The spooky thing is, you probably won't even notice. To lose one's certain foothold now and again is no bad thing. Like that fleeting moment when you find your head nodding off in the car then jerk yourself awake.

And what to do with a million pounds and loose change? I expect we've all considered it once or twice since the lottery came along. I'd already tackled that question once, although my windfall came from a stiff, not a ticket. Now I would get to do it all over again. Only this time, I would do it differently. I slept on the matter, and decided not to tell a living soul. With one exception.

'Keith? It's Helen Robbins.' Keith sounded surprised and more than a little irritated to hear my voice, and reminded me tersely that I was supposed to go through the call centre now and speak to the value-range staff. 'Yes, I know,' I said politely. 'I just wanted to call you personally and tell you that you can shove your poxy account right up your—'

EPILOGUE

I DON'T HAVE TO work any more. It's a nice position to be in, leaving me entirely free to lapse back into my previous lackadaisical lifestyle. Being a far more practical sort these days, I was standing outside shivering on the pavement for a good ten minutes before the bank on the corner opened its doors for business. I sat in one of the open-plan booths, filled in the forms and bravely handed over the passport containing the cruellest picture of me ever taken.

'Will you be making a deposit today?' asked the friendly cashier.

'Yes,' I said, and handed her the cheque. She did a double-take.

Glancing back up at me with fear in her eyes, she fumbled for her key fob and quickly locked the desk, nervously smiling, 'I'll just go and get the manager.' I returned her smile and said nothing. Minutes later, she reappeared with a steamed dumpling of a man trotting by her side.

'Miss Robbins!' he exclaimed as though having missed me desperately for years. I shook his sweaty outstretched hand. 'I'm so sorry. We should have used my office for this instead of—'

'Please,' I assured him. 'It's not important.'

He was already ushering me towards his door. 'Do come in! Do come in!' he puffed, reaching for his phone. 'I'll just get Giles in here too. I expect you'll be wanting some red-hot investment advice.'

An hour or so later, sliding my trusty key back into the familiar latch, I casually dropped my handbag by the front door and hung my coat quietly on the rack as usual. The deafening banging and crashing could mean only one thing. I wandered through to the kitchen.

'Oh, for heaven's sake get out of the way and let me,' I said.

Rick pulled the fat cigar from his smiling mouth, beamed wider than a mile and handed me the metal milk jug. 'You're late, Hell.' He grinned with sparkling eyes.

Of the two of us, I think it was probably me who laughed the longest.